QWUEDEVIV CREWS

we come with peas

Qwuedeviv Crew 52: We Come with Peas
Copyright © 2013 by K.F. Martin

For information contact:
grimalkin.bookhouse@gmail.com

Book and Cover design by K.F. Martin
Graphic Title Design by Devin « Shea » Lowell

ISBN: 979-8-9898980-0-8
Third Edition: December 2023

QWUEDEVIV CREW

we come with peas

K.F. MARTIN

Grimalkin Bookhouse

An imprint of K.F. Martin

Dedication
To my supportive family. Without their love and support, I would be lost. Dad (Howard), Mom (Carrie), and Brother (Seth). Love you guys!

Prologue

THERE COMES AN IMPORTANT time in life when one is forced to make decisions. Life or death decisions. Now, those of us in leadership have to make these sorts of calls more often. To put it simply, do or die. I would call it DoD, but if you say that, it just sounds like you can't pronounce dude, which I can. Anyway, doing was a mighty vague option, but dying...that was just unacceptable! So I did what any good, noble lieutenant would do. I got away from the crash site and headed for the nearest available cover as fast as possible. But that's a topic of its own! You see, the thing about cover is, it is, yet again, really vague.

How was a commanding officer like myself supposed to know what adequate shelter was when they'd just crash-landed on the planet they were supposed to invade?

I suppose I'm getting ahead of myself; I do that a lot thanks to my superior intellect...stuff. Anyway, I'm Second Lieutenant Smiley, commander of Qwuedeviv Crew 52. I'll spare you the details, but we're pretty much the coolest, most luxurious species around. The Earthians refer to our kind and many others as "aliens," but we can discuss all of those boring social stigmas later. Right now, we have more pressing matters.

1

The More Pressing Matters

*T*HINGS GOT OFF TO a bad start for me. One moment, I was perfectly content in a free fall plummet towards Earth and the next thing I knew, I'd crashed in the wrong—I take that back—actually, my entire crew had failed to land in the proper spot and thus left me stranded and alone. Not to worry though, I was perfectly capable of taking care of myself.

The landing had been a little rough, and I'm willing to admit I was a little bit shaken. When I made my way towards Earth ground, everything was spinning. The world was an odd smear of green, blue, gray, pretty smileys, and brown. Even though my kind isn't known for our amazing sense of smell—no nose you see—my gills were detecting high levels of smoke and...dirt.

Once my Visual Scanners had transmitted the signal to Command Center to disengage Spinning Doom Mode, my field of vision was, shall we say, significantly clearer. The blue was now above me. The brown, nearby where the crash site was. The gray appeared to be their civilization structures...and...hold on a second. I distinctly recall receiving a report in regard to "pretty smileys," there were certainly no pretty smileys anywhere. I knew pretty smileys—I had a couple on my ears, back, shoulders, and feet. Someone was feeding us false info! Huh! Well, I'd have to look into that later.

For now, I had gotten Earth readjusted properly enough to make sense and needed to plan my next move. Under normal circumstances, one might have expected the crew's leader to search out said crew; however, this was not a normal circumstance or time. Besides, I was certain they would want their commander to be safe and I agreed with the concern they surely would have shown. That aside, it was big, open and well, quite honestly, I wanted to hop back in my box, seal off the panels and go into lockdown mode. In other words, I was a tad bit apprehensive about being out here.

It was time to find a better place to set up base. I did my best to keep out of the line of sight for this planet's inhabitants. Surprisingly, they seemed to show a great lack of observation in noticing anything about the crash.

That was fine—my drop pod would explode before they could use it for anything. It wasn't the most discrete method, but there was no way I could pack the thing up on my back and carry it along with me. My biggest concern right now was...well, me.

Thus far, I still hadn't come across any Earthians. Perhaps they didn't venture out until later in the day. Although I had no real perception of the current time, I was making a guess at it being early. Even though I could see stuff, it had a darkish hue to it and either my fur was thinning or it was chilly out there. I'd add that to the qualifications for a proper base.

Safe. Secluded. *Heated.*

I continued walking along streets I had never seen before. Buildings towered to both sides. I hoped they didn't have security cameras or something similar. Otherwise, I was in a great deal of trouble. Security work wasn't my specialty.

From a tourist perspective, it seemed to be a nice little community of some sort; lots of little grassy patches in the front of each house. I guess each Earthian could have a nice rolling turf for summer. I'm sure they liked to warm their bellies in the sun just like any other creature.

Anyway, base. Base yes. I needed a suitable base. There was one main problem with this whole procedure. I wasn't sure how one went about obtaining one of these things or how to tell if they had already been taken.

Wait. No, no, no scratch that! I was an invader! I didn't need permission. I'd just take what I wanted. Choice base interior and exterior knowledge was not my specialty, but I figured the bigger the better. That concept tends to work for most things. The bigger the explosion, the more damage— our tactic experts think they're so smart. Really, they just get a fancy title to state they have a brain! This is why I would never settle for being a Tactical Advisor.

Anyway, it was around this time that I discovered exactly what I needed. This house was taller than the others and nearly double the size. It also had a little fence around it that couldn't possibly have kept anything in or out. There was a space to crawl through underneath it and obviously space above as well to climb over. So there I stood, standing where I stood, staring at the stood. Er, fence. I was stooding in front o—ahem— staring at the fence, which I stood in front of.

It didn't take long for the obvious choice to come into clarity. I would squeeze myself underneath it. Those reasons wouldn't be as clear to someone like yourself because you don't have access to all the top-secret files. However, if you did, you would understand that this was the only logical conclusion.

Before I initiated Stealth Crawl, I checked to the left and right to ensure no one was following me. No one was—just in case you were curious. So Stealth Crawl was activated. All at once my limbs lowered me to the ground. It was even colder against the pavement, which prompted me to hurry up. Something odd happened though.

Instead of slinking under in one smooth stride, I uh, only got about halfway. Strange. I yanked and tugged and pushed and pulled, but it seemed my faulty uniform had snagged on the chain link of the fence. This was severely problematic, especially since there was no one around to help me!

My tail swished back and forth. Us felines tend to do that when displeased, you see. I was, in fact, rather displeased and I had full intentions of letting the fence know it. Interfering with a lieutenant's plans was very reckless and rude. I pulled and pushed again. The fence continued clanking and clattering—making a whole ruckus of noise rather than freeing me. I was preparing to rip the whole thing apart for scrap metal with my sheer strength when a light flicked on in front of the house.

I froze.

Had the Earthians been alerted to my presence? I pushed the gray hood of my uniform back and angled my ears forward. I heard a frog croak somewhere—I think that's what the Earthians called them—but nothing more than that. Huh. False alarm, it must have been a decoy motion-sensing light.

The struggle resumed. Clank. Clatter. Tug, tug, clank, clank. Clash. Earthian defense equipment defied all logic; after all it was only logical that if I couldn't go forward, I should be able to back out the way I had come. My patience with the illogical fence had run out, but before I could punish it for its acts of tyranny there was a strange *cht cht cht* noise coming from the yard. I was still in the midst of deciding what it was when the *thing* attacked me. A whole torrent of water right to my face! The horror! Earthians were ruthless beasts!

I hit the Reverse and Retreat directive, but the fence wouldn't let go. Trapped! My fur fluffed up in an instant.

"Alright, Beast! One more move like that and I'll—"

Before I could finish, the water monster had spun and struck again. I let out a yowl and went into overdrive on the escape directive. The fence clanked furiously as I unleashed my raging wrath. Vicious yowls that should have sent any creature running mingled with the clashing of a fence and the sputter of the Water Beast. What we had on our paws was an all-out war.

Let's get a couple of things straight here. I was in horrible danger. The beast had a thin body that was laced through the whole yard—a serpent of some kind. More notable still was the metallic gleam of its head. This beast was none other than a vicious mechanical land serpent. A soulless machine with a taste for shooting concentrated beams of ice at anything that entered its lair.

I knew my time was up. This was the end, but I'd go down fighting. In the years to come I'd be remembered in Qwuedeviv history. I'd be a hero. Kittens everywhere would strive to be like me. I would have raised the standards of what it meant to be a lieutenant by leaps and bounds.

The world was becoming blurry. It was only a matter of time now. A sudden screech drew me back. It appeared that my battle with the ice-shooting mechanical land serpent had distracted me from noticing possibly the most hideous creature I'd ever seen. It had slipped and fallen on the wet grass, shouted something in its native language and crawled back towards its home.

It struck out and, with incredible speed, wrapped its skeletonous hand around a lever. As it turned, the mechanical land serpent's ice ray diminished. The creature then got back on its paws. My mouth dropped open, and with renewed strength, I was prepared to get out of there, even if it meant leaving behind some of my uniform and a good chunk of fur.

This new creature was tall—more like the size of a highly unpleasant unit in my crew called Spork—but it was even *uglier* than Spork. Its face was completely bald and misshapen with an odd protrusion between its eyes and mouth. It had a little fur on its head but everything else was *bald*. Never in my entire career had I seen such a grotesque monster, but I couldn't force myself to look away.

Upon closer inspection, I noticed even more scary details. Its tiny, round ears were far too low on its head and it had too many fingers. Worse still, it had no tail—not even a terrifying hairless one. Krillfish! This thing made Spork look beautiful!

The creature raised one grotesque hand to adjust the squarish glasses hiding its eyes, and then it took a few steps toward me. My heart was pounding on the inside of my chest, knocking to see if everyone at Command Center was still alive. Command Center was a bit preoccupied though and couldn't give our Circulatory System commander a prompt response. Fear can have a powerful effect over an individual and all at once, I began emitting a terrible wailing sound of a yowl—a um, well it was a cry for help. Someone had sounded the alarm!

The creature waited until I had uh, given up that particular endeavor. It was probably going to eat me or try to steal my fur...or my tail. My poor, luxurious tail!

"What *are* you?"

I gazed at the creature again as it moved closer. I needed to get a story together and quick. It could be my only chance of survival.

"You look like a giant...cat."

"*Yes.*" I finally managed to answer with a bit more enthusiasm than intended. "I am a Giant Cat."

None of my kind had ever accused me of being a giant, but I was perfectly willing to be a Giant Cat in the Earthian culture if it meant I got to keep all my fur and respective limbs.

The creature placed its hands on its hips.

"Cats don't talk though, and they don't wear clothes or have humanoid figures."

"Then why the heck did you say that?"

The Earthian adjusted its glasses again.

"Well...uh...I...I suppose I don't know."

Silence. Actually, the silence carried on for a surprising length of time as the creature stood there staring at me. I decided to take the chance and work at freeing myself. I mean, if it was gonna just stand there, then I didn't have much to lose. I twisted and squirmed, but all it really did was get my uniform situated rather uncomfortably. For a stupid short fence, the darn thing sure was strong.

"Wait," the creature gasped.

Somewhere deep inside my kitty soul, I knew that was a wait of ill fate, a wait of destruction. It was the wait of all waits. The wait that would—

"You're...you're like some kind of alien. Some freakish cat alien!"

That was oddly enough, a very good and close guess—maybe minus the freakish part. If anyone was freakish, it was the furless creature with a mechanical pet monster; it made me wonder if all Earthians were accustomed to regular alien visits though.

"Oh my gosh...you are. Are we being invaded?"

"Yes. I mean no!"

This Earth creature was confusing me. Of course we were here to invade! But it wasn't supposed to know that. Before I could add additional lies of security, the creature had already started off on some kind of mental breakdown. It was squealing and yowling.

"Oh...ohhh no." Its hands went to the unruly fur on its head, grasping large clumps. "Why me? Why out of everyone in the world...this is bad. I have to tell someone; the cops, the government, my employer. Alien invasion. Aliens! I knew they'd come!"

I was beginning to believe that I might have stumbled across my first "Human." It fit the description. Loud, obnoxious, stupid, high-strung, ugly. I had trained long and hard for such an occasion though. Well, encountering a Human—not so much the death by ice-shooting mechanical land serpent.

"Hey. Hey, Human." It took a few tries, but I got its attention eventually. "Don't worry about it. We come with peas."

2

The C.C.K. Routine
Never Fails

THAT SHUT IT UP for a moment. After much research from studying Human Entertainment Media we had discovered stating you came with peas always settled Human uncertainty. The phrase comes from ancient Earthian civilizations that were primitive. Well, more primitive than their current state that is. The offer of peas served as a uh, promise that they hadn't come to steal food I suppose. Earthians love peas.

As luck would have it, I had managed to find an even more primitive Human though. I had assumed that the creature would be impressed with my rather powerful declaration of possessing peas, but much to my surprise, and I'm sure the surprise of all of Command Center, their entire culture was lost on this one. That was clearly a problem on Earth nowadays. No one had any respect for ancient Earthian culture.

"Peas?" The Human spoke up at last. I could tell it was trying to sound as if it knew what it was talking about, but I knew it didn't. "Why...why are you telling me this?"

I rolled my eyes—it's a gesture reserved for complete fish-brains like this individual. "You were freaking out. It's supposed to calm you down. *Duh.*"

Again there was a pause as its tiny Human brain tried to process this info. "Is that your way of saying you're friendly?"

Maybe there was hope for the Human civilization after all. It had only taken an alien from another planet to explain the truths so long forgotten. It made me happy to know I had helped a species that would have otherwise been doomed by their flawed memory—not enough to change my mind about taking over their planet and enslaving their species or anything of course.

"But you just said you were invading."

Funny how the Human brain works. Couldn't remember their main food source and its history but clung like a little earth monkey to the word invade.

"Did I? I don't think so."

"You did."

Know-it-all Humans were not something I intended to tolerate. I had tried the nice approach. It had failed. It was thus time to move on to other, more forceful methods.

"Look, Human, if you go tell anyone, do you know what they'll do?"

"Well I do believe they may question my sanity and—"

"*Aside* from lock you up in a crazy house, they'll take me away and do all kinds of horrible tests and experiments. Then my species gets all upset and comes down here to blow yours off the face of the planet. Is that what you want? To single-handedly be responsible for your entire species' destruction when all we ever wanted was to observe and learn?"

Kekeke that gave it something to think about! And so it did. I was beginning to wonder if Humans entered a state of sleep with their eyes remaining open. It seemed to be a sort of weird trait in my opinion, but certainly not unheard of. Besides, there were always those cyborg things that sort of looked like Humans in movies. I wasn't sure if they were actually real or not, but I was willing to consider the possibility.

After I grew bored of lingering in my own thoughts, I decided to prompt the Human along some.

"Besides, how could one alien kitty cause any trouble?"

More pondering. The Human really liked doing that.

"I suppose..."

That was close enough to an answer for me. No ordinary Qwuedeviv could have pulled that off like I had. The Human had been outsmarted and now it stood at my mercy—subject to my superior intellect and charming disposition.

A light breeze picked up that ruffled my tail fur and furthermore reminded me of the ice shards strewn about my furry gray face.

"Your mechanical land serpent struck and attacked me. My face is now very cold and wet. I—"

"Oh. You mean the sprinkler?"

I checked to confirm we were discussing the same violent creature and nodded—it was a strange name for such a beast.

"Yes the 'sprinkler' as you call it. I'm liable to sue. I mean, that was a totally unprovoked attack! I was just minding my own business, crawling under this here fence and—"

"You know, that's worth considering." The Human tapped at its chin with its sorry excuse for a hand. "Why *were* you crawling under my fence?"

That had not been the point I was intending to make at all. Me being under the fence had absolutely nothing to do with the unruly behavior of the land serpent. Here we were having a discussion on owner responsibility and the Human had to go off rambling about why I was stuck under a dumb fence.

"It's none of your business!"

"It's my yard!"

The Human flailed its arms. Honestly, the gesture confused me so I decided to dismiss it and carry on.

"I see that. The fence I was willing to forgive—it's the mechanical land serpent that needs—"

"You're an *alien*, trespassing on my property at six in the morning and you're telling me I have no business asking why you were trying to stuff your furry little hide into my yard?"

I could hear commotion down the street now. Other Humans must have been alerted by this one's yowling. This was not good. My chances of convincing the whole Human species that I came with peas were very, very poor. It was time for a new strategy.

"Alright, forget the suing. Just remember what could happen if you keep yowling danger to everyone."

That quieted it down fairly quickly. It sighed and then a sort of gentle smile collided with that ugly bald face.

"Alright, I get it. You're probably lost and confused. Something scared you and you didn't have time to think about how you'd never fit through that gap."

I...well no, that wasn't exactly how it had gone. The getting stuck part was right but was it really that obvious I wouldn't fit? I had thought I'd aligned it pretty well and...huh. Oh well, I'd worry about that later. Command Center would certainly be receiving a complaint in regards to their slacking conduct.

For now though, I had the perfect opportunity to unleash the secret weapon. This weapon has been known to captivate its victims long-term—sometimes for life. No kidding, it's that powerful. It's something I like to call "Cute, Cuddly Kitty."

The key is to let one's eyes widen and expand to maximum capacity. Direct eyes upward at subject. Works especially well when light sources reflect off of said eye, creating an adorable sparkling effect. Keep mouth relaxed and in a pitiful frown, ears should slump to the sides a tad, and the finishing touch is one tiny, kitten-like "mew." Gets them every time!

Just as expected, it worked even with the Human. It knelt beside me; gaze no doubt locked on my adorable face.

"Aww...you poor little thing."

Yes, that was right. I was a poor little thing. Mercy and pity were proper responses. The next step would be the Human's great regret for the way it had treated me. It would wish to give me its home and loyalty to make up for the inhospitable treatment it had displayed.

I was ready to receive my prize, but much to my horror, it stretched out its bald hand. I hit the fence in an attempt to go backward—Humans were a terrifying species. One moment, they seemed slow and helpless; the next, they moved with light-ning-fast refluxes...reflexes... Something like that. The point is I didn't receive my so richly deserved reward—instead, the crea-ture reached out and stroked the fur of my forehead. Yes, you read that right—they had skipped touching the hood of my uniform and had gone straight for the luxurious fur.

There are a few things to keep in mind about my species—the first of which should be we don't like being touched. At all. Especially by Earthian aliens. I actually added that last part there, but I'm sure other Qwuedeviv would agree with me.

"It's okay." the Human tried to assure, reaching then for the fence and the back portion of my uniform. "Let's get you out of this mess."

Yes! Let's! That sounded much more to my standards. I couldn't see what the Human was doing exactly, but the wiring stopped clawing my back, and a few moments later, I was able to back out from the gap easily. Granted, I was still on the wrong side of the fence, but it was a step in the right direction...or a step back in the wrong direction for good reasons or something. The point was I was free to take the next course of action, whatever it may be.

There was a moment of awkwardness as I stood there, poised to run. The Human watched me in return. It seemed I would have to solve this problem or it wouldn't be solved at all.

"So. You plan on letting me in?"

"Not really."

That was not what I was expecting at all. What had happened to the "poor kitty" thing? Now they weren't even going to let me into the house?

"But...but your people. The horrible things. Don't you remember—"

"If you're an alien I'm sure you have some kind of cloaking device. Let's be realistic here." The Human tilted its head to the side and adjusted its stance. "There has never been an alien species that didn't have some kind of fancy gadgets for that."

"Yeah, but—"

The Human was already walking away back towards its house. This was...not good. Time to change tactics yet again. Sometimes all of our elite military training and knowledge is too complex for common species' understanding. In these cases, you must switch to a more primitive dialect. That was my intention now. Ditch the commander status and appeal to cute factor.

I hurried to the fence once more and clung to the chain link. It was actually easier to climb than I had expected. Turns out you don't even need claws to climb the links—fingers fit right into the slots. Had a bit of trouble with the legs since they were covered by my footwear, but I'd manage. It wasn't the most graceful of maneuvers I had ever performed, but it also wasn't the worst I must sadly report.

My foot snagged at the top and I toppled over the other side. I caught myself with my paws before I hit my face though.

The Human stopped and looked back at me. Now was my chance.

"Look, I—I won't take up much space. I promise to be good! Please?"

The Human continued its staring and feet shuffling as it rubbed its arms—guess it was cold too.

"I don't meow much and you'll never find a more loyal friend."

We might call that a stretch of the truth. My species wasn't the most...loyal to the species we planned to invade, but that was a detail I intended to leave out.

The Human slouched which really didn't do anything for its already lack luster appearance.

"Alright, fine. You can come in—for today. But the first sign of trouble you give, you're out, understand?"

I grinned, which made the Human take a couple of steps back. I had forgotten about the "creeping-out" effect our teeth had and made a hasty effort to correct this mistake.

"Uh-huh. I mean yeah! Thanks!"

Little did the Human know that it and its pretty little house would mark the first success of our invasion. Kekeke. Be good! How ridiculous!

3

I Set up My Command Post

*O*H YEAH, *I FORGOT* to mention. My invasion crew—we were actually labeled as a scout crew, but I'm pretty sure that was just a mistake in the paperwork; they meant to label us as the main invasion force. My point is I got to work fast once I had established headquarters. I had a lot of responsibility here as the overseeing leader of this entire operation.

There were just a couple of simple things I had to keep in mind for this whole thing to be a success. The first was keeping all knowledge of my true intentions away from the Human. This wasn't particularly difficult because Humans aren't very smart. The current one, for example, had left me all alone after only a few minutes of welcoming me into its home. It had grumbled something about not wanting fur on its furniture, but I had ignored that. I mean, seriously. Having any of my fur lingering was a luxury. I was doing it a favor.

Maybe it could collect the fur fragments and glue them to itself. At least then it would be a little prettier. Do you think all Humans are bald like that one? I mean...I was beginning to believe it might be a concern for me. What if Earth had some kind of environmental chemical that made fur vaporize? Would it affect Qwuedeviv fur, too? I couldn't remember a time when I had been without fur, nor did I want to. I'd be a monster—an ugly rat-cat alien doomed to a life of shame.

Anyway, setting aside those concerns for the moment, the Human had left, which meant I had an opportunity to begin our invasion efforts. First, I secured the room. This consisted of running around and assuring the Human was out of range.

As far as I could tell, it was gone. So I returned to the side of the sofa and flopped down on it. Superb. It was much softer than my box had been. I could get used to this. They had a flat-screened monitor...looked like quite a few boring books and some bound image manuscripts out too. Earthians! This one had its own house and couldn't find anything more interesting to use it for than boring reading material.

I had gotten a little carried away with Detail Inspection and had for the slightest, most briefest portion of a nanosecond forgotten to stay on Human Alert mode and wouldn't you know, the Human snuck in at that very moment.

"What the—"

My fur nearly stood on end.

"This isn't the sofa you meant, right?"

"I never even specified the..." It paused right there, bald face twisting into a scowl.

I decided it was probably best to let them feel like they had won—for now. There was no need to get myself kicked out of the house after all. I folded my ears down against my head, gave my best "kitty is sorry" look and crawled down from the luxurious furniture. The Human shook its head and left, sipping at something in a mug as it went along.

My ears perked up once it was gone. I hadn't wanted to sit on its stupid sofa anyway. It was time to investigate the rest of the house. Seemed to me I ought'a tour my new base to know where I should set up my personal headquarters, so I wasted no time.

There were quite a few rooms along the way. The halls were kind of narrow, but most of the rooms had plenty of space. My whole crew could probably fit in here...if they had survived...and if I ever saw them again. If not, it'd be plenty of space for me!

I ventured into one room down the hall where the door was partially open. The room was nearly empty like the others. There was a bed, a few boxes—looked like a half-done unpacking or packing job. I dunno how you'd really tell; it looks the same both ways. Oh well.

The room in question was pretty dark thanks to some kind of window blanket thing, but it seemed like there was light on the other side so...

How had I gotten so sidetracked? I had been looking for something else originally. I was just sure of it! Well the window had a nice view anyway. Overlooked what I presumed was the backyard. Lots of stuff out there. Some more grass, a pool, a fence and then beyond the fence were some smaller houses in the distance. Huh. Very interesting.

My tail started flicking back and forth. Seems it does that when my subconscious head thing gets thinking. I'm not so sure about that thing. Can't trust it. I mean it doesn't share its thoughts with me but makes me do stuff. Soon enough, it'll be taking over my job or something.

Back on the subject of Room Inspection though, I decided to proclaim that room inspected and declared it secure and...yeah that's what I was doing...I pranced on to the next with confidence. All the rest of the rooms checked out fine and...pretty much boring. Nothing to play with—er I mean work with.

By now my clothes had dried. Thankfully, aside from my face, my fur really hadn't gotten wet, which was good because us Qwuedeviv, ugh, get our fur soaked, and it takes *forever* to dry. That aside, it probably would have put a wave in my velvety, soft, bluish-gray fur! We couldn't have that happening; I look bad in curls.

· · · ● · ● · · ·

"Here, kitty, kitty, kitty!"

I heard the voice in the distance. Sounded like that Human again. Troublesome thing. It had barely left me alone for any real time and here it was, whining again. How was I supposed to do my job when I had to look after a Human all day?

I blinked my eyes against the warm rays of sunlight that had penetrated the window covering's defenses. Dawn had given way to daybreak. With a grumble directed at no one in particular, I scurried out of the room, tail and ears both up in a gesture of friendliness.

Instead of answering directly, I replied with a simple, "Mew?" as I reached the railing.

The Human was on the floor below. When it saw me, it smiled. From the looks of it, this Human was gonna be easy to manipulate.

"I have to go to work, Kitty. I'll be back later this afternoon. Be good, okay?"

I purred and rubbed the side of my face against the railing. Humans fall for that cutesy stuff really easy. Sure enough, it worked. With a smile, it departed, but just before the door closed, I heard, "And stay out of trouble."

Puh-lease, like a lieutenant was going to listen to that! I heard the rumble of a vehicle fade into the distance. I was now officially free for the day.

My search went into overdrive; I had already searched the house, now to set up points of interest. What I really needed was some kind of beacon. A beacon my crew could find and follow. Unfortunately, I had left that all back at the box when I had gotten terrifi—erm, when I had to abandon ship. Kinda regretted it now, but I figured the furballs would manage. Besides, I was starving and tired; even commanders needed to relax.

I headed to the kitchen, climbed the counter and opened the cabinets above the sink. There was some canned junk up there, but nothing tasty. I tried the ones below next, but there were only some bitter-smelling cleaners. Either the Humans had no taste or the treasures were in the fridge.

I pried that open next. The choices weren't too amazing; a half-eaten sandwich, some cold, O-shaped spaghetti things, and a huge supply of soda. Pondering just what kind of madhouse I had stumbled upon, I scooped up the bowl of cold noodles in sauce and headed for the sofa. I set the bowl up there, then crawled up, found the nearby primitive remote, pointed it at the screen in the center of the room and commanded it on.

It was around that time I realized I had forgotten my desired eating utensil. Yet again, I had to abandon my post to retrieve it. By the time I had reached the kitchen, I discovered my tail had been dipped in red sauce. I flicked it a bit to get the excess off before returning to my search.

I had to go through a lot of stuff to find a proper eating utensil. They weren't under the table, not in the glasses, not in the fridge…finally found some in the sink. They even had some unidentifiable mystery snack stuck to 'um still.

They were all different shapes; straight and long, slightly curved and pointed, round and scoopy. Wait, round and scoopy! I felt the fur along my spine begin to rise as I realized

I was staring at none other than a spoon. I breathed cautiously, hoping it wouldn't detect my fear and then slowly backed away, snatching a fork up in the process. I darted away from the scene and dove back onto the sofa.

The bowl of cold O's fell over and a good portion seeped into the cushions...oops. I scooped up the remainder with my paws and—eh, it was a little messier than expected. I glanced at the screen while licking my paws.

Some kind of cooking feed it seemed. They were making a pie or dessert thingy. It looked tasty—much better than this meal. I'd have to look into it. Maybe the Human could cook up some, although I had my doubts based on its current kitchen content. CKC for those of you familiar with codes.

I shoved another forkful in my mouth and tried not to think of the flavor much. They weren't good, but I'd had worse. Besides, I needed to recharge my strength for future invasion efforts and leaderly stuff.

Those cold, canned O-noodles could kind of grow on a cat. After a while and a lot of browsed live feeds, they didn't seem half bad. I guess I was pretty hungry because when I looked back at the bowl, it was empty. Well, no bad guest house manners here! I gave the bowl a thorough licking with my blue tongue and set it on the counter. It was really a superb job I had done—not that I was one to brag.

With a pleasantly full belly, I headed back upstairs to the room with the big window. I sat there between the window blankets and the corresponding window and began to lick my face and paws clean. I take pride in my hygiene, you see. It's a very good trait to have. A commanding officer must always look sharp and admirable. That aside, fur gets sticky and sticky fur is a pain—it attracts dirt, small bugs, and a million other things.

It took a good while to get myself to a satisfactory level of clean, but when I was done, even the sharpest of Qwuedeviv officers would have been put to shame: high-quality gray fur, compact and plush—like snuggling up in one of those fancy microfiber blankets or something. It was no secret that I had in my possession some of the finest—if not the finest—fur in all of Qwuedeviv history.

Don't think for a second that being in possession of such valuable material was easy either. How would you feel if you had to keep your gold-plated diamonds sparkling when they happened to be your shoes or something?

Somewhere in the time span that I had finished cleaning, I had ended up on the bed. It was pretty comfy despite my initial thoughts. It was one of those kinds that seemed to melt under your paws wherever you set them down. It was probably the kind on Human commercials that the kits can bounce on and not knock over the glass of grape juice, things I had learned from my research material prior to crash landing. I curled up in the center and sank in. It felt amazing. I yawned briefly and rolled onto my back—a short nap could be nice.

4

I Should've Stayed Home

"*K*ITTY!" *THAT WAS CLOSE* to my name but...
"KITTY!"

My ears perked up; fur frazzled as I was jerked from the
ever-peaceful realm of sleep. At first, I thought we were under
attack. I rolled off the bed and scurried to try and get underneath it. I was about halfway there when I heard the voice again.
Clarity began to return after I had rammed my face into a boot
of some sort. I hit all drives into reverse and pulled myself out
just as I heard the voice again. The Human! Right!

So it turns out the "short nap" was a little longer than
I had intended for it to be. My superior lieutenant intellect
and training told me this—I basically saw the light was fading
outside and could assume that if the Human was back, its job
was probably over. You do some basic math here and multiply
the square root of the hours the Human had been gone by the

number of boots stuffed under that bed and you come up with the answer—it had been some hours.

I stumbled into the hallway, reaching out for the railing I couldn't quite seem to get. It kept moving away from me or something. This is why you shouldn't wake up a Qwuedeviv so abruptly. We have sensitive equipment that must be calibrated slowly and with care.

"It's too early for all that shouting," I mewed once I had reached my destination—the rail.

I opened my eyes to half-slits and flicked my tail once. I could see the Human scurrying about below. It seemed rather frantic. Of course, I had no idea if this was normal Human behavior or not so I just yawned.

"There you are!" It called out as if it had found me.

My ears felt heavy—like at least ten pounds per ear. They were like weights. I shook my head without much of a result. "Me?"

"Yes, you! Come here!"

There were certainly nicer ways to address your guest and future ruler— but I wasn't gonna complain much. I'd let it off easy this time and we could work on the tone later. I made my way back to the stairs and plodded down them with feet that also had to weigh a ton a piece. It was amazing how sleep could change the weight of things so quickly. Eventually, I made it over to where the Human stood, tapping its foot impatiently.

It was in the living room, standing remotely near the sofa actually. The live feed monitor was still on and—one of my ears drooped. Seemed I might've forgotten to cover up a few tracks of my previous endeavor. When I got to thinking about it, it just *might* have had a lot to do with why Grumps-A-Lot looked a bit irritable.

I decided to play it cool and casual, so I stood beside him, tail still behind myself and innocent brown eyes gazing up. The

Human was quite a bit taller than me—that's why I had to look up.

"Did you do this?"

I followed the path its finger was pointing to the sofa where, huh, go figure, there was an orange sauce smear that seeped down into the sofa cushions. I had to think about this one a bit. Naturally, admitting to having any part in this was out of the question.

"Umm...no."

The Human raised an eyebrow. "You didn't do this?"

I glanced at it again and shook my head.

"So you're telling me you're innocent."

"Yep."

"Even though no one was home aside from you."

"Uh-huh."

"And you expect me to believe it?"

"Exaaactly."

There was an awkward pause as I stared at it and it likewise glared at me. We carried on that way for quite a bit longer than I realized was even possible; must have been about five to ten minutes and then finally?

"Well, I-I don't believe you."

My ears folded down. "You don't? I'm hurt! To think that I would be so rude as to disregard the rules."

"Get out!"

My ears perked up about this. Perhaps it had forgotten the dilemma I had with being outside. I took a few steps back and frowned. Maybe the sad eyes would help me here again. It was worth a shot anyway. I had just gotten them worked up into their ultimate state when an annoying ringing noise sounded from the other room. The Human looked at me, glared, and then dashed for the communication device.

That was fine with me. Meant I had a few minutes to think of what to do next. I could run and find a new place, but it was evening, probably swarming with Earthians, and then evening would lead into night which was...dark. Kind of like Spork's face when I told it I hadn't done the paperwork I was supposed to.

Have we discussed Spork? If not this is a topic we should cover. Spork is a unit in my crew—our interrogation officer, as a matter of fact. The job description in itself says a lot as to the character of it. Spork has a habit of sort of...well, I guess co-leading the crew, and when it gets something set in its mind, there really isn't any changing it; nor a desire to. Spork is tall and mean. The quick version, if it didn't even happen to show up, let's just say I wouldn't exactly miss it. How did I get off on that topic though? I was supposed to be plotting how I'd get out of this.

Toooo late. The Human was already back. I made a run for it, but I'd hardly gone any distance when I felt a hand tighten around the scruff of my neck. This was bad. I was tugged back, which sort of forced me to stumble along backward too.

"Out! I said you were going out!"

"But I don't have anywhere to go!"

"Too bad!"

"Remember the fate of the world—the fate of your friends, family—"

It opened the door.

"You can't do this to me!"

"Sorry, Kitty." It grumbled.

I clung to the doorframe as best I could, but it wasn't long until my grip faltered. I was slowly being yanked out into the cold, cruel world and—

"Mew!"

I lost my grip and we both tumbled. I ended up on top of the Human who had apparently broken my fall. But...I was almost certain that unless outside had obtained a barrier that looked like walls we weren't "outside."

"You can stay in here if you want," the Human huffed as it got up and dusted itself off.

I scrambled to my feet and looked around. I had neglected to notice the Human had turned on a light before we fell through.

The room was colder than the others had been and seemed a lot less friendly. There were metal benches with all kinds of strange, menacing tools and bottles. I didn't like the looks of this. It reminded me a lot of the areas Spork worked in. That was quite alarming.

Now I don't consider myself easily frightened, but let's just say this had gotten me shaking. I knew what Spork did to people. This Human...had I really messed up that bad that the Human was gonna—

"I'm sorry! Really! I know I shouldn't have eaten the food on the sofa or even been on the sofa. I'm really, really, super sorry!"

It just shook its head and turned away. Before I could follow, the door slammed shut. I was left all alone in the scary room. That was all part of the process. Spork did it too; leave them alone for a while, let them dread it. Well, I was certainly dreading it as I paced around.

There was a concrete floor, dim lighting, a whole display of violent tools— oh and a transportation vehicle. There was a car in the center. After coming to terms with my fate, I decided to look at some of the labels to see just what kinds of horrors awaited me. The first read "tire shine." Odd, but I didn't like it. I set it down, let a long yowl escape and then flopped down on the concrete.

A puff of dust rose up around me. It tickled my gills and made me sneeze. I stayed there for quite a while considering my fate, my crew's incompetence, and a number of other depressing thoughts. It was unfortunate that someone like myself would be needlessly sacrificed.

• • • ● • ● • • •

I must have dozed off for a while. It was to be expected after all the work I had accomplished within the day. I was pretty cold and stiff upon prying myself up off of the cold concrete. I don't recommend sleeping on concrete if you can avoid it. The cold seeps right through your bones to zap all of your life energy.

My life energy had been sufficiently zapped and I had to limp around a bit to get all of my various limbs functional again. Perhaps I had dozed off for more than "a while." I wasn't entirely clear on what lengths of time had gone by. I had no clock in the prison cell and no light of day could penetrate these walls of iron.

I yowled a sad song with no true words. It would have had words if I could've thought them up, but I'm not the best song-writer on the spot. I need a little more time to think these things out. It was definitely a song about the sadness and depression that hovers around a 'deviv caged like an animal. Touching song.

Near the end of the...hm, not sure which verse, had been singing it for quite a while, something strange caught the corner of my Visual Scanners. I rotated the position of my head to track the "something" to its source. Strangely enough, it appeared to be light. Furthermore, this light appeared to be coming from a small gap beneath a primitive, manual-rising panel door.

The door began to rise. I took a few steps back to give it some space. At once, blinding light attacked my eyes. I hissed and scrambled back after tripping over a can or two that I had knocked down during the performance of my song and brief but fierce rebellion against my prison cell.

Once my Visual Scanners adjusted the brightness and contrast ratio, I was able to make out a vaguely humanoid shape. Within a few more seconds, I could make out even more details about this individual. Unless I was mistaken, which is not often the case, before me was standing the Human who had placed me here in the long past early evening. Its head fur looked even more chaotic than it had during our last meeting.

It grumbled something as it fought with the panel door for a moment then sighed.

"Hey, Kitty."

5

Or this Home Could Work

I WASN'T SO SURE how to respond to that. I mean, it had just locked me up, what I now assumed had been all night, leaving me to dread my fate. Now it had made it easy for me to escape and greeted me like we were buddies! I decided to welcome myself outside before taking any additional action. Better safe than sorry. At least this way if the Human decided to chase me, I'd have a better chance of escape.

I gave the Human a most disapproving glare, but it seemed oblivious.

"You hungry?"

Aha, so it seemed it was going to play dumb. I decided I'd ignore it, bet that would teach it. It finally seemed to pick up on what I was doing and frowned.

"What's wrong, Kitty?"

"First off, my name is *Smiley*, not Kitty—"

"Smiley? That's a weird name. I've barely seen you smile the whole time."

I grabbed the hood of my uniform and flung it back, leaned my head forward, and pointed at the smiley faces on the backs of my ears. "This is why!"

"Well, I suppose that makes sense. Why are you so ill-tempered all of a sudden?"

"You locked me in your torture chamber all night! Why do you think?"

"That's not a torture chamber."

"Oh really? Then what exactly is it, huh?"

"My garage," the Human stated as it walked inside said chamber. "Where I keep my car and such."

My ear twitched. A garage? Was that like a hangar? That would explain why the transportation vehicle was there. Why hadn't it told me that before? Some people!

"I know it's not exactly the best place to keep a house guest, but you messed up my house, Kitty."

"Smiley."

"Smiley." It repeated back. "So of course I'm going to be a bit upset."

"You kicked me out."

"I'm sorry, okay? You can leave if you want. I was trying to protect you."

I contemplated it right then, leaving. There had to be more alien-friendly Earthians in the area; on the flip side of that, there were probably a lot of less alien-friendly Earthians as well. Meh, what was a simple misunderstanding among friends? Any decent Qwuedeviv would give the guy a second chance.

The conversation in between there and the house wasn't all that exciting or interesting so I'll cut through most of that. We had gone inside and I was now sitting at a table. It was kind of too tall for me—obviously, no one had taken my kind into consideration when they had made it. My feet couldn't quite touch the floor, and the chair itself was kind of uncomfortable. Made out of wood. Who makes a chair out of wood? That's just poor design.

"Mmm," the Human exclaimed as it flipped the contents of a food can it had placed in a pan on the stove. "This smells great. You a fan of canned beans and sausage, Kitty?"

"I'm not sure I know what it is, Human, but I'm sure it will quell the savage beast."

The Human chuckled after that for some reason. Not sure what it found funny about the savage beast. I mean I very easily could have eaten it or something for all it knew. Well, in reality, I couldn't. It was far too big and I was far too small. Now Cloudy might have been able to do something like that, but Cloudy wasn't here.

"So tell me Kitty, er, Smiley, how'd you get here? No one seems to have noticed anything."

"Of course they haven't. I arrived in my drop pod. It self-destructed after I got here. Your Human news reporters probably suspect it was some delinquent Earthian kittens.

"You mean kids." It stirred the contents of the pan again. "But if your ride home exploded, how will you get back?"

You know, the thought hadn't really occurred to me until then. How *was* I supposed to get home? The drop pod was only meant for, well, dropping, not bringing me back. I had no method of communicating with Headquarters currently and I was stranded from the rest of my crew. How was I supposed to rule the planet singlehandedly and get back home to brag about it?

That sort of changed a lot of things and I found myself spiraling into a dark pit of despair. What was I doing? Sitting here in the enemy's house, waiting for breakfast. Krillfish! Was I a prisoner of war? What was I going to do? Hopeless ...helpless...

"I...I have no way home."

"No?" The Human was done cooking the food by now and had begun sliding off hunks of the stuff onto two plates.

"I have no communication with Headquarters. My drop pod was never meant to return home anyway."

"Oh...that's no good." It sat down at the table and picked up a fork. "Can't you use our satellites or something? Aliens always seem able to utilize those in movies and such."

"Perhaps my tech unit or mechanic could, but it's really not my department."

The Human shoved a forkful of the salty food in its mouth. "You said you were the only one."

"Only one here currently. There's a few others stranded somewhere. Probably dead."

"Oh..." It frowned, "Sorry for your loss."

I sighed and lifted a pawful of the gunk to my mouth and shoved it in. Even through the bitter tang of sorrow, it tasted pretty good.

"Well, they're bound to notice you're missing eventually, right? Then they'll come look for you."

"Not likely. Not with our numbers." I took several more forkfuls of the stuff. This Human food was tasty! I could get used to it for sure.

The Human thought about that for a few moments and then nodded.

"Well, you know I've kind of always wanted a pet. Kitties are cute and cleaner than dogs..." It turned to look at me. "Kitty, if you'd like, I'd be honored to have you as my cat."

Under normal circumstances, I wouldn't have cared. I'd have had no reason to. A Human offering a military officer their home as a pet? Huh! The nerve. But right then, I was lonely and desperate. I didn't want to be stranded on this planet all alone. I didn't want to become a science experiment for someone. And this Human...it...it actually *liked* me.

I'm sure my eyes were adorable and shiny because it felt like I was on the verge of tears as I leaned forward on the table towards the Human, mouth wide in a big smile.

"You...you wouuuld?"

It was a touching moment in the history of our two species. I launched myself into its open arms, and for a brief moment, we hugged. That is classified information by the way. No one is ever to find out that I hugged a Human.

It laughed, cried and petted my head. I purred. Yes, it truly was an amazing time. There was an awkward moment as it drew to a close. I um, eventually made my way back to my chair and sat down to finish my breakfast.

"My name's Cedric by the way."

"Cedric..." I repeated back. "Well, my name is officially Qyrvus Mur'rak. My actual name is Qrr'keke'qrr Mur'rak. Before you ask, yes, there is a logical explanation for it, but we don't need to get into that right now."

"So where does Smiley come in then?"

"Oh, that?" I smiled. "Simple! That's my earth name! We all have one."

"Handy. The other would be hard to remember."

I finished off my breakfast and purred. Maybe being an Earth house pet wouldn't be so bad. The Qwuedeviv military would be fine without me I was sure. They'd probably decide Earth was too dangerous for our kind and go invade another planet. Sure I'd miss being around my own kind, but...I was sure Earth had plenty to offer a poor, blue-gray Qwuedeviv like myself.

"Please don't take this wrong, but what are you exactly?"

"A kitty of course!" I purred.

Cedric scratched at its head a bit. "I meant more like...if you had an actual species name or something."

"I'm a Qwuedeviv."

"A Qwuh-what?"

"Kweh-deh-viv." I repeated, slower this time so the Human could follow the sound.

Cedric tried repeating the name to itself a few times. None of the pronunciations were exactly correct, but it was close enough and Cedric seemed proud of itself anyway. That was fine with me; let the simple-minded Human feel it had succeeded.

"I guess I'll need to pick up a few things for you then..." its voice trailed off as I presume it was making a mental list of the things needed to support a pet properly.

Well, good, a responsible pet owner was a good thing to have, and I was proud that mine seemed to be taking proper initiative in this endeavor. It happened to glance at the clock on the wall then.

"Where does the time go?" it whined as it sprang from the table, hitting its knee in the process.

I watched as it hopped around for a bit, yowling in pain. Once it had gathered its composure, it obtained an unmarked black briefcase and tied the laces on its shoes—they had previously been untied you see.

"Sorry Kitty, er, Smiley, or whatever it is you want to be called. Can't be late for work."

6

Smiley—Me! Because
I'm Adorable!

FROM THE SHORT TIME I had been here, it seemed Cedric did a lot of work and running. Perhaps he even ran for work. Yes, I said he. Turns out, unlike us, Qwuedeviv, many Humans use gender-exclusive pronouns regardless of whether they're on active duty or not. Seemed like a pointless complication of life to me, but that was what they did. I wasn't entirely up to date on every little detail of Human behavior you see.

I had had better days, but I had also had worse. At least I had a place that was confirmed to be my new home. That was always something to fall back on—less satisfying than invading, but better than death in my opinion.

I took the time while Cedric was gone to better acquaint myself with my new home. It was mostly a lonely and boring day as I had pretty much already discovered all there was to see on the first day. Nothing had changed that much so after a brief walk, I lounged on the sofa and took a few naps.

Occasionally, I'd poke my head over by a window and see what the world was up to. The world never seemed to be up to anything in my range of sight though. Life around Cedric's home was boring. It didn't even have all the neat lit up pathways and such like the base back on Qwuh-9 did.

I was actually thankful when Cedric returned that night—I never expected to crave and need the attention of an inferior Earthian Human, but I had to do what I had to do, and what I had to do was be this Human's friend or pet or whatever.

He sighed as he pushed the door open. Both arms were occupied by what appeared to be a couple of paper bags. A set of crinkly, noisy bags dangled from his hands as well. He was also balancing his car keys on the top of one finger and paper documents in his mouth. I simply watched him walk by into the kitchen and then followed after him.

Almost all of the Human's supplies made it onto the counter when he flopped them down with a huff, all aside from the bag of fruit, which rolled across the floor. One Earth Fruit rolled near me so I decided to drop to all fours and bat at it a bit. Instinctual battle training I'm sure.

My tail flicked back and forth as I hunted the stray fruit right up until Cedric came and took it away, mumbling something about its slippery properties. That fruit was not slippery at all for the record. It was Cedric's faulty grip on them that had been problematic. I decided against correcting the mistake for the time being though.

"Smiley Kitty," he eventually acknowledged with what seemed to be a halfhearted smile.

"Do you have work every day?" I asked.

"Most days," Cedric replied as he moved about the small kitchen, unpacking a variety of things, "why?"

"Because it gets boring here."

"You've hardly been here for a day, how can you—"

"Trust me, I can tell."

"Well, what would you normally do during the day?"

I supposed invade planets and plot world conquest was not the proper or acceptable answer so I skipped that one.

"Oh...I don't know."

"I got you this."

Cedric was holding out some sort of extra soft earth creature plush with long feathery tails. It certainly didn't look like anything I had seen before but I had to admit those feathery tails were tempting to bat at. I reached out towards it...and batted at the tails instead. Cedric let it drop to the floor as he stood up to finish his unpacking again.

Poor Human had a short attention span. One moment he was playing with me—er training with me—and the next he was preoccupied with his food rations.

"What do you even do when you go away?" I asked as I gave the toy another bat. I stopped it from getting out of my reach with my left paw and then gave it two quick bats with my right.

"Computer stuff—I work as one of the On Call Computer Repair Specialists."

"That's nice."

"You don't have a clue what that is, do you?"

"It's not like I spend all my life researching Humans."

"I'm not sure if that clarification is comforting or concerning," Cedric answered.

I personally didn't care which he felt it to be. I had decided I'd welcome myself to look through the goods he had brought back. After all, seeing as I was now a member of this squad, I had the right to put out a search warrant on the rations and claim anything that seemed particularly delicious for my own consumption.

I rummaged through one of the bags he wasn't in the process of putting away. It was mostly canned stuff and a thing of socks, but by the third one I had found something that looked promising.

"Cookies," I proclaimed and took the little plastic case out.

"Mm, yeah," Cedric replied as he reached up to put something in one of the upper cabinets—he sure was slow at putting stuff away, "it's for the work meet—HEY!"

He had turned around right then and had noticed me sitting there I guess. I had been gnawing at the side of the plastic for a bit—didn't seem to be a simpler way to open the darn thing—as I had been supervising his slow progress.

I stopped gnawing so I could reply.

"What?"

Gnawing resumed.

"They're for the work meeting tomorrow," Cedric sighed and pushed the corner of his glasses.

I stopped gnawing on the container of deliciousness and frowned. I thought the cookies were much more suited for me than work, but...I held out the container to Cedric who only sighed again and shook his head.

"I can't take it like that now."

I looked at the container of cookies. What was his problem with it? Yes, it was chewed around the edges—well, somewhat deformed, really—shark teeth can do a number on plastic. The important thing, though, was the treasure inside—which was perfectly safe still. Yes, so it had a bit of alien saliva on it. It'd be dry by morning!

"You might as well eat them now," Cedric grumbled and took the plastic container.

He opened it up, set some of the cookies on a plate, and handed it back to me. I purred a thank you and took the plate, tossing a cookie into my enormous, deadly jaws. The cookie had no chance and was crushed immediately. It was actually one of the tastier earth foods I had eaten so far. They made an excellent sugar food that was for sure—better than the ones I had tasted on my home planet even.

Cedric set aside one of the bags and complained quite a bit as he hunkered down and sat a short distance in front of me. He rested his elbows on his knees and supported his chin with them. I wasn't sure if he wanted me to share the cookies he had just given me, but I knew for a fact that he had more of them—I'd much prefer him to go eat those instead of mine, so I made no acknowledgment of his subtle hints.

"It's strange," he mused in a wistfully distant manner, kind of like he was some old guy with great knowledge now, "you're so much like us."

My ears perked up as I munched another cookie. I couldn't hear much of what he was saying after that second one; something about cookies being normal and more alike than the Humans had realized. *Munch, munch, munch,* had to feed the inner savage beast.

"So I've got a question. Would it be safe to assume that the media grossly exaggerates what the truth is about aliens?"

I was busy chewing on the most delicious chocolate chip cookie I had ever wrapped my mouth around in all my life when asked this. I gave a subtle shrug and nodded. Sure. Sounded good to me.

"So aliens really aren't out there plotting to take over Earth and all that invasion junk." Cedric shook his head and chuckled. "I should have suspected as much really. It only makes sense."

"Hmm," I mumbled in response.

That wasn't exactly true, but if it was what he wanted to believe, eh, easier for us to invade when we did decide to.

"So are there several other alien species among us that have been here for years and all that? I bet there are."

Cedric was one of those intellectual nerds. The kind that probably had no friends because no one had a clue what they were talking about. The kind who came home after finishing work that no one understood to make themselves weirder by coming up with alien theories.

"I don't keep up to date on all they're up to. Maybe."

"That's crazy."

I could think of something else that was crazy at the moment. Really, I had little interest in the subject he had chosen to talk about, but I figured I should at least humor the guy if I was going to be living here from now on. He was sort of functioning as my superior officer for the time being and the alien questions would get old fast.

"So do you have any amazing skills?"

"All my skills are amazing," I stated through a mouthful of half-chewed cookie.

"What can you do anyway? Aside from getting stuck in fences and devouring cookies like a beast."

"Plenty," I replied, "you'll see in time."

"I guess that's true. Besides, you've got a lot of adjusting to do, moving to this new planet and all."

"Very much so."

At that moment, I realized the whole plate of cookies had been depleted. This fact was rather disheartening, as I had quite liked the delicious little morsels. Gone so quickly. I licked around my mouth, capturing a few spare crumbs in the process.

I briefly wondered if my new lifestyle of sitting around all day and doing nothing but eating and watching the daily soaps would have negative effects on me, but I shrugged it away. It was probably nothing.

"Hey, Kitty, we should probably get a room prepared for you, huh?"

I nodded to this as well.

Cedric didn't invite me to help pick out my room upstairs. I hoped he'd choose a good one, although really, they all looked pretty much the same to me, and none of them had seemed particularly better than the other.

A little while later, Cedric invited me upstairs and showed me to a room down the hall. It was pretty much at the opposite end of where he was, I noted. This probably held some significance; like perhaps he didn't want me to be near him, or perhaps he was planning top-secret military strategies.

My new room was pretty boring, although I'm not sure why I expected anything more from the most boring Earthian on the face of the Earth. It had a forest green bed and a shelf that was totally empty. That was another oddity about Cedric I didn't quite understand. He was just one Human living in this huge house—he couldn't possibly use all the rooms or for that matter, need them.

Back on Qwuh-9, we packed rooms to their maximum capacity. There wasn't any of this scattering around of resources. We just crammed as many Qwuedeviv and supplies into a room as possible without starting a big fight or riot. Yes, this was definitely odd.

"So...what you think?"

"Not the best décor," I stated, paws clasped behind my back as I inspected my new living quarters, "sort of drab color scheme."

"Seriously? I welcome you into my home and you're gonna—"

"Hush, hush, my Human companion. You asked for my opinion, did you not? As a lieutenant, I won't sugarcloth it, or whatever it is you Earthians say."

"A lieutenant?"

"Of...earth plantology...of course," I replied, and then grinned to assure him all was well.

He blinked a few times and shrugged.

"The room shall do splendid, Human."

"Why are you calling me Human? My name's Cedric."

"Of course, Fredrick." I steadily admired my new room and contemplated all the amazing things I could have in it if only I had my mechanic still.

"Cedric..." I heard him repeat again.

"Yes." I turned around partially so that I could see him. "Cedric. Let us go feast upon more cookies and bask in the glory of our success."

7

I'm Struggling for Names Here

FOR THE RECORD, ME and Cedric did feast on delicious cookies in celebration that night. Oh, the feast we did have. Actually, I had done most of said cookie devouring. Cedric didn't eat many of them—not that I particularly minded. He was too concerned about carbs catching up with him or something like that. I, on the other paw, was totally fearless of these "carbs".

Back to important matters, morning had come around and Cedric had gone off to work much like he had the other days. Once again, I was alone with nothing of interest to do and no one to bother. To top it all off, I didn't even have any cookies. That made things significantly less thrilling.

I resorted to watching the local Human live feed again, "TV" I believe Cedric called it. It had this rather antique remote device that would let me sift through channels. It was wireless, but that was about all that could be said for it. Human technology seemed to be rather outdated in comparison to our own—not that it was a huge surprise.

Sadly, there wasn't anything very interesting on this picture panel today. The Local News had been on one channel. Probably Cedric's favorite channel—he seems to prefer the boring channels. Anyway, there had been what I assumed to be a Human parental figure on this TV, complaining about the education quality its children were receiving and just what standard it should be at.

The way I saw it, this entire problem could be solved if the parental unit just taught its kit whatever it needed to know. That was the problem with Earth parents. They didn't bother to do any training. What was this society coming to? I had been here two days and already saw the deterioration of the planet I loved.

Did I say loved? Of course I didn't mean that. It'd make no sense. I'm a Qwuedeviv invader. Naturally, we hate Earth, so the previously mentioned statement would be void. Incorrect. There was a falsity in the recording of my—just don't read into that too much, okay? I was misquoted by lovers of Earth who wanted to perceive me as a different kind of being entirely.

After the news was over, I turned it off. The TV that is, not the news. The news was already off. I mean over. Moving on. From there, I pranced into the kitchen while humming the tune of an Earthian afternoon soap opera.

I figured I might as well clean up around the place while Cedric was away. Plus, I had learned you could input number codes on this thing he called a phone—mentioned in a previous log—and it would connect you to another Earthian. Sometimes Earthians called Cedric too—usually about work.

I was attempting to wash the dishes without actually getting wet when the phone decided to ring. I dropped the dishes right there—on the floor as a matter of fact. I'm pretty sure they broke but that was beside the point. I grabbed the phone and hit the talk button.

"Hellooooo," I greeted as I held the phone to the side of my furry face and hopped up on the counter to sit.

The Earthian on the other line was talking fast. I wasn't sure what they wanted me to respond with. I hadn't learned all of the Earthian language and this guy talking so fast was not helping at all.

"So how about lunch at three?" I had heard a Human reply with that on TV. The Earthian on the other line raised their voice even more. The nerve of some people.

"I don't have to tolerate this. I'm an independent citizen; I know my rights!"

I disconnected the call and set the phone back in its cradle with an angry swing. Earthians these days just had no manners! I could hardly believe how rude that Human had been. Maybe Cedric was the only nice Earthian on this planet. Was he the last of his kind? I watched a movie about that once!

Those thoughts only preoccupied me for two minutes max. After that, I was totally bored again. Washing dishes no longer sounded appealing, not that it really had to begin with. It was even less so now though with the broken glass and such all over the floor. I'd leave that for Cedric to deal with when he got back. It was his house after all.

Next, I tried reading one of the many magazines; those were the bound image manuscripts that he had lying around. Never again. Who knew they could cram so much boringness into a few thin pages? I'd have to help him discover better uses of his time at some point. Slave species or not, this was pathetic.

On a search driven by pure boredom, I opened a few of the books he had around and found nothing interesting in them, so I decided to infiltrate the Human's Headquarters, also known as his personal room. This was a total breach of etiquette but sometimes boredom called for breaking a few normal protocols. I was sure Cedric would rather me be in his room than die.

I pushed open the door that hadn't been fully closed to begin with and ventured inside. There was a pair of fuzzy slippers right by the door. They actually looked pretty great to roll on top of, but I resisted the urge for the moment. I figured I could find better than that.

His room was surprisingly boring like the rest of his house. He had a giant bed that I immediately set out a search warrant on and investigated. It was plush, softer than my bed was. Figured. Cedric was holding out on me. Then again, he was the owner of this domain, so I supposed it only made sense. Later, I'd overthrow his rule and become supreme leader, then I would take his room.

I hopped on the nearby dresser from there and knocked a couple of picture frames over in the process. That was his own fault for not leaving a pathway for me to walk on.

I didn't find anything at the end of the dresser though, so I went ahead and hopped off of it. It was then that a bluish light caught my eye. On the other side of his bed—the side I had just been on previously—there was a blue light emitting from a device. It was a primitive Earth computer by the looks of it. Now there was something that could probably prove interesting.

I pushed the screen open the rest of the way and poked at the screen a bit. It hadn't gone into a power save mode yet so I didn't have to put in any password—score! Cedric had left a whole surplus of interesting links open so I spent a good bit of time investigating them. He seemed mighty interested in aliens.

One was posting on a message board, asking hypothetically what others would do if they were confronted by an alien. Another asked what the survival chances were when befriending an alien. There was also an email addressed to "mom," and a whole list of alien and pet websites, an odd assortment for sure. There were also a few things about laws and alien sightings. My ears twitched.

So! All this time Cedric had been plotting behind my back! I knew I shouldn't have trusted the Human. On the other paw, he fed me, gave me a nice place to stay, and generally protected me from all the outside threats, and as far as I could tell, he wasn't acting on anything against me here...so given the options...I decided to pretend I hadn't seen the computer and moved on.

Eventually, I concluded that Cedric's room was boring, too; left with nothing but my thoughts and a house that was emptier than one might have realized. Trust me, if you had to sit there and act like you were reading for as long as I had to actually sit there and do nothing, you would be bored out of your skull. Seriously, it was that bad.

So instead of boring you out of your skull, I decided I'd fill this part with a little bit of info about myself. Second Lieutenant Smiley, as I mentioned before, kin of Dr. Leech, Supreme Major General of our whole species. That was no little deal ya know. Pretty much made me a celebrity.

Now, our species was a bit different than what I had observed here. I wasn't entirely sure how this Earth's leadership worked but ours was run by our military. In fact, my entire species is one big military.

We invade every land we come across—that is our skill and mission in life. Why? Well, I can't say I know for sure, but it's what we do. Earth was on that list as well. Hopefully the Earthians wouldn't mind much; after all, it's nothing personal, it's just what we do.

8

Never Trust a Cactus

*T*HIS LITTLE TALE *I'M* telling you could get drab really fast. The following days I didn't have a whole lot to report. This "work" that Cedric partook in made him have a similar schedule each day. He would make some kind of breakfast for us in the morning and then head off to work, remaining there much of the day. Speaking purely from an observational military standpoint, it wasn't the best of choices he could have made. With so much time away from his base, it could have easily been taken over by another Human or an alien kitty.

After some time, I had gotten him trained to remember to make me some food for lunch and dinner before he left instead of just breakfast. I suppose I could've figured it out myself, but that wasn't particularly interesting.

Every day had been nearly the same as the one before. Sit, eat, look around, observe the occasional life form outside of the household, and bat at the toys Cedric had picked up at the local pet shop. Life felt very...lacking. It was good that I had a place to stay now, but it didn't take away the lonely feeling. I had never considered myself the needy type. I didn't need company; I was like a one-cat wrecking machine. At least I thought I was up until this point, but it turns out the lack of company made everything boring beyond words.

I rolled off the sofa to pace the house another time. I had lost count of all the times I had done so. Nothing ever changed and the interior was a little dull in comparison to what I was accustomed to. Unlike the halls of the Academy, which were kind of rounded and white with various colors running through the walls in circuit-like patterns, Cedric's were a flat off-white—kind of like he hadn't painted in a while. Knowing his lack of motivation for most household chores, he probably hadn't. I mean the guy would wait until he had run out of clothes before doing his laundry. That should say something.

I wandered through the kitchen, which was equally dull. I hadn't visited many true kitchens on Qwuh-9, so I couldn't say how they compared, but I assumed these Earthian ones were far below standard, just as their walls were.

I continued onward. The kitchen stopped shortly after and led to a little entryway for the other door. I made a right turn from there. Cedric's house kind of looped in a circle and there were a lot of halls. I was currently positioned in one of said halls—one that went both right and left. I knew there were a couple of random rooms in both directions, but rooms were currently not on the list of objectives.

I headed left down the hall. It was boring and plain—not even a single picture. Clearly Cedric had no decoration crew for this base of his. I paused near a room with an open door—the utility or laundry room or something like that. I had heard Cedric refer to it as such. Said room had a window in the rather beat-up-looking door that led to the exterior. I couldn't see out of it as well as I would have liked to, so I found a stepladder to stand on.

Outside looked like a lot more fun to be amidst than in Cedric's house. It was more colorful for a start and secondly—Great Northern Sea Cucumber! There was the strangest Earthian plant I had ever seen before right there on the back deck. It looked so strange that I wasn't even sure it *was* an Earthian plant. It could've been an invader from another planet—trying to steal *our* planet out from under our paws.

No plant was going to take Earth out of Qwuedeviv possession while I was around. Oh, I also wouldn't let them take over Cedric's base either. Cedric may not have known the first thing about military tactics—odd that they had set him up as commander, come to think of it—but *I* did. I could tell a threat when I saw one.

Another look was required. This "plant," or potential alien, was greenish. This was a customary Earth plant color, but that proved nothing. You see, Earthians also depict aliens as being these large-headed, black-eyed, green things. This plant alien was not only green, but it also had *hair* or something that at least looked like hair. Very strange, and you know what I always say about strange things; they need further, skillful investigation.

I didn't suspect wandering in the backyard would be too dangerous. I was capable of handling the plant alone and I couldn't see any other threats. So for the very first time since I had arrived, I headed out. There was a conveniently placed door there if you recall, so I simply moved the stepladder and used it—the door, not the ladder.

I pushed the door open just a bit and stopped to listen for uninvited guests or lurking Earthians. I didn't see any, which was probably good. I didn't suspect Cedric wanted stray Earthians in his yard.

With all precautionary measures taken in this military operation, I flung the door open wide and happily frolicked out into the open. It was a tad cooler outside than it had been in the house, but nothing too bad. The suspicious plant hadn't moved. I approached it quickly and sized it up.

It was one of the bigger ones I had come across so far—not that I had really been outside if you recall. From its rounded pottery vessel to its alien-plant head, it reached my shoulders in height.

"Hello, Plant; I am Second Lieutenant Smiley, Commander of Qwuedeviv Crew 52. State your alliance."

I waited. It didn't answer. I waited longer. It still didn't answer. Huh. Some commanders...

"Hey! Friend or foe!"

I gave it a jab with a finger.

"Meowch!"

Sharp pain pulsed through my finger. I retreated a safe distance, clutching my injured arm. I checked to make sure the plant hadn't followed before tending to my wound. Those of you with weaker stomachs may not want to read this part. These are the kinds of things that can traumatize a soldier. I won't blame you if you just want to skip this section and move on to a happier log. Maybe try a couple down from this one.

Are you sure you're up for this? Well, we'll see.

When I looked down at my paw, there was a sharp spike lodged in my finger. It was probably poisonous. I was probably doomed. Twenty-four hours max.

"So, you're a foe." My ears pinned down as I bravely and carefully closed my fist.

If this was the end, I wouldn't go down without a fight. My time on Earth had been difficult and it seemed its inhabitants had no intent of showing any mercy.

"You just messed with the wrong cat." My finger was throbbing by this point, but I ignored it. "If it's a fight you want, I'm just the Qwuedeviv to give it to you!"

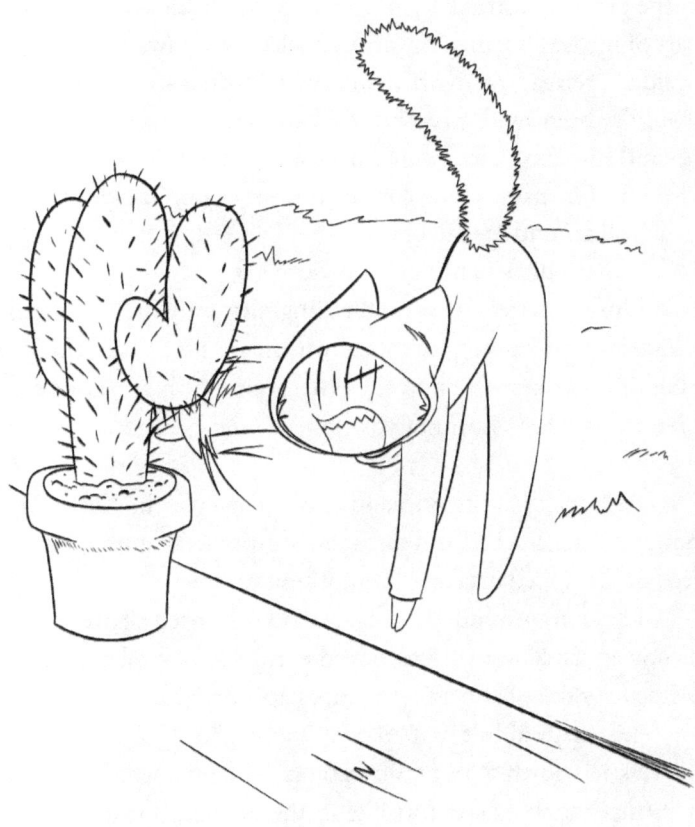

Everyone at Command Center cried for me to stop; they didn't want their hero to go down in such a gruesome war. I shut out their pleas and launched myself into battle.

First contact was brutal. I knocked the alien plant over, but in the process, it struck with lightning speed. All at once, every part of me was hurting: my arms, my legs, my paws, my body. I decided a retreat was in order and twisted with swift grace. Or it would've been swift grace, but the dumb thing snagged my tail fur and launched itself at me from behind. I didn't have time to avoid it. The plant made connection yet again. Prickling pain struck all around my tail base.

"That's dirty fighting!" I yowled.

Unfortunately, it was still clinging to my tail. I started panicking and running chaotically in an attempt to confuse it. Half of its strikes were hits, the others misses. I battled bravely, unleashing a fury storm of yowls, hisses and occasional bats at the beast.

At last, it lost its grip and crashed against the house. Its pottery vessel cracked and dirt spewed from its wound. Within seconds, it tipped over and lay motionless.

I held my ground, panting. My body burned all over from its poison darts. Many were lodged in my fur. Several more had pierced my skin. With a slight limp, I approached.

"Plant...it didn't have to be this way..."

I knelt down to rest my paw on its battle-damaged warship in a final touch of comfort like in the movies, but it had the nerve to push one of its darts in further. I jumped to my feet with a hiss and kicked the pot as hard as I could. It rolled a bit and more dirt fell out.

Feeling satisfied, I left it on the deck and went to live out the remainder of my hours. I figured I had nothing to lose now so there was no need to go inside or watch out for Earthians. Cedric would miss me, but he'd get over it eventually.

I found a nice tree to stand beside. It offered shade from the nonexistent heat. You see, it was actually beginning to get dark. It was fitting really. The sun of my life was setting, too. So I stood there—couldn't sit thanks to the poison darts embedded in my uh, well, the seat of my uniform; also known as Hindquarters.

I thought about the good 'ol days back on Qwuh-9—my home planet. Every day we practiced battling. Every day, I received notable mention for my incredible resolve to get the mission completed, even if it meant sabotaging the others. Ah, my younger days—the good 'ol days for sure. Back when Dr. Leech or any of the others could probably have found a cure for this.

I wiped a couple of tears from my eyes. I liked to imagine they were from fond memories, but I'm pretty sure it was because my tail had just brushed against the tree.

"Smiley?"

I turned my head slightly with a light, pained smile. It was Cedric. I must have been fading out not to have heard him coming.

"Hello, old friend." I looked to the sky once more.

"Old friend? We only met a week ago!"

I didn't reply—that's what they do in movies to make things more dramatic and heart-wrenching. His heart should be thoroughly wrenched.

"Is something wrong with you?" He was making his way over now from the back deck. "You're acting weird."

I lazily looked back at him. "Military life does that to people."

"Don't be ridiculous—you were fine this morning." Once he reached my location, he squinted his eyes. "Wait a second...military life? You told me you were here to observe and learn."

It seemed the poison had weakened my resolve not to disclose my true intentions, my true identity, and my top-secret credentials of being amazing. It was probably for the best that Cedric knew who his friend truly was before death though.

"There are many things about me you do not know," I sighed, "Poison darts. I suspect I only have a few hours to live."

He raised an eyebrow and marched back to the porch. I couldn't say I blamed the guy. It was hard news to take so suddenly. Soon his life would be empty and have no meaning. He also would have failed to have properly secured his home for a pet. His negligence had led us to this.

After he had gathered his composure and set the fallen enemy back up—with less dirt I could bet—he began heading my way again. I breathed heavily as I struggled to come to terms with the dramatic end.

"You messed with the cactus? Why?"

I assumed "cactus" was the alien plant's name.

"It struck first. It was merely protocol to—"

"My mother gave me that back when I moved out. I've kept it alive all this time—don't kill it."

How disgusting! Here his best friend was on the verge of death and he chose to side with the enemy.

"You...I...I can't—" I coughed, carefully clutching my throat.

"You're being dramatic. That's what."

Without warning, he reached over and pulled a dart from my side.

"Mew! Erm..." I looked both ways. "I mean, um, meow...yes."

"They're just cactus needles," Cedric continued with a roll of his eyes behind those reflecty glasses. "They aren't going to kill you."

"No?" Command Center issued the order to raise one ear into Alert Position.

"No. But they *could* cause a nasty infection. We better get them out."

9

This is Why You Shouldn't Trust a Cactus—The Extended Edition!

GETTING THE "CACTUS NEEDLES" out was not a fun process. We had worked on the easier ones earlier, the ones in my paws. I wasn't about to trust the Human to deal with the others though. No one was permitted to touch my tail, and Hindquarters was a sensitive region.

"But they'll get infected," Cedric insisted again, "and sore. Then we'll have to take you to a vet or wherever you take an alien cat and get you treated."

"Don't care."

"Not to mention you won't be able to sit."

"I've always preferred standing."

He huffed and tried to grab one stuck in my tail fur anyway. I got out of the way and hissed.

"Oh, come on."

"No!"

He crossed his arms and stood there rigidly, tapping a foot.

"Well, obviously, you just *want* to hurt then. Is that what it is? Do you *want* to have to go to the vet and get strapped down to have infected cactus needles pulled out? All because *someone* was being too big a baby to let their friend help them?"

Yes, as a matter of fact, because I was nearly sure that wasn't what would happen.

"And then have the vet suspect you might be an *alien* cat and ship you off to the—"

"Alright, alright fine."

Cedric nodded and sat down on the sofa, motioning for me to come over. I did, but I was a little confused when he patted his leg. Unless his leg could make miracles happen, I wasn't sure of its importance. He seemed to catch on and lifted me up by my scruff until I was standing on tiptoe. He pulled me towards his legs, so naturally, I braced my arms against said legs and pulled back.

"Smiley!" Cedric growled, still trying to pull me forward. I shook my head to both sides and struggled to keep back. "I'm trying to help you!"

"Are not!"

"It's the easiest way to reach the others!"

You know what? Suddenly, that sort of made sense. I struggled less after that. I was a bit unsure if I liked it or not, but I would tolerate it for now. It didn't seem like the best position to run from if needed though.

"Just make yourself comfy and don't worry—it shouldn't take long."

I rolled my eyes and grumbled as I got myself situated across his lap. I had the sofa to rest on as well—so it wasn't too bad.

Cedric started with my tail. They weren't really stuck in it, just tangled. Occasionally one would poke me, but not often.

"You know, you're a weird little alien." Cedric chuckled. "Don't they teach you about stuff before they ship you out?"

"We're the ones in charge of finding stuff out, remember?"

I picked at a poof of lint on the sofa as I half-grumbled the response. Cedric was mighty chatty for the current circumstances. I wasn't nearly as amused.

"Oh, right, so not everything you told me was a lie." Cedric pulled out one of the ones that hadn't been positioned in my tail. It didn't feel good, so I growled.

"Well, you're certainly the right cat for the job."

"Naturally—mew!"

Another there. This could be a really long process.

"Calm down. It's nothing to get worked up about."

"Oh yeah? *You* try getting cactus needles stuck all over your—" He pulled another right then. "Meowwww. Shouldn't you have, like, some no-pain surgery meds? I shouldn't be awake for this! What are you? Pokeyoo?"

"Wuh? I don't know who or what a Pokeyoo is, but it's a few cactus needles. Trust me, you'll live."

"Easy for you to—mew!—say! You're not the one—mew!—okay, seriously, stop!"

He did and I scrambled off his lap a good distance away so I could scowl safely.

"They're all out anyway."

"You monster."

"Thank you works just as well."

"Uh-huh." I rolled my eyes.

He just yawned and looked at the clock. It was pretty late by now.

"Goodnight, buddy. Try and stay out of trouble, okay?"

I had been lost in thought when he'd spoken up.

"What?"

"I said, be good. I'm going to sleep."

"Oh. Right. Sure."

I nodded briefly to him and headed into the guest room on the base level. Cedric slept upstairs so down here seemed like an ideal spot to keep the lights on unnoticed. It was time for some research.

It didn't take long to gather all the necessary supplies. I just had to take Cedric's laptop he had specifically asked me not to touch. With that and an adequately well-lit room, I settled into my box, pulled the laptop on my belly, and got to work. In case you were curious, yes, my injuries all felt significantly better by now.

Cedric had this odd picture set as the desktop. It was a bunch of people who looked like him, his family, I guess. I typed in "cactus" after the browser had pulled up. Cactus brought up tons of results, but it seemed I was on the right track. They totally resembled each other.

About two hours later I had gathered enough information. I honestly wished I'd had my tech unit there—or anyone. I'd have them write it down to send to our official Headquarters back home on Qwuh-9, but I didn't even own a notebook.

I set aside the computer and crawled out of my bed to turn off the light. Research makes a kittyshark tired and I'd need all the rest I could get for the next day. Maybe my injuries would feel better too.

10

Mr. Smith is an Ideal Athlete

"*KITTY? HERE KITTY, KITTY.*"
My ears perked up but I was still face down on the pillow in my favorite cardboard box.

"Kitty." I heard again.

I grumbled and pushed myself up partially. Cedric hadn't quite picked up on the fact I wasn't *exactly* the same as their Earth cats. Oh well, another day.

I crawled out of my bed. Command Center and such didn't seem fully coherent yet, so I had to rely on my own intuition. I navigated through the door and blinked a few times to get my Visual Scanners working— eyes that is. Or, well, that is the closest thing I can relate my high-tech properties to. A doctor would call them the same exact thing in fact.

"Right here," I replied and waited to hear him again.

"Oh, there you are." He appeared from behind and picked me up before I could protest. "How are you feeling today, Kitty?"

"It's Smiley," I grumbled and batted at his hand when he tried to pet my head, "and I'm fine."

"Great." He set me down and patted my head.

I glared at him. He didn't seem to be paying attention though. He probably wanted to tell me he was going to work. That meant I had already overslept. Ever since I'd gotten to this pathetic planet, I'd had this sleeping issue. I slept a lot, but then come to think of it, I had had that problem back home too. Guess it wasn't the planet and perhaps just my— never mind that.

"Kitty?"

Cedric was still standing there, weird creature. "You sure you're alright?"

"Fantastic," I replied.

He gave a half nod. "Well then, I better go to work. Breakfast is on the table."

"Yes," I answered, blinked and looked up again. "Have a great day."

Cedric gave me a second glance and nodded.

I waited until I heard the click of the front door and his car pulling out. Now it was my turn.

You probably thought today's mission involved cacti, didn't you? Sorry to disappoint you, but no. I had only gathered the information to know how to deal with them just in case they decided to launch a counterattack.

No today, I had decided Earth didn't look so intimidating. I would venture out and see it for myself; I wasn't gonna just sit around a house for the rest of my life. After adjusting my uniform and pulling the hood up, I headed out into the unknown.

Cedric's neighborhood had seemed equally as boring as he was from my time peering out of the windows. Upon leaving the front steps, my opinion hadn't changed. The lawn monster was dormant for the time being, but I still crept by with care not to wake it. Cedric insisted it was merely a "sprinkler" for watering the grass. I wasn't sure I believed that.

For the first time in quite a while, I left the front gate—Cedric had left it unlocked, so I didn't have to crawl over the top or under the bottom. The point being, it was a lot more pleasant this time around.

After I got out of the place, I headed down the street. I had done this once before when I first arrived here, but I really didn't remember many of the details. That was fine with me, though; made it more scenic and such.

Now my whole objective today was classified. A lot of my life is classified as you may have noticed. This tends to happen when you are a figure of significant importance. However, the important part of today was that I knew what my objective was.

I made a few turns here or there and trailed along empty roads—this was all good for me because I wasn't supposed to be seen by the enemy. Many of you might wonder why I was out here then. Night would have seemed like a better time to travel. Yes. To a common Earthian's brain, it would seem that way, but trust me, that was not the case, or I would have done so. You don't need to question my judgment. This was what I had been trained for.

After a few more roads, I happened upon a dilemma. There were more frequent Earthian sightings. Some were driving Earth vehicles and others simply walked. This would have intimidated a lesser Qwuedeviv into retreat. Not me.

Whenever an Earthian would get near me, I could hear it. So when I began hearing it, I would just dart towards the nearest hiding spot. It took a little longer this way than if I had just been prancing along, but as Commander Easy Cheese would say: "Wars aren't won without lunch." Words to live your life by those are.

After I made it through the more city-like portion of the Earthian grounds, I came across a most peculiar place. It was all fenced off from the rest of the Earthian camp. The space was decent-sized, but I could see the end where the fencing started making a giant loop. Closer to where I was, there was a set of structures.

It all appeared to be made from processed native trees as opposed to a more efficient material. The structures themselves had no evident purpose from my observation—nothing beyond holding in place a slab of plastic that was connected to it by two ropes.

On said plastic piece sat an Earthian kit. It squealed in either terror or joy—I wasn't sure which—as its parental unit pushed the roped plastic. Perhaps it was an Earthian training exercise; it was a bit hard for me to figure out without the expertise and knowledge of Cheeseburger. Oh—that was our weapons developer and mechanic. The guy who builds and fixes stuff when we whine enough.

I crouched behind a fallen tree that had been abandoned beyond the camp. Observing these creatures could prove useful to Headquarters later. It was partially my responsibility to see to it since the rest of my crew was currently MIA—Missing in Action.

Around the Earthian kit and parental unit were several other structures. There was a horizontal ladder that was suspended in the air by two sets of pillars on either end—not sure how that would help very much. Then there was a ladder leading to the top of a plastic thing. The purpose of the exercise was unclear as well. The kit would climb to the top, slide down with a squeal, and repeat the process. Strange.

I made an intentional effort to avoid the kit and parent and rounded the curve of a big pond that was beyond the Earthian kit's playground. Just beyond my current location, a cluster of Earth trees welcomed me to the protection of their cover.

I wasn't too familiar with Earth plants, but they were darkish green and needly. Since they provided more cover and possibly more interesting things to look at, I headed that way.

I wove back and forth between the trees, making only the occasional stop to pounce upon a pitiful seedling. The ground beneath the Earth trees crunched like cereal as I walked on their needle-leaf sheddings. Speaking of cereal, I could go for some of that at the moment. I hadn't really considered bringing any food along with me. Now it seemed like a grossly overlooked preparation step. This was the sort of thing that happened when a crew lacked its Tactical Advisor though. Oh well, couldn't do much about it now.

Eventually, I reached the edge of the Earthian deep forest. I forgot to mention earlier, but it was totally a treacherous journey, and I came close to dying at least nine times. Savage aliens attacked once, and another time, the plants came alive and tried to swallow me whole. No joke. My superior, invaderly skills saved me though and now I was ready to face my next obstacle.

Prepare yourself for this; it may come as a shock. It could cause your heart to beat too many miles per hour and then you wouldn't have good fuel economy. Back to the topic at paw, if you don't mind, the risk of needing to pay a few extra dollars for fuel, I had just stumbled across a top-secret Earthian base.

Orangish-yellow battle buses were all aligned in their vehicle hangar—obviously a primitive model but nonetheless dangerous. They likely contained elite troops that all civilizations feared. That is why HQ chose someone as qualified as me after all. Anyway the orange battle buses and so forth were all aligned and so forthly forthingly...forth.

It was time for an investigation. I scanned the area with my high-tech Visual Scanners and attuned Ear Radar to pick up all frequencies. All checked out clear. It was time to move in and get a closer look. My ears lowered against my head in preparation for Sneak Mode as I lowered into a crouch. Keeping my tail just from brushing the ground, I crept closer.

The super-secret base was a surprisingly boring building. It had "School" written in large print along with a giant name that was probably known only by the coders of Earthian language—which is called Earthanese by the way; I know all these things.

The building itself had a lot of papers posted in windows and on plastic-covered boards. Most of it seemed to be indicating proper behavior of Earth kits with little visual graphs of horrible things like sharing and taking turns.

I hurried on before the brainwashing techniques could permanently damage my mind. In fact, I was in such a deep, mental struggle that I didn't notice I had run straight into danger. I should have suspected that the Earthians would pull such trickery on an innocent cat. They couldn't be trusted.

Just on the other side of the building was a field of caged kits. They squealed and pranced about in a horrifying display of total lack of control. It was a madhouse. Kits were kicking at sand in a giant box; others kicked at a ball that other kits wailed and chased after. Everywhere I looked there was another Earthian kit doing *something*.

Turns out I had been mistaken. It wasn't a secret base at all—it was Earthian Kitten Training Grounds!

In the midst of my horror and realization of the terrors that might befall my luxurious pelt if such a grubby-handed little beast was to grab hold of me, one of the previously mentioned beasts managed to breach our first line of defense and positioned itself right along the—

I hissed and spit like any fearless soldier would. Tail Fur puffed up to twice its size, which was just about maximum capacity on the intimidation scale.

That little beast had grabbed the fencing of the—oh. False alarm. Do you recall I mentioned the Earthian kits were caged behind fencing? Yeah, it couldn't reach me, thus there is no reason for you to be alarmed. Don't worry.

The Earthian kit may have startled me just a tad, but I recovered with unmatched swiftness.

"Looook!" the kit shouted and stuck its stubby finger through the fencing. "It's like Mr. Smith!"

Three additional kits scurried over to join the first. Two of them agreed that I looked like Mr. Smith while the third declared I didn't look like Mr. Smith at all. I wasn't sure who Mr. Smith was and had no intention of finding out.

"Kitty!" a higher-pitched Earthian kit squealed.

That sound could've ruptured eardrums. I shook my head, gave a light hiss, and backed up some. Their screeching had disrupted the calibration of my Auditory Radar System.

I wasn't one to hurt the kits if there was an alternative, but I wasn't going to let them defeat me either. Suddenly the other kits became interested in what was up and flocked over to the fence where I was. I issued another warning hiss. In a large group, they were a little more intimidating, you see, even with the fence between us.

All the kits began yowling then, reaching through the fence, murmuring "kitty kitty" in some babyish voice amongst other chatter. They could have been talking in code for all I knew, and I was growing increasingly uneasy.

"Mr. Smiiith!" another yowled.

Others soon joined in the chant for Mr. Smith, and before my very eyes, a large figure began making its way towards us. Mr. Smith towered over the children. Actually, Mr. Smith towered over me too. Instinctively, I tucked my ears down so they wouldn't be as visible. Think Earthian. Think Earthian.

The taller figure moved closer to the fencing, pushing aside a few of the kits in the process. I took a wary step back, prepared to run at any indication that Mr. Smith suspected I wasn't a fellow Earthian.

The kits were still squealing and hopping about. Terrible little distractions they were. My unease was increasing. Standing there in the open in a stare-down with Mr. Smith did not seem like a good idea.

The Earthian had a brownish-orange shirt on and the weirdest rainbow-visored helmet ever; hadn't seen an Earthian with one of those before. I also hadn't met an Earthian instructor though.

Mr. Smith grasped the top of the fencing and then...then Mr. Smith did something I didn't know Earthians could even do. He hopped the fence!

Mr. Smith could've easily been an athlete. He had the leg reach for almost any sport I could think of. That Earthian man—or what I was assuming was a man, based on the "mister" portion—had just cleared the final barrier of safety that I had set up. Well, I hadn't actually set up the Earthian fence, but it was still acting as my protection. If I hadn't already given the okay to unleash full fluff mode, I would've ordered it then. Since I had already efficiently covered that procedure though, and since it had had very little effect on Mr. Smith, I instigated full-scale retreat measures. There was a time to fight and there was a time to run like you'd never run before. Now was the latter.

11

I Get a Fancy Collar in this Chapter!

*A*CROSS THE PARKING LOT and back towards the forest that I had pranced through earlier, I charged onward in an all-out sprint. I probably didn't look like anything more than a bluish-gray blur. Mr. Smith was chasing and calling out to me. I couldn't really understand what he was saying but I also didn't want to.

I slipped on some of the needly leaves from a tree and went tumbling head over heels for an unknown length of time. Felt like an eternity. When I had finally stopped my helpless roll, I caught sight of Mr. Smith—upside down. Or rather, I was actually upside down, but whatever.

He had stopped at the edge of the Earthian parking lot. I guess Earthian Instructors couldn't travel on the dirt like I could. Lucky break. I didn't want to take any chances of him following after me though, so I broke out into a full-on sprint clear back to Cedric's yard.

Everything on my journey back flew by in one giant smear. If I ran past other Earthians, I didn't recall it at all. All l knew was my legs had never burned so bad before. My chest...it...well, it...it felt like it might explode at any—whew, you know, that was really a long run; perhaps I should've paced myself a tad more.

I grabbed at the fencing of Cedric's yard to hold myself up. Just a moment, that was all I needed to catch my breath. Yeah, that. That was all.

"There you are!"

I jumped with a sudden burst of energy and fluffed up. In one smooth turn, I had flipped direction entirely and now stood poised to confront my attacker—eyes aglow and sharp teeth bared. Command Center was ready to unleash everything they had on the enemy.

The only thing wrong with the whole deal was that it turned out to be Cedric. He wasn't exactly a threat; I was kind of thankful to see him after all of this actually.

I barely had time to look at him before he wrapped something around my neck and snapped it closed. I tried looking down at it but couldn't quite make out what it was.

"It's a collar."

I cast him a glance. Whatever was around my neck made a slight jingle.

"It says you're a legal pet basically."

"They let you have aliens as pets?" I asked once I had calmed down some.

I was still in the works of getting my fur flattened down, but that's just a consequence you have to deal with when you activate an expensive piece of war equipment like myself.

That aside, I didn't care how legal I was now. I had more important things to worry about. Things like Mr. Smith suddenly appearing at the gate and wanting to take me away to the labs or the government or the president of the world.

"Erm, well, not exactly," Cedric clarified, "you're listed as a Russian Blue."

I raised an eyebrow.

"It's a cat breed here. You kind of look like one with all the dense, blue-gray fur..." He must have detected I wasn't buying it because then he added, "A mutated one."

"Really?"

"Well..."

"I don't think so." I tugged at the collar some, but it wouldn't budge.

"Nooo, don't do that!" Cedric pushed my paw away. "If you get lost, it has my address—so you can get back."

"Hmm..." This was worth considering. "I suppose that makes sense."

Cedric stepped back to admire his choice. I tried looking down at it as well, but—no big surprise here—I still couldn't see it.

"So uh, does...does it look good?"

Funny how the entire topic of Mr. Smith had momentarily left my mind like that—almost like I had forgotten or something which, of course, I hadn't. I was just humoring Cedric so he didn't feel so bad about his life; that was all.

"Oh yes," Cedric said in the way he did whenever making a technical analysis he knew the proper answer to. "It complements the gray-blue fur."

"Considering this is coming from the guy who wears casual socks with his dress shoes, I'm not sure how to take that fashion compliment."

He chuckled and grinned.

"It's pink with black paw prints and trim."

"Not a bad choice," I agreed.

"So where were you?"

"Oh, yeah, about that." I finally let my ears perk back up. "I went exploring today and a monster found me! It was big and ugly and had like...razor teeth and eight eyes—like a spider! Its name was Mr. Smith and it wants to eat me."

"Wait...what?"

"The monster."

"Mr. Smith?"

"Yeah!"

"Wants to eat you?"

I nodded. Seemed my Earthian friend was finally catching on.

"And where...exactly did you meet this Mr. Smith?" Cedric asked.

Before I could answer, he had, oddly enough, tucked a finger under my new collar and tugged me along. Not really wanting to choke, I followed as he led me back inside and over to the sofa. He flopped down there with a sigh and rubbed his forehead. Cedric always seemed exhausted and tired.

"You need lemonade."

He opened one eye, barely visible from between his fingers, to look at me. "What?"

"Lemonaaaaade," I replied, moving myself closer to Cedric. My ears stayed perked up as I gave him a light smile. "It has mystic healing powers. I saw it on TV."

"Smiiiiileeeeey."

"That's me!" I purred and curled the tip of my tail.

"So where did you meet this Mr. Smith guy?"

Back to that topic, it seemed. I went ahead and gave him the story clear from the beginning when I had left the house and breached the Earthian defenses, eventually reaching the school on a "tour" of local plant life. Had to change the story a tad so he didn't get suspicious of me.

Afterward, he rubbed his forehead, gave a subtle sigh, and stood up.

"He was probably just wondering what the kids were so excited about. It probably isn't anything." He looked back at me and prodded my muzzle with one finger accusingly. "But you need to stay inside, little kitty."

For each syllable, he poked my poor muzzle, which I didn't think was necessary.

"Fine, fine. I will. There wasn't anything worthwhile out there anyway."

Cedric was in good spirits up until he ventured into the kitchen, where I had, uh, not exactly been the neatest Qwuedeviv on the face of the planet. Dishes had a tendency to become broken whenever I decided to wash them.

"Smiiiiley," he grumbled and bent down to pick up broken shards of glass. "I swear sometimes you're like taking care of an infant."

"An experience I assure you have not experienced," I replied.

That got me a glare—a glare of his eyes that is, not the usual glare of his glasses that he had. He muttered something under his breath as he went to obtain the dustpan and began hastily—and not very efficiently, sweeping the glass shards up.

"You missed some."

Another glare. He certainly was moody today.

"Then why don't *you* come over here and clean up?"

"Negative on that, Private. Lieutenants are above such things."

"What..?"

Oops. Simple slip of the tongue. It could've happened to anyone, but of course, it didn't choose to happen to anyone. It chose to happen to me, which was unacceptable. No one listened to me about it though.

"TV." I fumbled as I took a few steps back. "I learned it on some show—anyway, I uh, need to go do important things."

"Important things? Really? Smiley, you don't have any—"

"I'll catch up with you later. Good talk."

With that, I slipped away, ignoring Cedric's attempts to call me back.

I found my cardboard box and flopped down in it. Today had been a stressful day; first town, then Mr. Smith, and now Cedric was probably suspicious too. I burrowed my fuzzy gray face down against the pillow in my box. I hoped Mr. Smith really wasn't anything to worry about like Cedric had said. I had hoped for a lot of things in my short, distinguished life that hadn't happened though. When I was a kitten, I had hoped to become a space slug and eat all of my friends. It didn't happen. I was pretty disappointed.

12

It's Just Like in the Movies!

I WAS AWAKE BRIGHT and early—I think noonish or so. I had already started the day out right by munching on a bowl of sugared flakes and had every intention of going outside to frolic in the yard. The land serpent was out of commission after I had cut it open with scissors the other day.

Oh yeah, some time had gone by since the previous log but nothing had been particularly noteworthy. In fact, despite how intense and life-changing the events that day should have been, life had gone completely back to normal. Mr. Smith had never hunted me down; Cedric hadn't even asked me more about my resources and knowing such coded military language. No, he had more important things to rant about apparently.

Things like telling me to clean up after myself. Wash the dishes. Use the lint brush on the chair if you're going to in-sist on sitting on it. Wash your clothes every once in a while.

Don't stand on the table. Wash your paws and brush your teeth. Toothpaste isn't an acid paste to ward off intruders. No, it doesn't go on doorframes or in water to add flavor either.

It was just one thing after the next: don't do this, don't do that.

"Smiley!!"

I paused, paw still resting on the door. To ignore or not to ignore...

"Yeaaah?"

No response. I had learned that meant he wasn't going to finish until I went and found him. I really didn't understand that logic. I mean me and my crew yelled at each other all the time. In fact, we were really good at yelling at each other. Cedric needed to work on his.

When I arrived in the guest room, which is where he was, in case you didn't know, Cedric was standing near my bed—my cardboard box. It was filled with its usual plush pillow and pile of blankets.

I smiled at it. Such a good bed.

"I told you that you needed to start taking on a little responsibility around here."

"I doooo. I wash the dishes."

"*Lick* the dishes. That is not clean."

"Picky."

"Look, is it so much to ask that you keep your room clean and not terrorize everything else in the house?"

"Yes."

"Smiley..."

"No."

"Then why is there torn-up paper scattered from here clear out to the living room?"

Hmm. Seemed Cedric was right. Little torn bits of paper formed an artificial snow barricade all around my box. It was pretty thick, gradually thinning as it made its way out of the room, down the hall, and into the other room. What we had here was a top-secret file: mysterious torn paper bits.

"Maybe it was aliens."

Cedric gave me a somewhat incredulous stare as he lifted his glasses momentarily.

"Yeah. I think you're right. And I think its name is SMI-LEY."

"If it is, it's purely coincidence," I purred.

"Smilllleeeeey."

"Whaat? It's true! I didn't have anything to do with—"

"Smilllleeeeey."

"Okay, I might've had a little to do with it, but only a very, super-tiny, hardly tangible, not worth mentioningly small amount."

"Smi—"

"Okaaaay, I had everything to do with it! But ya gotta understand. Caffeine that late at night is a disaster waiting to happen! You don't know how many moths and shadows I hunted. *You have no idea.* I got *bored.*"

He sighed and shook his head as he often did. "Look, just get it cleaned up."

"But housecats don't clean up after themselves!"

"You're not a house cat!"

"You said I was!" I insisted as I followed after him.

"Ughh...you're smarter than a house cat!" After a moment, he added, "debatably."

The phone rang then—my saving grace. I had been saved by the phone more times than I could count by now. Cedric was a popular person to a lot of people. After I had gotten my phone privileges taken away, they were also a lot less angry. He never wanted to share any of his stuff.

Well, while he rambled on the phone, it was the perfect time for me to slip outside. I crept out of my room and down the hall to the door at the front of the house. I had just reached it when I heard him call from the kitchen again. My ears folded down against my head as I rolled my eyes and turned. Cedric was quickly approaching.

"I just got done telling you to clean up that—"

"But Cedric..." I frowned and looked up at him sadly.

"No. Now."

I heaved a sigh and sulked my way back towards the trail, occasionally glancing over my shoulder to see if Cedric looked like he had regretted being too tough on me yet. He didn't. In fact, he had the nerve to tell me I better hurry my furry behind up. How rude.

I knelt down in the hall and started gathering up the small bits of paper. It was boring and, furthermore, not work that was fit for a lieutenant. It was horribly demeaning, and I had reason to suspect that this would leave a scar for life.

Once Cedric decided that I was working all right, he announced that work had called him in that day. Today was normally a day off for him, you see.

"I'll be back early this evening." He turned towards me briefly as he was closing the door. "You better have that all cleaned up by then."

"Yes, Your Highness," I grumbled as the door shut.

I picked at a few more pieces of the paper but soon decided I had worked enough for the time being. I had a lot of hours until Cedric would return so I might as well head outside and enjoy a little fresh air. Fresh air is good for the body and mind.

I placed the papers I had already picked up in a neat little pile then scurried outside. Much of the fresh air I had previously mentioned existed outside, and there it was to greet me upon my triumphant exit. There and air, it was delicious. I stood near the railing of the deck for a bit, where the sun was just catching some of my fur and giving it a fantastic coating of warmth.

After a little bit, I ventured down into the grassy part of the field, not the parts that were asphalt or concrete for parking the car, but the areas around it. The grass tended to home a lot of small Earthian bugs. These bugs were fun to hunt and frighten as they would fly and provide an even more exciting chase.

The delightful bugs were sparse during the midday sun though. I found a couple of the hopping kind and batted at them for a while—it reminded me of my training back on Qwuh-9, except the two were nothing alike. Nevertheless, it was far more amusing than picking up papers—which, of course, I was still going to do later, but...

I turned around and nearly fell on Hindquarters. It was just like in the movies where everyone else notices the impending doom but you're totally oblivious to it. How long had I been poking at those bugs? Why hadn't I heard anything? And why was Mr. Smith suddenly standing mere feet away from me in my yard..?

13

It's all Standard
Military Protocol

*S*O *LET ME RESET* the scene here. Me in the yard, minding my own business. Mr. Smith, in my yard, not minding his own business. Let me walk you through, just briefly here, what would have had to happen in order for Mr. Smith to be in my yard.

Mr. Smith would have needed to leap over yet another fence without alerting me. That should not have even been possible. Let me tell you, though, this had very much happened, and Mr. Smith was very much here.

"Uh! Mr. Smith! I uh, wow, funny meeting you here. What uh, what brings you here?"

"Furbrain."

"Oh. I see. Well. You know I think we just got off to the wrong start." I began backing up as I spoke, trying to create a little distance between us. "You see, I think you're great. I mean, I'm your biggest fan. I love—"

He was still getting closer at a pretty rapid rate. I had already made it halfway around the house and was nearly in a backward sprint.

"Now let's...let's not make any hasty decisions. I uh, whoah—"

Tripped over a decorative plant there. Horrible place for a plant now that I think of it, just rotten. I fumbled over it though and kept moving back.

"I'm sure we can work this all out without any confrontation...or dissecting."

I was in the backyard now, which, although decent in size, seemed by far too small when stuck near Mr. Smith.

Mr. Smith was a scary guy. Brownish orange shirt, black pants, blue helmet with a rainbow visor, and a long, thin, gray tail that split near the tip into two, each with a magenta eye. Scary man as I was saying.

It was then that I made the wrong move. Or, well, to be fair, I couldn't have helped it. Maybe if Cedric hadn't been so adamant about keeping his lawn green with those sprinklers. Maybe if he'd just come outside and get a little exercise doing it by hand. Maybe if I hadn't been walking backward, just maybe I wouldn't have tripped over those very sprinklers.

"I'm sorry I was spying on your elite forces at the training facility! I only wanted to assess what levels of opposition we had and perhaps steal them all for myself. I eat three square meals a day and remember to floss fairly regulaaaarlllly!"

Looking back now, I'm not entirely sure what importance that last part had in the matter. Naturally, good hygiene is fundamental for a good soldier, but it seems almost misplaced now. Perhaps some of Command Center had been out to lunch when typing up that directive; I'm not sure.

"What's your problem?"

I put my tears, final moments, and parting words on hold for a second as I glanced up at Mr. Smith again. That was not the response I had been expecting you see. Perhaps something more along the lines of, foolish alien, I will now eat you with my fangs, etc.

Mr. Smith did not seem prepared to eat me though upon secondary observation. He was just standing there, arms crossed and tail slowly sweeping back and forth. Wait a moment. I was quite certain Cedric did not have a tail. Cedric was an Earthian Human, Mr. Smith was supposed to be an Earthian Human as well, but Mr. Smith had a tail.

Hey...you know what? Mr. Smith wasn't as Human-looking as I recalled him being. You know that blue helmet I was talking about? Well, there were two rather tattered, large gray ears sticking out of it—oversized cat ears, not round stub Human ears.

I had to consult Command Center on this matter. The multiplication just wasn't adding up enough numerators, or whatever that Earthian saying is. Numbers weren't adding up, I think that's what they say.

One set of long ears and one thin gray tail equaled two, which only confirmed my theory. One plus one equals two. It does not equal Earthian and it will likely never equal Earthian. So, through a series of complex mathematical formulas you see, Command Center and I had scientifically deduced that Mr. Smith couldn't be an Earthian Human.

Mr. Smith grasped his blue helmet with two hands and gave it a bit of a jerk. It came up and off with a hiss. Removable faces were certainly not a feature of Earthian Humans. That was just another confirmation that I had been right all along with my scientific hypotheses.

The whole helmet removal thing really wasn't all that impressive. Not like on the movies when the steam and fog clear from around the face and suddenly their identity is known. This guy had no sense of flashy style, no appreciation for proper movie effects, and no love of popcorn. This guy happened to have a gray face and two sets of gills behind either currently pupilless magenta eye. This guy, as a matter of fact, was neither Mr. Smith nor an Earthian.

"*Spork?*"

"You're not too quick are you...*commander.*"

You'd have thought someone offered it a bitter lemon—that's an Earth fruit—when it said "commander" based on the expression it made. Total disgust. From any other Qwuedeviv I would have questioned their sanity. Spork was a different story. Spork was chronically disgusted by life and all who were granted existence in it.

"You know if you have something against me or my leadership, you should take it up with me."

"I *have.*"

"Oh. I see. Right. Well in that case—"

"You're the last one I would have expected to survive," it grumbled.

"Aha." I found a rock in the grass and sat on that. "Always there to lend encouragement, Spork."

It half growled in response. Didn't seem to give it full effort even.

"Wait a second." My ears perked up as I studied the other Qwuedeviv. "Why is your sense of style all ugly now? And more importantly, why is your name Mr. Smith?! What have you done with the Spork I know and love!?"

I uh, squeaked as it grabbed me by the scruff of my neck and brought me up to eye level. Had been totally sudden and unexpected. You gotta give people a warning when you're just gonna snatch them up all of a sudden like that.

"It's a disguise. Something us Qwuedeviv tend to practice when scouting, Lieutenant."

"Ohh, right. Very good, I was just, er, testing."

It dropped me without any warning. I landed rather hard on my uh, rear. Didn't feel extra good. Poor Hindquarters.

"Why did you run?"

Had to dig that one out of a deep folder. Running ...running. Running wasn't something a brave lieutenant would do. I happened to be a brave lieutenant thus the Running File was not something we kept lying around at Command Center. It was filed into the deepest depths, likely never to be accessed or used.

My head flopped to the side some as I entered a deep state of concentration. This requires a Qwuedeviv to personally search through the files of their mind to find the proper folder. In such a state one's expression may lose a few points on the intelligence scale, usually visible in the eyes and open mouth.

Spork must have meant that deal back at the school. It had appeared like I was running for my life at the time you see. Easy mistake to make. It was actually a tactical fallback. See, I knew Cedric's yard would be a much better and safer place to meet than the school grounds so naturally...

"Never mind. I don't want to know what kind of mind-numbing excuse you're contemplating."

I gave Spork a bit of a frowning glare.

"For your information, Corporal, I was doing no such thing! In fact, I—"

Just then, the facts and pieces of the puzzle started falling into, uh, the puzzle piece spots.

"Wait a second...you were teaching Earthian kittens..." The sudden shock had to be evident in my eyes as I took a step back. "You're a traitor!"

Spork growled and swung its tail to the side. "I was blending in with society *and* gathering information on how prepared those *kids* are for war and battle. What have *you* done, *commander?*"

"Ah, that."

I laughed nervously as I tried to think of a logical excuse for the matter. Before I had a chance to answer, Spork noticed my collar. Spork was significantly larger than me as I may have mentioned, so it had to kneel down to my level in order to get a better look. It reached out with one of its dark gray paws and flicked the little jingly bell. It made the usual adorable jingle that always brightened my day. It didn't have the same effect on Spork.

"What *is* that?" It grumbled and tugged on it.

"It's a uh—mew!" I rubbed my neck a little. Spork was anything but gentle. "...collar."

Spork gave it another sharp tug. This time it yanked my head forward with it. It didn't feel particularly great, but I decided protesting was probably a bad idea. Many things that are normally very good ideas are null when dealing with Spork. In fact, if you want to be on the safe side, just assume nothing is safely secured as a "good idea" when dealing with Spork.

"A tracking device," it concluded.

One of its torn ears flicked.

"Are you a prisoner?"

I glanced at its face and was just about to answer when it hooked a finger under my collar and hiked it up. I had to stand on my toetips in order to keep from choking. Choking would be a bad thing, obviously, but I was actually even more concerned by how close Spork was getting to my face. It wasn't like it to lean down to be at eye level with someone. Grab them by the scruff of their neck or shirt and yank them off the ground? Yes. This? No.

"Spork, what are you—"

"Shut up."

Was kind of hard to tell what it was looking at since its pupils still weren't visible. That's something us Qwuedeviv could do—hide our eyes with one illusion or another. It's considered rude behavior to do so amongst other Qwuedeviv, but let's face it; Spork wasn't the politest Qwuedeviv to ever set foot on Earth, or anywhere else.

Anyway, more importantly, its head was right beside mine and it kept tugging at various portions of my collar like some kind of barbaric...I don't even know. Earthian I guess. They were awfully barbaric.

It was kind of hard to see what it was doing, which I wasn't particularly grateful for.

"But I—"

I squeaked and my fur fluffed up. Without any warning, Spork had bitten my collar. Yes, the collar that was still wrapped around my neck. No Qwuedeviv in their right mind would—Spork was just—my neck here, people. You know, sensitive place, easily punctured, necessary for life— right beside a mouthful of razor-sharp teeth.

"Spooooork!"

"*Shut up*," it grumbled all muffledish—for the record it sounded more like "shuh up," presumably because it had a mouthful of collar.

It pulled me to the left, then the right, then briefly up off the ground, and then down again.

"But my neck—"

"Ish whuh I trying not t' chew t'rough."

I mewled and folded my ears down against my head. This had the potential to turn bad very quickly with a mere slip of the jaws, and that aside, I didn't even fully trust Spork to begin with. I could only do my best to hold still and hope to survive.

Its muzzle kept bumping my neck every few seconds, minutes, hours—whatever it was. I mean, it made sense because it had to get close enough to grab the collar with its teeth but well, let's just say it was frightening. Terrifying even. And I might—just a very small chance—I *might* have uh, yowled my head off the entire time. Yes, it had requested silence while working, but doctors also requested cooperation, and they sure as all krillfish weren't getting that from this cat.

All at once I felt a snap and stumbled to the right. I ended up face down in the grass, round muzzle pushed into the dirt. I was kind of glad I didn't have a nose right then. Dirt would've totally gotten up it and caused a sneezing fit.

My neck was feeling rather breezy and cool. I wasn't entirely sure if that was a good or bad thing.

I pulled the levers at Command Center to order my legs into full dig down and overdrive mode, got my face out of its grassy burrow quick enough, and found myself sitting there.

Spork was still there, beyond the little blurry green lines in my vision. Shook my head. Grass. Some of it had clung to my muzzle from the uh, excavation of the lawn a few moments ago. Not wasting a moment, I started grasping at my neck with my paws. It was still there but it was hard to tell if it was in proper condition.

It was then I felt something damp against my neck. My ears flopped down as I ran my paw gingerly over it again. Yes, it was definitely damp. Now, perhaps those of you who do not have fur would not understand the highly complex issue at paw, but you see, when a furred creature gets a cut or, say, a life-threatening bite, the blood often seeps into the fur, and makes it damp.

I noticed Spork was *grinning* about this, almost like this was some form of humor or remotely amusing. I was disgusted by the total lack of professional behavior from my fellow soldier. I mean yes, we were supposed to be brave and strong and not cry when another falls, but krillfish, ya can take a moment to at least *look* upset by it!

I grabbed my tail and pulled it close. It was the only comfort I had in this cruel world. Who'd have thought my death would come at the paws of a comrade? A comrade who didn't even seem to care about the fatal mistake it had made. I wiped away a few tears and angled my best glare at that...that fiend!

"I'm gonna die! And all you can do is—"

"You're not gonna die." Spork shook its head and grumbled something—most likely rude—that wasn't quite audible.

"Oh yeah?" I hopped to my feet and let my tail go into Full Lash mode. That shows anger. "And just what do you think *this* indicates?"

I pointed in the general direction of the damp fur.

Spork came over to where I was standing at the slowest pace imaginable, paws clasped behind its back as it leaned forward to get a better look.

"Yeaaah. It's just drool."

"...what?"

Spork sighed and rolled its head or neck, or whatever you roll when your head moves in the fashion its had.

"Drool. Saliva. Spit, Smiley."

We shared a moment of silence as I ran that through my intelligence banks.

"You...spit on me?"

"Not intentionally, no." It raised one paw beneath its chin. "Not to say I don't think you'd deserve it."

I gave it another glare—a glare probably wasted on someone like it, but oh well. I felt my neck again and tried to massage the fur a bit.

"Krillfish, Spork. Why'd you have to use your teeth?"

"I didn't *have* anything else."

"You're telling me you didn't have some kind of slicey thing, really?"

"I came from the school," Spork growled.

"And your point is?"

"It's against regulation."

We both paused. I was staring at it with what I could only assume was disbelief. Spork had never been the rule-abiding type, so I didn't see why now would be any different.

"Have you ever even *considered* the requirements for blending in?"

"Of course!"

Another pause as we stared yet again. I had the feeling it didn't fully believe me.

I was sort of debating back and forth with whether or not I wanted to ask Spork about that—leaning heavily towards not asking. I never had to decide because as fate would have it, at the very worst of times, someone decided to return home. That someone, as you may have guessed, was Cedric, and I had every reason to believe that he and Spork just might not become the best of friends.

14

This is the Last Chapter, Mew!

I COULD ONLY STAND there and wait to see what would become of all this. Cedric was in the front yard—as he usually was. That's where he parked his car you see. I had heard the car stop, then the door to said car shut. I assume it opened as well, but I hadn't heard that particular noise and don't want to falsify this log.

Spork glanced at me briefly before making its way around the corner of the house and tromping over anything that really got in its way at all. Some people were nature lovers. Spork was not. In fact, Spork was more of the mindset of wiping everything clean planet side and starting over. That kind of thinking often didn't go over very well with the inhabitants.

I scurried along behind Spork wordlessly. What was I gonna do to stop it from neutralizing the threat of Cedric? I mean sure, Cedric was kind of a whiny individual and Earthian at that, but all things considered, he wasn't a terrible guy. I kind of enjoyed his company and it really wasn't very decent guest behavior to annihilate your host.

"Oh, Spork, there's like... a few things we didn't fully go over."

It vocalized something that sounded somewhere between a growl and a grunt but otherwise ignored me.

"You see, there's this Earthian Human—"

For a split second, I thought I might have Spork's attention. That split second vanished when Cedric started whistling. Spork's ears went up and its line of sight returned to the direction of the blissfully unaware Earthian Human.

It was one of the times I wished Cedric actually had friends where he worked so that he could have stayed out later; maybe gone to dinner or watched a movie with a female Earthian counterpart. But no, home early evening, just as he had said he would be. He was carrying an armful of luggage—looked to be some groceries and his tech stuff.

Spork growled. Its ears pinned down against its head and its eyes and gills began to glow with that weird whitish-pink light that seemed to appear whenever Spork got particularly disgruntled by something.

"Spork, he's not a threat. He let me stay at his home."

Spork was at least listening to me now. I could tell that by the fact it hissed quietly.

"He's been really nice to me." I thought about that for a moment then shook my head. "I mean aside from the times he made me do the dishes and clean up the mess I'd made."

"Like a slave?" Another low growl.

It was kind of impressive how Spork could still be understood yet never unclench its jaws or stop growling to do so.

"Yes!" The lights show of glows resumed. "I mean no! No! Nothing like that! I—"

A quizzical "Smiley?" from the house paused our discussion on the matter. Spork drew back into the cover of the tall tree-bush thing on the side of the house and then turned towards me.

"You told it your *name?*"

"*Well, yeah,*" I whispered back, "do you have a brain at *all?* What good is an invader name if you never get to use it?"

Spork exhaled in a hushed sigh since we were whispering and such.

"What kind of resources does the Earthian have?"

"A lot of canned food—"

It slapped the back of my head with its tail. "*Weapon and defense* resources, you worthless—"

"Smiley!" That was Cedric again, being unintelligent and not noticing that it was *odd* for me not to be there at the door to confiscate all the tasty treats.

"I don't think he has weapons," I whispered back as I tried to push my way in front of Spork while still staying in the cover it had found.

"I wouldn't trust you as an information source." Its eyes narrowed as it locked on some nonexistent target in front of us. "But," it unsheathed its black claws, "it's dead either way."

Spork stood from its crouch and resumed walking towards the front door. I hurried to get alongside it, but it pushed me back with one paw and made me topple over backward.

"I'd keep a safe distance, Lieutenant. This might get ugly."

That, of course, ended in a growl.

Cedric had presumably dropped off the groceries in the kitchen by now. My main basis for this guess was I could hear him going on about the paper that was still shredded all over the floor, meaning his eyes could now see the floor. Really, I had had full intentions of cleaning it up. I had just run across Spork in the meantime, and that had sort of occupied my time.

"Smiley!" I heard him shout, this time with a touch of impatience.

Once I had picked myself up off the ground, my ears pinned down. Spork was far too close to the house entrance for my liking. With no real time to consult Command Center on the matter, I darted ahead of Spork.

"Negative on that, Spork!"

It paused briefly, giving me a skeptical glare.

"I'm going in solo on this." Yeah, that sounded good. "Better...umm...cover...stuff that way. He won't suspect anything."

I was pretty sure Spork was going to disagree with me, but I decided to hurry away before I could hear its voiced disagreement. I had no clue how long it would be before it decided to come barging inside. That was inevitable. Spork was not very patient and tended to have an all-sufficient "I'll handle it" sort of attitude.

Anyway, until then, I had bought my Human pal a few more minutes to run or something. Still wasn't sure what the plan was once I told Cedric there was a monster here to eat him.

Cedric was standing by some of the shredded papers when I made my way into the house. Great! At least I didn't have to go searching for him.

"You promised you were going to be good," Cedric stated, his voice quieter than it normally was. He turned to face me. "I trusted you."

"I swear I was going to clean this whole thing up."

My tail curled and swished back and forth—this was a bit urgent, and he was making it difficult to get the info across properly.

"You always say that and then you never do."

"Cedric. Seriously. Another time. We have more important things at the moment."

"More important things?"

Cedric adjusted his glasses. He tended to do that when irritated, amongst other reasons. Adjustment of glasses usually indicated he intended to speak his mind. Right now, we didn't have time for his mind to be spoken though.

"Because clearly, my opinion doesn't matter anymore."

"That's not what I—"

"Well, it certainly seems like it."

"Oh, come on Cedric, I—" I glanced back to check out the Spork situation for just a brief moment. By the time I was facing Cedric again, I noticed he was holding something bottle-shaped—wider at the bottom, narrowing at the top. It also had what appeared to be a trigger and nozzle system on the top—primitive in design, but I had already covered how primitive didn't always mean ineffective.

"Uh...Cedric?"

"You have a bad habit of not keeping your word. A person's word should mean something—whether human or alien."

I took a hesitant step back. Cedric's hand was hovering over the trigger for the device, and I had a feeling this would not be something I enjoyed.

"Cedric, will you just listen to me?"

He smiled briefly. Something about the smile seemed off to me, though; it was weak.

"Of course, Smiley, I always listen to what you have to say, but right now, I need you to listen to me." He took a step towards me. "I hate to do it to you, Kitty, but I think you'll appreciate it later on."

How about no. I highly doubted the likelihood of that statement. Sounded a lot like the things officers back home would say. Regardless, it was a time-sensitive matter, and I was almost sure I heard something outside right then.

I needed to seriously speed this up. Cedric couldn't be reasoned with words, so I was going to have to take yet another approach. I pinned my ears back, stared him down for a moment, and then darted past him.

He pulled back the trigger of the tool in hand and a thin stream of water shot out, striking the wall right beside me. I had feared as much. Cedric had found himself a primitive Earthian water-launching device.

I heard it hiss a couple more times as I made my way to the staircase and darted up without a second thought. Cedric was following behind me now. Earthian Humans weren't all that fast or coordinated, so it took him a while to follow me up. It gave me a couple of moments to plan my next move while I was waiting. Unfortunately, I couldn't think of a move worth planning. Getting Cedric outside and safe from the top floor seemed unlikely.

I flattened my ears to the sides just in time as another hiss of water sped by and splashed onto the wall beside me. Cedric had caught up by now so the chase resumed. I took a hard right and Cedric followed behind me. Now overlooking the floor below, I noticed the door open briefly. Time was up.

I ordered a full stop on the breaks and slid to a halt.

"Cedric! You have to stop!" Had to dodge yet another stream of water, then another. "This is for your own good!"

"This is for yours too."

Sometimes people just don't listen to a word you're saying. This was one of those times. I retreated down the east wing of the connecting second-floor hall until I reached a dead-end. Now I hadn't the slightest clue what to do; I hadn't even made it through the part where I figured out why I had run up here to begin with.

"Cedric, no!"

I held a paw in front of my face partially to ward off the terrible stream of impending water, but also to try and show Cedric just how wrong this decision was. He was jeopardizing his own safety by confronting me as a Qwuedeviv. If Spork saw this...there wouldn't be a thing I could do for the poor guy.

Cedric held the bottle level. Conflict was evident. He didn't really want to pull the trigger.

"Look, I know it seems like I've been rude and stuff, but trust me! I'm only trying to protect you!"

"You always have excuses." His finger tightened on the trigger. "I thought we were friends."

"We are!" I tried to push back further, but I was already up against the wall with nowhere to run. "I swear by all great fish, I'm telling you the truth!"

Cedric shook his head. That had not been the sign I was hoping for. It seemed our fates were sealed. There was no going back now. I may have been known to exaggerate a fact or two in my life, but I assure you, this was not one of those times.

Almost on command, a dark form emerged from the shadows of the hall. Spork's tattered ears and glowing eyes were visible over Cedric's head. The Qwuedeviv moved silently toward us.

I felt my own mouth drop open as my tail twitched. I didn't want this! I mean, sure me and Cedric had had our scuffles, but I never wished he was *dead*.

Cedric's grasp on his primitive cat-torture tool loosened. He stood still for a moment, obviously catching on to the fact I was behaving weirdly even considering I was about to be sprayed with water. After he gathered his courage or whatever he had been spending that moment doing, he turned slowly.

Eye to eye with my interrogation officer, I knew he had to be terrified. Spork made no visible move. Its long tail whipped back and forth, and a growl had begun to rumble in its throat. Cedric was in serious trouble, and I had no way to help.

Pronunciation Guide

SPECIES
Qwuedeviv: KWEH-deh-viv

CHARACTERS
Qyrvus Mur'rak: K-eye-r-vus Mur-ack
Qrr'keke'qrr: Ker-kehkeh-ker
Cedric: Sed-rick

PLACES
Qwuh-9: Kwuh-Nine

KerFuFFLe'S LUNCHBOX OF COMMUNICATION

Mission: Rule Earth, Maybe
Problem: Corporal Spork

Second Lt. Smiley still believes its mission is to infiltrate and rule Earth. After all, who could possibly be a better choice for such a task? Smiley attempts to explain Crew 52's directive to Corporal Spork, but the shark-like Qwuedeviv isn't convinced. The only logical solution is to locate the rest of Crew 52 and reestablish communication with HQ, but that is easier said than done. The fur will fly and the search is on.

ABOUT THE AUTHOR

K.F. Martin is a lifelong cat lover and sci-fi enthusiast with an interest in deep sea creatures and military conduct. She authors and illustrates the Qwuedeviv Crew 52 series and lives in a rural mountain range with plenty of her own little kitty tyrants. Her other interests include drawing and sewing plushies. A couple of her other favorite animals are foxes and wolves.

• • • • • • • • •

AT WAR FOR THE BREEDER

PREGNANT WITH FOUR ALPHAS' BABIES

BOOK FOUR

BELLA MOONDRAGON
OLIVIA BHELLE KILDARE

ROGUE WOLF

PUBLISHING

For our friends

CONTENTS

CHAPTER 1: CLOSER THAN FRIENDS

BARBARA

It seems I have my work cut out for me. I had mistakenly assumed getting one of the Alphas to jump into bed with me would be easy.

The room assigned to me is so small, it's the size of my shoe closet back home. I made my demands about my living conditions quite clear to King Gene. How dare he give me such a shoe box for a bedroom?! He said this room is the best and used to belong to his cousin. I wonder if she ever felt like she was suffocating in such a small room. Just being in it is giving me claustrophobia.

A maid knocks and enters the room with a glass of water on a tray.

"Is it room temperature?" I ask the maid.

She nods nervously.

I take the glass of water and sip. "This is not 68 degrees Fahrenheit. It seems to be more like 71 degrees Fahrenheit," I say as I spit the water back into the glass. "Also, I clearly asked for water with cucumber slices. This water has lime in it. Don't you know the difference between a lime and a cucumber? Pathetic! Get out of here."

The maid scrambles out of the room. I walk around the room trying to think of a new way to get to one of the Alphas. If they are all as fixated on the Breeder as my last target was, I would have to know what makes her special. Alpha Tristan might have just given me a great idea with his insult. I will have to learn a thing or two from this Breeder in order to know the best way to get one of these Alphas for myself.

Being Luna has its own advantages and perks, but being queen will change my entire existence. It will give me more power over the lands. I can't lose this quest.

After putting on a decent pair of jeans and a blouse, I take off the dog collar for a little while. I moisturize my neck and put some baby powder on before putting it back on. I am going to have to talk to King Gene about wearing a dog collar. Wearing such a thing for the duration of my stay here is not going to work. Couldn't he have put it on my ankle instead? It is within his reach, for crying out loud.

"Do you need us to launch another attack on the capital?" I can hear my Beta, Robin, ask me through our mind-link.

"No. Lay low and see to things back home with the pack. I'll let you know if I need anything else," I respond.

I make my way down the hallway, wondering where to find this Breeder. I don't have to look for long, as I see a pregnant woman and a red-haired lady walking toward me. I plaster a huge smile on my face.

"Oh, my. You must be Rose. You are as beautiful as everyone says you are. Pregnancy really suits you," I compliment her. I continue to beam at her, trying my best to figure out why the Alphas seem taken by her. Her nose seems a little big and not suited for her small face.

"Who are you?" The red-haired woman steps in front of the Breeder protectively.

"Oh, I'm Luna Barbara. You are such a great maid, protecting your mistress like that. I am harmless, trust me," I assure them as I smile brightly at her.

"My name is Kelly Silver, and I'm not a maid. I am Alpha Eli's sister and your worst nightmare if you dare try to hurt Rose," the redhead warns me as she gives me a suspicious look.

Oh, wow. Two for the price of one. Maybe I can also befriend the

Alpha's sister and get in her good graces. This is going to be easier than I originally imagined after all.

"Oh, pardon me. I was about to ask why such a gorgeous girl is a maid. You look like a model. That red hair is pure fire. What hair dye do you use to get it so red?"

The girl scowls as she glares at me. Is she not one to take compliments?

"Parents' DNA is the name of the hair dye," she spits.

Dang! I was so sure she had dyed her hair. Who has hair this magnificent? "Oh, my bad. You are gorgeous, stunning even; both of you are simply beautiful."

Kelly gives me a look over before taking Rose's hand and walking away without another word. Bitches!

"Where are you going? I'm so bored and know no one around here. Could I join you guys?"

Kelly looks back at me from over her shoulder and says nothing. I take her lack of a response as a yes, and follow them. We walk into a room that is just as small as my own. A woman I recognize as King Gene's Beta's wife is sitting on a bed. I have met her once or twice at some functions.

"This palace is full of gorgeous women. You're Beta Adam's wife, right? I'm Luna Barbara." I smile at her. Honestly, all this fake smiling is making my jaw hurt and probably creating unwanted ugly smile lines.

"This is Shelby, and we had no idea you were a parrot, Luna Barbara," Kelly says sarcastically to me.

The insolence of this girl. Does she know who I am? "What do you mean?" I ask, still smiling.

"A parrot can speak, but constantly repeats the same phrases until it learns new ones," Kelly explains with a cold tone.

I bite my inner cheeks to stop myself from lashing out at her. I had to make these women believe that I was a friend, after all.

"I know who you are... the Luna who is a prisoner yet roams around the palace freely with servants at her beck and call," Shelby chimes in.

3

Dang! Is everyone around here so unwelcoming?

"Ahh, the king just wants to negotiate deals with my pack. After all, he could gain more from my powerful pack if he showed them that he's treating their leader well, despite the mishap. He and I are actually acquaintances. We've known each other for a long time," I admit.

"I see," Shelby answers lazily.

I can see that these two ladies aren't about to believe anything I say. I decide to focus on the person that they seem intent on protecting. If I gain her trust, the other two might soften up.

"How are you doing, dear? Are the babies kicking yet?" I ask.

Rose smiles lightly at me and nods. "Yeah. I just feel like an elephant."

"Oh, stop it. You look gorgeous. The belly suits you. Any weird cravings?"

She laughs. "Pickles and peanut butter."

"Oh, wow. I liked ice cream and hot sauce when I was pregnant," I laugh.

Rose's eyes open wide as she regards me. "Ice cream and hot sauce? That's really weird."

"Luna Barbara, why are you being nice to Rose? Also, why did you attack the capital and come here to brag? Why even attack if you and the king are close?" Shelby asks.

I swallow as I try to formulate an answer. "I'm generally a nice person. Also, I feel Rose and I have a lot in common."

Shelby raises a perfectly plucked eyebrow at me. "A lot in common? Like what?"

"Like knowing how it feels to have your child threatened; Emily did a shitty thing by trying to kill Rose and her babies. I can relate to how she felt, being terrorized in such a way," I empathize. I bite my tongue, realizing I had revealed a secret that King Gene had told me in private.

"How do you know about what Emily did?" Shelby continues to cross-examine me.

"Rumors travel fast. I must have heard someone talking about it somewhere," I offer.

"Weird. I didn't know that knowledge had traveled outside these walls. So, how were your pups threatened?" Shelby inquires.

"Well, see, that's why I attacked the capital and came here. My child went missing, and I believe King Gene has some intel on what happened to him. I came here to try to figure out what he knows. All I am is a heartbroken mother following the trail of my missing child. Being a Luna without an Alpha is hard. I would really like to find my son, and maybe hook myself an Alpha in the process."

I realize I have again divulged my mission without fully intending to. I do hope they only took the sob story about my so-called missing child and nothing about getting myself an Alpha.

"Hook yourself an Alpha? Here?" Kelly asks.

I feign a whimper as I try to blink hard so as to squeeze out some fake tears. It works as I feel a fat teardrop roll down my cheek. "You know, ruling a pack as a single woman is hard. I mean, this is a male-dominated kingdom. But I have to be strong, for my kids. We women are like tea bags. We never know how strong we can be until we're thrown into hot water, right? We have to stand together as women."

"Right..." Shelby says.

I can tell from her tone that she's not buying my story. I need to move on to act two of my script.

5

CHAPTER 2: SANDWICHED
BETWEEN ALPHAS

Eli

We are not in the greatest position. Not only do we have Alpha Stephen's men in front of us, but Reece and I also have to worry about Alpha Kane. As some of our warriors poured in from their previous locations near the castle, they warned us that they had spotted the other pain in my ass creeping toward us from the north.

The last thing either one of us wanted to be was a nice juicy sandwich for the other two Alphas to devour.

"What are we going to do?" Reece asks as the two of us look at a map in a few moments of civility. We've managed to keep Alpha Stephen's forces on the run, forcing them back away from the village where Rose grew up, but I have a feeling that's not going to last forever. Some of my troops are on their way right now to take a look at Rose's parents' house again.

During the last battle, we had some issues, and I swear I saw Alpha Stephen's men sliding their way back toward the new mansion, but I wasn't certain, and I was too busy ripping throats out of wolves to look more closely.

"We're going to continue to drive Stephen backward, toward his own lands," I say. "And as we go, we should be able to put some space between ourselves and fucking Kane."

"Unless he stays glued to our asses," Reece mutters.

I look at where Alpha Kane's troops were last spotted on the map, and I understand why he is concerned. They are within a few miles of our current location.

Asshole….

"Let's move the left flank of your warriors over here," I tell Reece. "That will give them the top of this ridge to anchor against. Then, as long as they are able to hold onto the high ground, Alpha Kane will have to run uphill to get to them."

"That makes sense," Reece says, nodding his head. "I just hope we can get that division you sent into the village back soon. We're going to need them over on the right. That seems to be where Stephen is amassing his reinforcements."

Reece is right, and we don't have the luxury of reinforcements. Unless we request warriors from Tristan or Mark's packs, and at the moment, one of them is making sure that whatever the fuck had happened in the capital the other day was under control, and the other is still defending the castle from Alpha Kane's lingering forces.

It seems like Alpha Kane is spread thin, but he may have other packs helping him.

Before I can answer Reece, I hear my sister's voice in my head. "Eli , can you hear me?" she asks, using the mind-link.

I wanna say no because whatever it is that Kelly needs is going to serve as a distraction, I just know it. But I feel compelled to find out what's going wrong. In my gut, I have a sharp pain that makes me wonder if something is wrong with Rose or our babies.

Giving Reece a sign that I'm using the mind-link, I try to keep my voice calm. "Yes, Kelly. What's up?" I ask.

"Thank the Moon Goddess," Kelly says. "Listen, this stupid bitch Luna that King Gene has prancing around the castle is almost as dangerous as Emily was. You need to get back here. I don't know that we can handle her by ourselves."

A wave of confusion washes over me as I try to process what she wants me to do. "Stupid bitch Luna?" I repeat.

"That's right. Luna Barbara from Shore pack. She's trying to seduce Alpha Tristan and Alpha Mark. She's a nasty slut!" Kelly sounds exasperated.

My brow furrows as I try to think about this. "You want me to stop fighting Alpha Stephen and Alpha Kane because Alpha Mark and Alpha Tristan can't keep it in their pants?"

"Yes! That, and I'm afraid this Luna is going to try to hurt Rose," she adds, sounding almost as exasperated as I feel.

"Kelly, Reece and I are in the middle of a fucking war. We don't have time to go back there to babysit the two Alphas who we sent back to babysit the pregnant lady. Tell those two motherfuckers they'd better keep their dicks in their pants, or when we get back, we'll chop them off. As for Rose's safety, if they spend time with her instead of with Luna Barbara, she should be fine!"

"It's not as easy as you're making it seem!" Kelly whines in my head.

"It is as easy! It's definitely easier than trying to fight two Alphas at once!" I shake my head in exasperation.

Reece asks, "What's going on? Is everything okay in the castle?"

Tuning out Kelly's pleas, I tell him what she's told me. Once I conclude my recounting, he is just as pissed off as I am. "I have no doubt that Alpha Mark and Alpha Tristan can figure out how to keep Rose safe. If they take shifts, or one of them keeps an eye on Rose while the other one keeps an eye–from a distance–on Luna Barbara, they should be fine."

"That's what I told her, more or less," I reiterate to my friend. "I don't see the problem either. Even as much of a sex maniac as Tristan is, I wouldn't expect him to cheat on Rose." The idea of him hurting her makes me want to punch him in the balls, even though I'm pretty sure he'd never do that.

"Isn't this Luna Barbara a prisoner? That's the intel I got from my men, that she'd been arrested for starting that riot in the capital. So... if she's a prisoner, why is she a threat?'

"Apparently, King Gene has given her free rein to walk around the castle," I explain. "It sounds to me like this whole thing is just a damn setup with Gene."

"Well, we can't go back now. We have to finish off Stephen before Kane's forces all end up on top of us," Reece declares, which I already know and agree with.

"Eli!" Kelly screams in my head. "Answer me, damn it!"

At the same time, I hear howls in front of me and howls behind me.

We've got company coming from both sides.

"Kelly, just make it work. It'll be fine. Tell those assholes to keep Rose as their main focus, and if they hurt her, I'll castrate them with my own teeth!"

That seems to get my sister's attention as Reece asks me, "Do you think I should pull my troops away from the line with Stephen and send them around behind us?"

I look at the map again as the sounds of howling turn to sounds of grunts and snarls. The battle is beginning again. We need to strip, shift, and get out here.

"I don't think we should split our main forces apart," I tell Reece. "Let's stick together and see if we can beat Stephen back before we turn around to face Kane. Alpha Kane might have more men, but they've all been fighting recently, whereas Stephen's smaller forces are mostly new to the field. Let's continue to combine our forces against Stephen while the line we've got behind us holds off Kane, and then we can swivel around and send everything after Kane."

Reece nods his agreement as we hear the battle drawing closer. In my head, I start to receive messages from my commanders.

Alpha Stephen's warriors are about to descend upon us.

We exchange one more look before Reece and I each strip out of the shorts we've been wearing and shift into our wolf forms. He runs off in one direction, to the left, and I head off to the right, each of us going toward where the main body of our troops are located. He's already given the orders we discussed for the warriors holding off Kane; I heard them moving into position while I was talking to Kelly. So even though we are in a precarious position, I think we can do this.

I think we are strong enough to defeat one Alpha and then the other, as long as Reece and I continue to work together.

The best way for us to make sure that everything goes smoothly for our sides is for Reece and me to tear out as many throats as possible. Both of us need to be killing machines.

That is, if we're going to get out of here alive.

CHAPTER 3: WORKING AT THE CARWASH

TRISTAN

It's killing me that I'm not out there with my troops, trying to hold off Kane, or even out on the battlefield with Eli and Reece while they battle against Alpha Stephen. I have some of my scouts out there, keeping an eye on the situation. If I need to, I can pull some of my own pack warriors away from their current positions and send them to my friends' aid.

I'm just not sure if they'll make it in time.

Mark is in with Rose at the moment, so I have decided to sit in the library and stare at a map of the area where my scouts have told me Eli and Reece have their men situated. I've tried not to interrupt the two Alphas because I know from my own experience how difficult it can be to concentrate on ripping the throat from a wolf while you've got a thousand voices in your head.

The map isn't doing much to help anyone. I know that Reece has his flank up on a high ridge that overlooks where Alpha Kane is positioned, and my understanding is that a battle has broken out on the line along where Alpha Stephen has his men. My mouth waters, and I can almost taste the aluminum flavor of blood and feel the meat as it tears between my teeth as if I was there.

While I am sitting at the table, staring at the map, trying to envision the battle as it unfolds, I hear the clack of high heels on the floor and see Luna Barbara entering the library.

She's not wearing the maid's outfit anymore, so I have to assume she's no longer trying to pretend that she's working here, rather than just being a prisoner.

But then, she's wearing very tiny jean shorts that allow her ass to hang out the back, and she has on a tiny, tight white tank top that doesn't even come to her belly button. I don't have to stare very long to know she's not wearing a bra.

I feel myself begin to harden, and I have to rip my eyes away. She is a very attractive woman, and I can't help the images of her on my bed using my magic wand, which I subsequently had to burn, to make herself squirm and moan.

I love Rose. I don't need to have sex with anyone else ever again.

Besides, Luna Barbara is clearly lost. She was obviously on her way to a car wash, perhaps one for charity, and she's just taken a wrong turn.

She's carrying a bottle of water. Maybe she intends to use that to go out to King Gene's garage and wash up his cars.

"Oh, hey there, Alpha Tristy," she greets me with a mischievous smile.

I don't know if I should correct her or let it go. Do I care if she knows my name?

"Whatcha doin?" She bats her eyelashes at me and stops in front of the shelf that contains a bunch of romance novels. She pulls one off of the shelf and flashes the cover at me.

It looks like the kind of book Reece would love, one of those bodice rippers, with a pirate on the cover and a woman with her boobs hanging out the top of her gown.

Now, even the imaginary woman on the cover is making me hard....

Thank goodness I wasn't sitting in here reading a romance novel, or I'd be in all kinds of trouble now.

"I'm just looking at this map," I manage to say as she comes over and plops herself down on the table next to the map. I move it aside. I don't want her bare ass cheek making an imprint on my map.

She takes the lid off her water and takes a drink, spilling it all down her front.

Her wet T-shirt becomes transparent, and I cannot will my eyes to look away.

She knows this, and smiles. "Oopsies," she purrs.

I clear my throat, finally managing to rip my eyes from her nipples.

"Thank goodness you didn't get your book wet," I say, swallowing loudly.

"Yes, but my shirt isn't the only thing that's wet, Alpha Tristy-Pooh."

I've had my name abused many different ways over the years, but Tristy-Pooh has to be a first….

"Are you, uh, on your way to wash King Gene's car or something?" I ask, willing my eyes to focus on the map.

She giggles. "Nope. But I wouldn't mind washing you!" She sits the book aside and pours more water out, onto her hand, splashing her boobs again, and wipes the water on my nose. I lean back, trying to get away from her as she makes, "vroom, vroom," noises like she's trying to start an engine.

I suppose she's trying to start my engine.

"You're gonna have to stop that," I demand, taking hold of her wrist and moving her hand away.

She adjusts on the table in front of me, spreading her legs. Her shorts are so short, I can almost see more than the folds in her denim….

"What's the matter, Tristy-Pooh?" she asks, sticking out her lip in a pout. "Are you afraid I might try to shift your rod?" A seductive grin takes over her face.

I push my chair back slightly, thinking I need to bolt. "Nope," I tell her.

"Are you afraid I'll make you blow a gasket?"

15

I shake my head, willing her to stay away, but she moves again, closer.

"Do you think that I might ride your muscle car too hard?" She winks at me.

"That's… stretching it a little," I say, shaking my head. "Why don't you just go read your book in your room?"

She turns and picks up the book, putting the water bottle down. I am afraid my map will get wet, but I don't move forward to rescue it.

"Do you ever read romance novels?" she asks in a sultry voice.

Again, I shake my head, deciding not to throw Reece under the bus.

"Well, that's too bad. I can read you a scene, and then, we can reenact it." She waggles her eyebrows at me.

"I really don't think that's a good idea, Barbara. I'm in love with Rose, remember?" I clear my throat.

"Oh, please. It's not as if she's not having sex with other men. Besides, I know how you like your toys. I haven't forgotten." Again, she's winking at me, and then somehow, she manages to reach into the pocket of her tight shorts and pull out a tiny pink thing I didn't even see in there.

How I missed it, I'm not sure, but then, I was trying not to stare.

It's a vibrator, the kind that a woman uses to lock onto her most sensitive spot. I have difficulty avoiding the images of her on my bed again, and if she was using that on herself….

The chair screeches as I push it back further along the stone floor.

She takes this as an invitation to straddle me, moving forward like a flash to occupy my lap, the vibrator on and held between us as she pushes her wet breasts into my face.

I need to get out of here! I need to push her off and run to the door!

Before I can move, she's leaning toward me, her lips parted.

And then I hear a familiar voice….

"What the fuck are you doing?"

I immediately push Barbara off and jump up, my eyes glued on the doorway.

It's Mark… but he's not alone.

Rose is there, too, and even from across the room, I can see tears glistening in her eyes. She feels hurt and betrayed.

Grabbing my map up off the table, I leap over Barbara, who is struggling to get up off the floor. Mark and Rose are both headed down the hallway now, but I rush to catch up to them.

"Wait, little flower!" I call, finally reaching them and managing to get in front of them, thanks to Rose's big baby belly. "It's not what you think!"

"Oh, that whore wasn't sitting on your lap?" she asks, folding her arms across her chest.

"Well, no, that part is true. But we have to think she's not really here for the reason she's supposed to be. I mean, King Gene claims she's a prisoner, but she's just wandering around the castle, free as a bird."

"You mean this bird?" Mark asks, raising his middle finger at me.

I deserve that, so I can't even pretend to be mad. "I'm so sorry, Rose. I should've walked out of the library as soon as she came in wearing another slutty outfit. I was just trying to help with the battle the best I can from afar." I show her the map.

"Well, I did hear her say that she was here to steal one of my Alphas," Rose exhales, her face still wearing a frown.

"Do you believe me, Rose ?" I ask, praying she knows how much I love her. "I'm so sorry I let it go on as long as it did without running out of there." I don't want to go into the details of what I was feeling. She doesn't need to know that. Maybe it's the thought of war that made me feel so animalistic that I was willing to spend so much time with the Luna when the only woman I love is right here.

"Yes, of course I believe you," Rose says. She leans up on her tiptoes, and I kiss her.

Then, Mark and I exchange a worried glance. All along, I've just assumed Luna Barbara was here to try to seduce one of us. Whether or not that was meant to hurt Rose or just let the Luna get her kicks, I didn't know. But now... well, perhaps Luna Barbara is here for more devious reasons altogether.

CHAPTER 4: THE UGLY FACE OF DEATH

Reece

The battle in front of us rages on even as we get intel from the troops behind us that Alpha Kane is taking a detour. He's spotted our lines of defense and has decided it's not worth it to engage us if he can avoid it, especially not now that he's limping so badly from the previous engagements he's been involved in against all four of us, as well as the king's men.

Alpha Stephen is being a bigger pain in the ass than I thought him capable of, and as we continue to rip the throats out of his warriors, they just seem to keep pouring through the thick trees. I have to wonder if he's not got help from another source.

Could there be other packs sending warriors to help Stephen?

It makes sense that he would have some allies, but anyone who would side with him has to think that he has a real shot at becoming the king. Perhaps he is telling everyone that he's going to marry Emily and that Emily will be the next Luna?

I don't have much time to think about it deeply. A large male wolf with fur the same shade as the night sky comes flying between two trees, his teeth bared, and I know he's bigger than me and fresh to the battle, so it's going to take all of my concentration to defeat him.

Bending my knees, I get ready for his advance, and he arrives swiftly, plowing into me with his head down, using it like a battering ram to hit me in the chest. Normally, when I am in this position, the attacker will go flying over my head, but this one seems to know that trick, so when he hits me, it's with his full strength.

My ribs take the brunt of the force, and I hear a cracking sound that I hope is just my ribs dislocating and not breaking. I have to ignore the sharp pain that radiates throughout my chest and makes it hard to breathe. Rather than standing there, letting the pain consume me, I have to fight back. I lift my head, my jaws open, and I find the most vulnerable place he has near my mouth–his shoulder.

I bite down hard and pull, and the wolf grunts in pain as he moves to try to get away from me, but it's not working well, as I have a vice-like grip on his flesh. When he pulls away, I feel the meat from his shoulder tear, and I am left with a mouthful of bleeding, raw, fur-covered shoulder.

Despite the seriousness of the injury, he doesn't back down. He comes at me again, saliva dripping from his fangs as he aims for my neck.

Spitting out the chunk of him I've torn free, I prepare to defend myself, my own teeth ready to do more damage, but this time, when he hits me, it's near the same place as before, and I am driven back-ward, onto my back.

This is the most vulnerable position a wolf can find themselves in. I scramble, kicking all four of my legs, trying to flip over, as he pounces on top of me, pinning me to the ground.

He is using his snout to try to get me to turn my head so that he can get to my throat. I refuse to do so as I use my back legs to try to break free of his hold, but it's too much.

He's bigger than me, he's stronger than me, and he hasn't been fighting for hours.

I think of Rose, back home in the castle, rubbing her protruding abdomen, thinking about Eli and me out here fighting to keep her family safe.

I think about my unborn baby. Will I have a boy or a girl? Will they ask about their dad?

I think about my parents. My mother, in particular, and how sad she'll be to hear of my passing.

I try to reassure myself that I at least died trying to do what was best for the kingdom and the woman I love.

I feel his warm breath flooding over my face and my neck and shoulder as he overpowers me. That saliva drips down, hitting me in the snout before it rolls off.

Continuing to fight is doing me no good, but I won't just lay here and die. My eyes close of their own volition.

Suddenly, I hear a whooshing sound, and the weight on top of me is removed. I open my eyes to see a ball of red fur flying over the top of me, the black wolf crashing into a large tree to my left.

"Eli!" I think as I leap up off the ground.

The other Alpha has taken the black wolf by surprise, but he's still not as big or strong as our common enemy, so I hop up and run over. Between the two of us, we are able to pin the other wolf down, and Eli allows me the honor of reaching down and ripping out his throat.

I taste the sour, warm substance as it coats my tongue, turning my mouth to aluminum. It only takes a few chomps to tear through his jugular, and with a whimper, the wolf grows still.

Forever.

With blood dripping down my jowls, I look at my friend. "Thank you."

Eli shrugs. "I figured Rose would be upset if you died." He winks at me.

I know he loves me like a brother, but we let it go at that. Battle means relying on one another, and while I hate ever being in the position of needing to be saved, I appreciate what he's done, and he knows it.

The two of us run back toward where the fighting has unfolded, and in the distance, we see Alpha Stephen himself. He's in his wolf form, but his fur is far too clean to hint that he's been fighting.

"Give it up, Alpha Stephen!" I shout using the mind-link.

"You know that Alpha Howard and Luna Karen are missing, don't you?" He has a gleam in his eye as he speaks.

"And you know that Rose is not fond of her parents," Eli replies.

I see Stephen's expression shift. He wasn't expecting that.

I don't think he has them. We've had lots of soldiers patrolling the village since we left, and I'm almost certain Rose's family has gone into hiding, but even if Stephen does have them, we can't rescue them again. We can't take them back to the castle with us anyway. All they'll do is cause Rose pain, and they don't even seem to care all that much about their grandchildren.

We've done our best to keep Rose's village safe, but her parents are on their own.

"You tricked me!" Alpha Stephen shouts. "I thought that Emily could help me to gain favor with the king or at least be good in the sack, but all she wants to do is spank me!"

I hide a laugh. I'm not sure what to say to that.

Eli has an idea. "Alpha Stephen, return to your pack lands, and beg King Gene for forgiveness. That's all you can do."

Alpha Stephen looks defeated as his wolves are pushed further and further back away from where we stand. He will have to make a choice soon. Retreat, or face the consequences of picking a fight with larger, tougher packs.

I get intel from my commanders behind us. Kane has shifted his retreat and is no longer angling toward us or Rose's village. The warriors from Rose's pack are standing their ground around her homeland, and they seem to be capable of defending their people against any attack Kane or Stephen may throw their direction.

Judging by the way that the other two Alphas are directing their troops, I think that Rose's people are safe for now.

"Run home with your tail between your legs, Alpha Stephen!" Eli shouts.

Stephen takes a look at us and then turns around and disappears between the trees.

We have been victorious. Now, we need to return to our sweet Rose.

~

MARK

I'M NOT sure what to say to Tristan, but Rose seems to have forgiven him. A few weeks ago, I may have wanted to beat the shit out of him for even entertaining Luna Barbara's advances. But after the incident with Emily, I have to be more understanding.

We are still standing in the hallway, and the two of them seem to be having an intimate moment. I think about walking away, but just as I am prepared to leave, I hear a familiar sound behind me.

The click-clack of high heels on the marble....

At first, I think it's just Luna Barbara. She wears those ridiculous shoes, too, but I know that cadence.

I recognize that precise sound, and it sends a shiver down my spine. My eyes widen as I see Tristan's head lift to look over Rose's blonde crown and down the hallway.

He looks terrified.

Turning around slowly, I hold my breath.

It is my worst nightmare.

A familiar voice, one that makes me inwardly cringe, makes an announcement that has my blood running cold.

"I'm back, BITCHES!"

CHAPTER 5: SEND A THIEF

Emily

I stand with my hand on my hip as I look at the people in front of me. They all stare at me as though I am a ghost. I can see the blood drain from the Breeder's face as her eyes fixate on me.

The sight of Alpha Tristan and the Breeder should be making me want to puke or tear her throat out, but I am more interested in the female standing at the end of the hallway. Was the bitch wearing my bum shorts?

Luna Barbara.

I should have known my cousin sent me away just to replace me with that evil bitch. So she was the one he was now sending to woo the Alphas and become the next Breeder.... While Emily was shackled to a man whose pecker needed me to sing *Get Up, Stand Up* for it every time we had sex–correction–attempted to have sex.

It wasn't as if my cheerleading and singing worked to get the old geezer's cock up. That thing was like gum; chewed up and spent. Nothing was ever going to bring it back to life, not even the blue pills he kept popping like Tic Tacs.

"Your droopy ass is stretching my shorts, Luna Barbara," I greet her coolly as I look her over. "And I doubt they are age appropriate.

Shouldn't you be dressing in… I don't know, maybe adult diapers or something? I have heard that accidents are common for women your age."

Luna Barbara looks at me and scoffs. "Hello, Emily. Tired of your old man already, or did he get tired of you? If I remember correctly, you have a gift of draining the very will to live from all of the people around you. Or did he find out that your va-jay-jay is a garage for every Tom, Dick, and Harry to park their wang in, Evil Emily?"

What a bitch! I launch myself toward Luna Barbara. I am ready to pull the obvious fake hair extensions from her scalp, but Alpha Tristan is quick to step between me and her. He catches me mid-flight, as I soar in the air, hands ready for a cat fight.

He slings me over his shoulder like a sack of potatoes, kicking and screaming. I would focus on how strong and macho the Alpha is if I wasn't bent on ripping the stupid smirk off Luna Barbara's heavily Botoxed face. I can hear Barbara's irritating witch laugh as he walks away down the hallway.

"Why did you stop me?" I scream when he puts me down in the sunroom. "Do you know who that woman is?"

Alpha Tristan shrugs. "Luna Barbara is a prisoner. The real question is, why are you here?"

"You'd better thank the Moon Goddess that Emily is back to save all of you. It's a good thing I came when I did because y'all need me," I exclaim.

Alpha Tristan looks at me and frowns. "Nah. Luna Barbara is a great replacement for you. We don't need two of you."

I can feel my heartbeat racing, and I feel I can't breathe. I reach down my armpits, and as soon as I can feel the clasp of my push-up bra, I unhook it. In one swift motion, I slide the bra from beneath my sleeveless blouse, taking in a deep breath as I feel my ta-tas free from the pressure of the tight undergarment prison.

"Why the hell are you stripping? You haven't even been here for five minutes and you are already trying to seduce me?" Tristan says as he covers his eyes with his hand.

I can't help but laugh at how panicked he looks; I playfully throw the bra at him. He moves away from it like it's a live snake.

"Sorry to burst your little ego bubble, Alpha Tristan. I am not trying to seduce you, so cool your little tantrum. I just needed to be free of that bra jail. Do you know how relaxing it is when women remove those things? So liberating. Anyway, back to the Luna Barbara issue. She is dangerous and has to go," I explain.

Again, he looks at me and frowns. He then gives me a crooked smile before saying, "Takes one to know one, right? Or is it because you're afraid she's better than you at the seduction game? I thought Emily wasn't afraid of a little competition."

I feign a smile at him. The guy is handsome but really stupid if he thinks Luna Barbara is here for a little *Bachelorette in Paradise* season.

"I see you don't know just how dangerous Luna Barbara is, huh? Do you think she's just here to grease your jean's zippers? Do you think she is lil' Emily who wants you to spank her to the moon and back? Little Emily who just wants love and attention? Whatever she might gain from you sexually is a bonus for her. What Barbara wants is power. Marrying one of you will get her to be the queen, but that won't be enough. Luna Barbara is a black widow. Whoever becomes king will never rule alongside her." I state my case.

I look at Alpha Tristan and hope the fear and urgency of the situation at hand are evident in my eyes.

"What's the worst that Luna Barbara can do that you haven't done, Emily? You've tried to kill Rose and our children. You killed an innocent woman. If you're saying Luna Barbara is more dangerous, what will she do? Cause global warming?" Alpha Tristan asks.

I can't help but pace up and down. The metallic platform stiletto heels I am wearing are beginning to painfully pinch my toes. I kick them off, and they make a thudding noise as they land on the marble tiles. I pay them no mind as I continue pacing barefoot. I need to make Alpha Tristan understand how dangerous this Luna is.

I try to find the words to drive my point across, but I can't. I stop pacing and look up at him, as I have lost several inches in height since removing my shoes.

Lacing my fingers together, I drop to my knees. I need to show him that I am not the enemy here... not anymore, anyway.

"I am not one to beg... ever, but I need you to hear me. I am so sorry for acting like a crazy bitch in the past—"

He cuts me off. "Psycho, deranged, monstrous..." Alpha Tristan adds.

In the past, I would have gotten up and given him a piece of my mind for calling me names, but I probably deserve that and more. Being treated like a sex doll for a flaccid prick, and being discarded and ignored by my cousin, had messed with my psyche... or maybe it had actually put the loose screws in my brain in the right place.

Alpha Stephen had not bowed to any of my demands. When I had asked him to spank me, he had told me his arms were tired and had ordered five of his best guards to take turns spanking me since I liked pain. They had used all their strength to spank my poor bottom, and I hadn't been able to sit without a doughnut cushion for a whole week.

When I had complained to him to tell his men to stop, he had laughed and said, "Oh, you want it harder, you say?"

I swallow as I remember the pain and fear as I got spanked mercilessly while shackled to the bedposts. He had then told me that he had given me extra spankings to keep in my bank so that I would stop bothering him. I had been the laughingstock of his whole household as I walked around like I had a hot carrot between my legs. Everyone had heard about the 'spanked madam of the house.'

When I called King Gene to complain, he laughed too. He told me that I was getting exactly what I liked. Spanking was supposed to be fun, not torture.

"You can call me any name in the book, but you need me here, Alpha Tristan. Compared to Luna Barbara, I am a toothless dog. All bark, no bite. You are all in danger with her here, including Rose and the babies. Luna Barbara will kill all of you to get what she wants."

Alpha Tristan looks down at me as I continue kneeling. "I hear she lost a child. A mother would never harm children."

I chuckle. The sound came out with an irritated twang to it. Nothing sexy about that. "You mean like the child she sacrificed? Luna

Barbara killed her husband after one week of marriage, all because she wanted to be the sole ruler of Shore pack. When he died, she was already pregnant. When she gave birth to a son, she found him to be a threat to her rule. Imagine that. A child she bore was a threat to her. He was an heir and bound to someday be the Alpha. She gave the baby to her guard and told him to get rid of it. The baby never suckled his mother's breast."

Alpha Tristan's eyes widen as he regards me. "You mean she killed her own child?"

"Yes. So, do you think she'll hesitate to kill Rose's children? They aren't even her blood, so she won't hesitate to kill them herself. Then she will kill whoever is king so that she keeps all the power for herself."

Alpha Tristan runs his hand through his hair. "Why would we need you to help us? And why would you even want to help us?"

I am quiet as I think about what to say. Should I tell Alpha Tristan about how the Alpha of Shore pack that Luna Barbara married and killed was my mate, the love of my life she seduced, stole from me, used, and killed? I was here without a man because of her. She had ruined my life. I had sworn my revenge years ago, and now I was going to take it.

"I have a score to settle with Luna Barbara. A drunken night is what made her Luna, a drunken night that was never supposed to happen if she hadn't spiked Alpha Ivan's drink, the night she got pregnant and used the pregnancy to force him to marry her. Listen, I know Luna Barbara. Only I can match her evil games. Let me help you, Alpha Tristan."

I can see his eyes soften a little as he considers my proposition. "When she's gone, how will we know you won't be a threat to us again or join forces with her and attack Rose? You both have the same agenda, after all."

"Same agenda? No. I am not interested in being a queen or Luna anymore; I don't want to kill Rose or her children. Do you know why I was so competitive and swore to not lose? It's because of Luna Barbara. After losing Alpha Ivan to her back then, I swore to never lose again. Honestly speaking, I don't even love any of you Alphas the way Rose does. I was just doing it to win. I wanted to win the game of love for once in my life. Luna Barbara messed me up real good. I became irrational when it came to winning. If I get my revenge on her, I can close that door for good. Mentally and emotionally. I am your best bet on this."

I stand up and look at Alpha Tristan. I can see he is still uncertain about whether to trust me or not.

"I don't know about this, Emily." Alpha Tristan sighs, shaking his head slightly in confusion.

"I am not the same Emily that left this palace a few weeks ago. Use me to protect what you love. Send a thief to catch a thief?" I plead.

CHATER 6: DREAM OF MY ALPHAS

ROSE

I don't know what to think about the situation with Barbara, but it worries me. Tristan shouldn't have been in there with that woman for so long.

And now... Emily's back?

The moment I saw her, a cold sweat broke out all down my back, and the little hairs on my arms stood erect; I even felt like my ass was sweating.

What the hell could that horrible monster want?

Mark quickly ushers me to my room, leaving Tristan to speak to Emily in the hallway.

"Come on," he urges in a gentle voice. "There's no need for you to stand around and watch that crazy woman face off against that other crazy woman."

I take a deep breath and let him lead me into my room. Mark helps me to get comfortable on my bed, propping my swollen feet up on a couple of pillows. I thought that a quick stroll down the hallway would help me to feel better, but it hadn't gone that way.

Mark gets me a glass of ice water, which I appreciate. I take a few swallows before there's a solid knock on the door. I think it must be Tristan, but when the door opens… it's not him at all.

"Reece! Eli!" I practically spill the ice water on myself, trying to sit up.

"Don't get up!" Reece insists as they both come over to kiss me.

Reece's lips find mine first, and it's clear he doesn't care that two of the other Alphas are there. He kisses me like a man who's just returned from war. And judging by the smell and look of him, that's exactly what he is. I don't mind that he didn't stop to shower first, though.

As soon as he pulls away, Eli kisses me just as passionately. I hear Mark grumble behind them.

"You're back!" I say, once I can breathe again.

"We are," Reece says, nodding. "We need to shower and probably get some sleep because we've been fighting most of the last few days, but we had to see you first. How are you?"

I'm not sure how to answer that question. "Luna Barbara is being impossible," I begin. "And Emily's back."

"Emily?" Reece's eyes bulge. "Really?"

I nod. "I don't know what to do."

Before anyone can say more, Tristan bursts into the room. "Hey! I thought I smelled you guys!" He hugs the other two Alphas, and all four of them sit down on or around my bed in the chairs by the window. My feet are still propped, and Reece, who is sitting near them, begins to rub them as Tristan tells us what's going on.

"Emily seems genuinely concerned about Barbara's presence here," Tristan says. "She claims to have changed."

"And you believe that nonsense?" Mark asks. "First, we catch you with Barbara, and now this?"

"Catch him with Barbara?" Reece asks.

Tristan waves a hand, dismissively. "It's nothing, just like when Mark was caught spanking Emily." Mark scowls at Tristan. "But seriously, Emily says she thinks Barbara is bad news."

"Well, maybe they're working together to get us to lower our guard," Mark suggests.

32

Tristan shakes his head. "No, I don't think so."

"No offense. I know I was put in a compromising position, too, but I don't really trust you at the moment," Mark admits to Tristan, coolly.

The dark-haired Alpha only grunts.

"Tristan, despite you being on guard duty off and on the last few days, we haven't spent much time together," I remind him. "Maybe while Reece and Eli go get cleaned up and sleep on this newfound information, you and I can have a little... chat." I try not to be too forward in front of the other men because I don't want to hurt them, but I hope that Tristan gets what I'm saying.

I can tell by his expression that he does.

"We'll be back later," Eli says first, catching my drift. Reluctantly, Mark and Reece follow, and I immediately miss my foot rub.

Tristan drags his hands down his face before he goes and locks the door. No one comes in much besides the other Alphas, except for Shelby, Adam, Kelly, and occasionally Vienna, but I don't blame him for being cautious.

Tristan kicks off his shoes and plops down on the bed next to me, making me shoot up a little and land back where I'd been lying. I giggle, and he smiles at me. "Whatcha wanna do, little flower?"

I grin at him, and he makes a move toward unbuttoning my top without me even bothering to answer his question.

With my big belly, it's hard for him to get me undressed, but if there's one thing about Tristan that always rings true, he will not give up. Eventually, the two of us are naked, and he is gently taking his time, kissing me all over.

"I've missed you," he murmurs into my neck as his large hands cup my breasts, and he begins to roll my nipples with his thumbs and first fingers.

I moan, wanting him inside of me. "I've missed you, too," I tell him. I wonder how this will work best with my enormous belly. I haven't quit having sex with the Alphas while I've been pregnant, but I feel like my stomach has swollen in the last few days.

My babies have been eating well. All of them will come out smelling like peanut butter....

Tristan rolls over onto his back and guides me on top of him, and I trust he knows best. I doubt he's ever had a belly of this size on his chest while making love to a woman, but he is an expert.

He lifts me up, and I come down with his cock buried deep inside of me. He feels so good, I have to close my eyes. My head falls back, and I begin to move my hips. His hands are still working over my breasts, and I feel myself losing all grasp on reality.

When he lowers a hand and slips it inside my folds to find my most sensitive area, I cry out in ethereal moans. The harder he rubs me, the more I buck against him, the further over the edge I fall.

I know Tristan is waiting as long as he can to join me in euphoria, but he can't hold out forever, and eventually, he is filling me with his warm essence, and his grunts of satisfaction let me know he is as blissful as I am.

Carefully, I remove myself from him, his hands gently guiding me to the bed. He tosses a blanket over me, and I pull it up, getting cozy as he wraps an arm around me, kissing my forehead.

"Thank you, little flower," he says. "That was amazing."

"Thank you," I murmur. I am spent now, but I want to speak to him. I want to know why he thinks Emily might be forgivable. I ask him, "What did Emily tell you exactly?"

He sighs and readjusts on the pillow, and I can't help but lift a hand to brush a dark curl away from his sweaty forehead. "She told me that Barbara killed her own child, amongst other horrible stories." I stare at him in shock. I remember her mentioning having a baby. I had no idea she had killed the child. "I don't know. You guys are probably right about Emily. She just seemed genuinely worried."

"Worried that someone else will become queen," I counter, shaking my head. "Tristan, even if I could forgive her for trying to kill me—twice—we have to remember that an innocent woman, a sweet grandmother, died because of her actions. She tried to seduce Mark. She went after Reece strongly, too. That woman is a selfish witch, and I don't think she's changed her ways simply because Alpha Stephen has a limp member."

"You're right, beautiful," he assures me, caressing my cheek. "I've been all mixed up lately. I've been away from you too long. But I will say, I'm certain that Barbara and Emily have no love for one another."

"Well, that could be a good thing because maybe they'll spend their time going after each other. Or maybe… they'll just drive the rest of us even crazier than we have been lately." I don't want to think about it. I'm too tired.

I snuggle up against Tristan's warm chest, and he holds me close, playing with my hair and kissing me softly. As I start to drift off, I hear him whispering, "I love you, Rose."

"I love you, too," I mumble. Or… at least I think I say it. I might be asleep.

Then, I hear him singing a soft lullaby, but he's not singing it to me. He's singing it to the babies, and it makes my heart melt. If I were awake enough to cry, I probably would. But instead, I drift away, carried to dreamland by the sound of Tristan's rich tenor.

I hope I dream of my four Alphas and our babies and not those evil witches that have invaded the castle.

CHAPTER 7: OH, MY LORDT!

ROSE

After I awake from my nap, Tristan is dressed and sitting next to me, apparently just watching me sleep. "Hi," he greets me.

I smile up at him. "What are you doing?"

"Well, I was trying to sleep, but Eli and Reece are driving me crazy. They want to see you," he replies.

I can't help but sit up quickly. I've missed them so much. "Help me get dressed?"

Tristan immediately hops up and helps put the clothes back on me that he stripped off a little while ago. I am so big now, I actually do need help getting dressed, unlike before when Vienna helped me just because she was supposed to.

"It's always more fun taking your clothes off than putting them back on," he admits with a sly grin before he smothers me with a kiss.

Once I'm dressed, he lets the other Alphas in, and soon enough, all four of them are back in my room.

Reece and Eli smell so much better. I throw my arms around them and kiss each of them, and I kiss Mark, too. I've missed them all.

We talk for a while about how the battle unfolded. Tristan and Mark have already told me about my parents, and it is unsettling, even though they've never treated me like loving parents should. This time, I hear about how Reece and Eli gallantly fought to save the villagers of my pack.

"Now, our troops are surrounding the village to make sure they're safe until your parents can get an army together," Reece explains to me.

"Thank you all for fighting for them," I say looking at each of their faces.

They are all smiling at me, happy, lovingly gazing at me, and as my eyes go from one face to another, I can't help but feel my heartstrings tugging in four different directions. The next thing I know, I'm breaking down in tears. Reece puts an arm around me. "Rose, what's the matter?'

"I don't know what to do," I manage to confess between sobs. Eli hands me a tissue, and I try to stop crying, but I can't. "I will never be able to live without any of you!" I cry.

"Oh, Rose, honey," Mark says, "don't worry about that."

"You'll never be without any of us," Tristan assures her.

"But… I can't marry all four of you," I remind them. "It's not fair to you."

"It wouldn't be fair for any of us to be without you or our babies either," Eli points out. "Rose, we've already talked about it."

I look up at them, still wiping away my tears. "You have?"

Reece says, "Yes. And we intend to all stay with you, darlin'."

My eyes bulge a little. "All of you? You're sure? But what about whoever becomes king?"

"We'll figure that part out. But we're never going to leave you, little flower," Tristan affirms.

I feel better. I have no idea how that would be possible, but I know they'll figure it out. I trust my men with my everything, my life, and the lives of my unborn children.

I know, though, as a soon-to-be mother, that I really need to learn how to become stronger and defend my loved ones myself. Maybe Kelly can give me some fighting lessons before I deliver the babies.

"Rose, you're tired," Eli points out. "You should get some more rest. We just wanted to see you."

I try to argue with him, but I'm yawning now, and I know he's right. I should go back to sleep. I'm also hungry, but I decide to sleep for a bit and then eat dinner.

One by one, they come over and kiss me goodbye, and then, they leave, and I feel a sense of relief knowing I'll never be without any of them.

Unless Emily or Barbara find a way to cause even more trouble in my life than they have before.

∼

Reece

With Rose sleeping, the four of us move into Eli's room. Kelly and Shelby are there, but they wrinkle up their noses at us annoying boys and take their girly party elsewhere.

I sink down onto Eli's couch and pour myself a drink. I have earned this after so much fighting; I still remember how close to being dead I was. Thank goodness Eli had gotten there when he did.

"What are we gonna do about this?" Tristan asks, taking the bottle from me.

"We need to figure out how we're going to divide this kingdom when this is all over," Mark says, matter-of-factly.

"What do you mean?" Eli asks, taking the bottle next. He politely fills a glass for Mark before he fills his own.

"Well, I think it's pretty clear the four of us should plan on ruling the kingdom together. Regardless of who the king declares is next in line for the throne, we are all tied to Rose. We all want to protect her. Let's just divide it up." He says this like it's not a big deal.

"You know we'll have to convince the citizens that this is a good idea, right?" I ask. "What if they don't want four kings?"

"We don't have to call ourselves kings," Mark counters, shrugging. "We can have one king and three... dukes or something."

"Dukes?" Tristan repeats. "I once had a dog named Duke. Sweet boy. Dumb as a brick. Couldn't sit to save his life. Used to poop on the side of the house."

We are all looking at him like he's lost his mind, and since his comments have nothing to do with what Mark is talking about, we all know we should just skip this discussion altogether.

But I can't help but ask, "How the hell does a dog take a dump on the side of the house?"

"Do you mean in a side yard?" Eli asks, trying to make sense of it.

Tristan shakes his head. "No, he would go up on his front legs, kinda like this...." He puts his hands down on the floor and pushes up but his ass never leaves the chair. "Then, he'd lift his leg, and kind of shimmy backward...." He does all of that without actually standing.

We continue to stare at him for a long moment before Eli turns to Mark and decides, "Let's go with lords?"

"Yeah, yeah, lord is a good title," Mark agrees.

"Besides, you don't want to be Duke Mark," I add, laughing. "Sounds like a character on a stupid sitcom."

"Or a porn star," Tristan chimes in.

We stare at him with almost the same expressions we had on our faces when he was talking about his dog shitting on the siding. He seems unbothered.

Mark gets up and walks over to Eli's desk. He comes back with a piece of paper and a pen and plops it down on the coffee table. "Okay. This is the kingdom," he begins. He draws a spiky-looking building near the center of the crudely drawn kingdom. "This is the castle."

"Are you suggesting we should just divide the kingdom into quarters?" Tristan asks. "Because we need to find a way to keep our own packs in our area."

"And we need to make sure no one gets all of the crappy packs," Eli adds.

They both have good points.

Mark sighs and stands up. "Let me get a pencil."

40

For the next hour or so, we debate about the best way to divide the kingdom into quarters. We talk about how we will go about settling disputes, what to do about natural resources being located in certain areas, and how to go about writing and changing laws.

It's all very Civics 101, but by the end, Mark proposes, "We should all take a blood oath to agree upon what we've discussed here."

Not only has he been drawing and redrawing our lines, he's been taking notes about what we've agreed upon for the rules of our co-lordship.

Eli pulls out a pocket knife, and one by one, we make a little slice in our thumbs and put a red print on the white paper. Eli hands out bandages, and we sit around admiring our work.

"Does this make us blood brothers?" Tristan asks with a laugh.

"Something like that," Mark says, grinning back at him. "I can't think of three finer fellows to be co-lords with," he adds.

"Co-lords?"

We had all been so busy adoring our work, and maybe a little lightheaded from losing a few drops of blood, that none of us had even heard the door to Eli's room open.

We are all wide-eyed, staring at one another as we swivel our heads toward the door.

From my vantage point, it's hard to see him over the back of Tristan's chair, but I don't have to see his face to know who has walked in on our scheming plan. I recognize his voice and can tell by the level of anger that it can only be one man.

King Gene!

And when he steps into my line of sight, he is fuming. His face is red, and he has his hands on his hips in fists.

"Mark! Come with me, now!" he growls and storms off.

Mark swallows hard and gets out of his seat, and I don't envy him one bit. But we have his back.

He's one of our co-lords, after all....

CHAPTER 8: IN THE KING'S FAVOR

Obediently, I follow King Gene out of Eli's room and down the hallway to his office. I try not to act nervous. I feel like we haven't done anything wrong. We were just discussing our options. The cut on my thumb where I sliced it to sign the agreement in blood smarts a little, but it's nothing.

Just a little flesh wound.

When we enter Gene's office, he walks around on me, closing the door and lifting his head as he pushes up onto his tiptoes to look into my eyes. "We have a problem, Alpha Mark."

I swallow hard, assuming that problem is that the four of us are plotting against the king. Technically, that was treason, even if we were just hoping to put our plan together after one of us became king.

"What's that?" I ask him.

"Luna Barbara," he begins, and I relax a bit, which puts me closer to his height, though I'm still a foot and a half taller than him.

"Right," I nod. "She is being a bit of a... a... nuisance."

He shakes his head and strokes his chin as he turns and walks over to his desk. Oddly, there's a tray sitting there with two glasses of what looks like wine poured, as well as a decanter. One of the glasses has a

43

blue tag around the bottom and the other one has a yellow one. They are the kind of silicon tags a person might use at a party. It seems odd to me, but everything King Gene does these days seems odd to me.

Is he going to offer me a drink? Are we going to sit down and have a chat about what to do about this newest pain in our asses? I follow him across the room.

"Listen, I know she's a slutty bitch. I get that she's already thrown herself at Tristan a few times. I don't know why. Personally, I think he looks like a bear."

"A bear?" I repeat. "You mean, his wolf looks like a bear?"

"No, no. As a human, he looks like a bear. All that hair. And he's so… big." He shakes his head and it seems like a shiver goes down his spine.

I don't know what to say to that. Tristan could be a bit bearish, I suppose. "Well, what would you have me do, Your Majesty?"

"I would like for you to go sit in Luna Barbara's room with her. She's in a private wing now, where I tend to keep all of my prisoners who are on house arrest. Sit with her. Have a drink. Chat with her. See if you can figure out what her goal is. She has to be up to something."

"Yeah, she wants to seduce one of us so that she can try to take over the position of queen. She's trying to replace Emily, which, by the way, you do know that Emily is back, right?" I ask him.

He pinches the bridge of his nose. "Of course, I know. I have no idea how she got into the castle when I specifically sent her away myself. The last I checked, I was still the king, not one of you… blood brothers." He looks at the bandage on my thumb, and I feel compelled to explain, but I don't. "Don't worry about Emily right now. Our first objective is to find out what Barbara is up to. Have a drink with her, loosen her tongue a bit, and when you're done, report back to me."

I don't want this job. I don't want to have anything to do with this assignment at all. I am already the one who tried to get information from Emily. Now, I'd have to do the same to Luna Barbara.

And the incident with Emily was still a problem. I can tell when

Rose looks at me, even though she said she forgave me, that the memory is still painful.

But he is still the king, and he had just walked in on us talking about what would happen after he is done being the king. I can hardly refuse.

"Fine," I agree. I see a look of relief wash over his face. "What's with the tags?" I ask as he gestures for me to pick up the tray. I feel like a glorified waiter.

"Oh, she, uh, only drinks out of glasses with a blue tag," he says with a shrug. "It's just one of those things." The king rolls his eyes. "Don't you hate it when you have to do stupid shit to appease stupid people?"

I look down at the tray in my hand and think... if he only knew. I don't bother to answer.

King Gene gets the door for me, and I carry the tray through. He escorts me down the hallway himself, which is really odd. Why not just send a servant to show me?

Maybe he wants to make sure that I do it and don't abandon the mission.

We arrive at a suite in a different wing. I keep note of where we are going. It's the north wing of the castle, one that's fairly far away from all of our rooms. I count four doors on the left side of the hallway until we reach Barbara's. I think it's a good idea to know exactly where she is, just in case.

Gene knocks on the door and then shouts, "Barbara, I'm opening the door!" He pulls out his keys and unlocks the door and then whispers to me, "I have to keep this locked or she'll be out and about all over the place again."

"Does that mean you're locking me in?" I ask him.

He shrugs. "Use the mind-link when you're done, in a half-hour or so, and I'll come and let you out."

I want to believe him, but there's something in his eyes that makes me wonder what the hell is actually going on.

The door is unlocked, and before Gene can open it, it's flung open from the other side, and Barbara is standing there, smiling at me.

"Well, if it isn't Alpha Mark!" she purrs. "Are you gonna have drinks with me?"

My eyes dart to Gene, and he smiles up at me. "Uhm... yes," I say. "Drinks so that I can get to know you as an amicable leader of another pack," I explain.

She only grins at me, and I swear her canines look even sharper than they should considering she hasn't shifted at all–or has she?

"I'll see you two later," Gene says, parting with us and practically pushing me into the room. The wine splashes a little.

As I cross the threshold, I hear the key turn in the lock behind me.

With a giggle, Barbara takes the glass with the blue tag off of the tray and gestures for me to take a seat at a little table set up to the left of the door.

I let out a sigh and set the silver tray with my glass and the decanter down. The only other furniture in the room is a large four-poster bed with a red satin comforter thrown across it. This setup reminds me a lot of Emily's room, though I don't see any handcuffs.

Yet.

"Well, have a drink, Alpha Marky," she urges, tapping my arm playfully.

I'm definitely going to need a drink or two to get through this conversation. I pick up my glass, the one with the yellow tag, and smell it before I take a small sip. It smells fine; it tastes fine.

I suppose I'm just nervous. "So, Luna Barbara," I begin, leaning away from her. "Tell me about your pack."

As she begins to answer me, I hear Tristan's voice in my head. "Well? Are we all screwed?" he asks. "Is King Gene taking you out back to tan your hide for causing an insurrection?"

"No," I assure him. "He didn't say anything about it at all. He's got me in here with Barbara, trying to appease her."

"In where?" Tristan asks me as Barbara goes on and on about how she felt it was necessary to attack the capital to make a point to King Gene. I nod and continue to sip my wine, glad I don't have to say much. Tristan won't just shut up!

"Her bedroom!" I growl back at him. "In the north wing, fourth room on the left."

'Why are you being so specific?" he asks me.

"In case you guys need to know where she's at at some point, and I'm not around to tell you. Now, shut up! I'm trying to get information from her."

He grumbles, "Be careful. Take it from me, she's a vixen."

"I know," I tell him as Barbara says something about her husband's death.

"That must've been very hard on you," I say apathetically, taking another drink of wine. My glass is almost empty. I'm just trying to drown her out.

"It was awful," she confides, batting her eyelashes. It looks like she's trying to whip up some fake tears.

I open my mouth to respond, but suddenly, I'm feeling super lightheaded. I set my glass down and wipe at my brow.

"Marky, are you all right?" Barbara asks me, but she doesn't seem really concerned.

Sweat is rolling off of my forehead. I stammer a few times, trying to get some words out, but something is definitely wrong.

Barbara is smiling wickedly at me. "You look awful, Marky. Are you hot? Perhaps we should get you out of those clothes!"

My eyes flicker closed and the wine glass falls from my hand, bouncing off of the table and spilling on the carpet. I note how the purple-red liquid looks like... blood.

In my head, I reach out to Tristan. He is the easiest to find since I just spoke to him.

As I slouch in my chair, Barbara gets up, that smile still on her wicked face.

"Help..."

Everything goes black.

CHAPTER 9: DEFINITELY NOT WHAT SHE WAS THINKING

Barbara

"Oh, dear. Alpha Mark looks a bit... unwell," I say to myself as I watch him slump into his chair. His eyes are closed, and it's clear the drugs I told King Gene to give him have taken effect.

Looking at him, I can't help but run a hand along my breast, pinching my nipple as my hand slides deeper. I slip my hand beneath my skirt and along the crease of my damp panties.

He is delicious, and I can't wait to devour him! I'll just need to drag him over to the bed. Soon enough, he'll be all over me.

I only have one question... what about the aphrodisiac?

It seems like that should be working now, too. Otherwise, he's just going to lay there like he's asleep, and that will not help with our plan.

Not even a little bit!

"King Gene," I call out, using the mind-link. "Mark is definitely under the influence of the drug I told you to slip him."

"Brilliant!" the king replies, and I can even hear him laughing maniacally through the mind-link.

Mark is so hot, I want to rub up on him. I need him to take me, though. What's going on?

"Yes, but what about the aphrodisiac?" I ask King Gene.

49

"That should be working now, too. Don't worry, Luna Barbara! King Gene knows how to follow through with a devious scheme. I never fail!"

"But," I begin, biting down on my bottom lip as a ripple of longing passes through my body. "He's not trying to seduce me. He's just… sleeping. And drooling a little."

"I'm not sure I understand," King Gene defers. "I did what you told me to do, Luna Barbara. I put the drugs in the cup with the yellow tag."

"Yes? And the aphrodisiac? You put that in, too, right?" I ask, desperation making my voice a bit high-pitched even to myself.

"Yes, of course!" he screams. "I'm not an idiot, Luna Barbara! I put the aphrodisiac in the glass, too."

My pussy feels like it's beginning to vibrate between my legs, I want this fine man so badly.

That's when it occurs to me what has happened, and the flames of passion are nearly replaced by fury.

"Did you put the aphrodisiac in the glass with the yellow tag, too?" I ask him.

"Why would I do that?" he asks. "That doesn't make sense. I put the aphrodisiac in the glass with the blue tag."

"Why would you do THAT?" I demand. "You gave the aphrodisiac to me, you blundering fool!"

"Hey! I'm still the king here!" he hollers.

"Not for long if you keep acting like this!" I tell him.

Despite my anger, I want Mark so badly, I can hardly stand it. I wonder if there's a way to make him hard despite his drugged state. I can at least rub up on him.

It's not like I've never forced a man to take me before. I am the Luna, after all.

With a sigh, I ignore King Gene in my head and take hold of Mark. Thankfully, my shifter strength makes me stronger than the typical woman. I am easily able to get him out of the chair and drag him over to the bed.

"Are you almost into position?" Gene asks as I mount Mark. His pants are still fastened, but my panties are sopping. I want him so badly, my hands are shaking as I start to unhook his belt.

"Why do you ask?" I demand from the king.

"Because! I can't hold them back much longer!"

"What?!?" I demand. "You have to! I don't even have my underwear off!"

"Make it look good!" he insists.

A second later, the door comes bursting in.

ROSE

"WHERE ARE WE GOING?" I ask as Tristan leads me by the hand down a hallway I've never visited before.

"I'm not sure what's going on, but I don't think we should leave Mark alone with that sneaky vixen," he declares.

"Don't trust him after the spanking incident?" Kelly asks from behind me. The other Alphas and Shelby are also with us.

Halfway down the hallway, we see King Gene, coming our direction. He has a strange look on his face. "Wh-where are you going?" he asks us, stammering.

"Oh, nowhere," Tristan deflects with a shrug.

"It looks like you're going somewhere," the king repeats, backpedaling as we are about to overtake him.

"Nope," Tristan insists. "Just a stroll."

King Gene turns on his heel and comes along with us. "Are you... looking for someone?"

Tristan says nothing, only shrugs.

"Because... I saw Mark earlier! He was walking down this hallway, hand in hand with Luna Barbara!"

My eyebrows raise as I turn to look at the king around Tristan's massive frame. "What?"

"That's right. He left my office and came down here to see her. I think... they're having a sexual affair!"

"Well, if that's the case, King Gene," Tristan begins, "I think we should rush to her room right now and see what we can discover."

I feel my stomach lurching into my throat. Surely, that can't be the reason Tristan is dragging me down the hallway at such a fast clip. If Mark was cheating on me, Tristan wouldn't want me to see that for myself, would he?

Wouldn't he want to protect me?

But then... if I saw Mark with another woman, it would devastate me. And Tristan might secretly want to have me to himself. That would mean he'd have to eliminate the other Alphas one at a time.

It doesn't sound right; I know I'm extremely hormonal. Maybe I'm jumping to conclusions.

"Yes, yes," King Gene exclaims. "Let's catch him in the act. I have keys! But first... can we slow down a little? I have a bunion on my big toe, and this hurts so badly!" I see his eyes shifting around and wonder if he's speaking to someone. Maybe he wants some of his guards to join us.

In case I try to kill Mark.

"Don't worry, Rose," Reece reassures me over my right shoulder. "I'm sure Mark isn't doing anything suspicious. After all, we thought the worst with Emily, but we were all wrong."

I nod, but I can't speak. If I open my mouth, I'll start crying. Maybe Tristan just wants to take all of the attention off of his slip-up with Barbara.

We come to a halt in the hallway. How Tristan knows this is where Mark is, I'm not sure. "Go ahead, unlock it," Tristan tells the king.

"Yes, yes," he says again, and he pretends like he can't find his keys.

With a sigh of frustration, Tristan plucks the entire keyring from the king's pocket and stares at it for a second before he chooses a key. I'm assuming he is looking for the master key, which happens to have a little red rubber covering over the top.

Tristan plunges it into the door and flings the door open.

What I see takes my breath away.

Barbara is on the bed, her legs spread wide, her skirt bucking as she rides Mark–hard.

"Oh, my Goddess!" I proclaim, rage and embarrassment filling my entire body so that everything has a crimson hue to it. "I can't believe this! First Tristan, now Mark!"

"Hey, little flower," Tristan declares, turning to look at me. "I might not be a saint, but I didn't do that."

Barbara turns her head toward us, her breasts flopping around so that it's obvious she doesn't have a bra on under her slinky top, and smiles.

"Dear Goddess!" King Gene exclaims. "Alpha Mark is having an affair with Luna Barbara!"

He sounds robotic, and I can't help but wonder why.

But I'm too angry to think through any of that at the moment. I want to turn around and stomp off, but Eli's arms come around me, and he pulls me to his chest. "Tristan, how did you know where Mark was?"

"Distress call," Tristan says, which gives me pause.

A moment later, Reece walks around us, and I turn my head to see him shooting over to the bed. "Son of a bitch," he says as he knocks Barbara off Mark. "He's sweating profusely! He's burning up! Tristan, give me a hand!"

"He's just got a passion fever. That's all," Barbara says, up on her knees. I think I see that she's still wearing her panties when she moves, and as Reece and Tristan haul Mark up off of the bed, his belt is the only thing unbuckled.

They're right. He's sweating a lot, and his head is lulling to the side as they move him over.

"Must've already blown his load and is having trouble keeping his eyes open because he's sooo tired!" King Gene adds.

I don't know what to think about any of this.

Barbara cries, "That's exactly right! He sure has! Many times! Bye, bye Marky! See you soon."

Mark can't even raise his head. We head out of the bedroom and down the hall, two Alphas carrying Mark. The king stays behind with Barbara.

Tristan looks me in the eyes and says, "Rose, he's not cheating on you."

"What the hell's the matter with him?" I ask, my heart leaping into my throat for the second time in just a few minutes as concern about Mark overcomes me.

Tristan sighs and says, "He's been drugged."

CHAPTER 10: SIMMER DOWN!

Rose

"Drugged?" I repeat Tristan's word out loud, mostly to myself. It makes sense, considering how awful Mark looks, but I'm worried. After all, the chef was drugged—poisoned—and she died. "Is he going to be okay?" I ask.

"Probably," Eli assures me, his hand on my shoulder. "It's probably some kind of a roofie, something that was meant to make him sleep so she could set it up like they were having sex."

"But, I have to wonder, the way that Barbara was all worked up, maybe she was supposed to give him something else, too," Reece says.

I look at him in surprise. "Like what?" I ask.

"Like some kind of aphrodisiac," Tristan responds for Reece. "Maybe she accidentally gave it to herself." He chuckles under his breath. "Goes to show that even the best-laid plans don't always result in anyone getting laid."

I turn and look at him, raising an eyebrow, but I don't say anything. How can he be joking at a time like this?

"I've summoned Dr. Penderghan," Shelby announces, running a few steps to keep up with us since she's been slowed by her mental conversation, I assume. "She said to take Mark to his room, and she'll be there shortly."

I turn to my friend and look into her eyes. "Thank you," I say. All of the anger I felt before has melted away. I know now Mark would never do anything to hurt me. I'm still not sure what he was doing in Barbara's room, but I'm assuming it had something to do with the conversation he had with King Gene right before then. The other Alphas had just come into my room to tell me that King Gene had walked in on them scheming and summoned Mark away.

"Why did you bring Rose to see that, Tristan?" Kelly asks, walking next to her brother. "What if Mark really had been having relations with that bitch?"

Tristan shakes his head. "I knew he wasn't up to something he shouldn't be doing. He told me he needed help. We were in the middle of a conversation, the lot of us, and I just figured we might as well all go together. I wasn't going to leave Rose there all alone"

That makes my heart swell, and at the same time, it makes sense to me; I'm glad Tristan brought me so I could see for myself what we are up against.

"King Gene was involved in this," Reece snarls. He doesn't seem any more worn out than the rest of us though he's carrying another grown man with one arm. "He must've been trying to set this up so it looked like Mark was cheating."

"He's been trying to poke holes in our relationships with Rose all along," Eli replies, sounding equally as angry. "Now that he realizes we are potentially organizing against him, he's probably even more worried. He doesn't just need to worry about what to do about Rose. He's going to have to contend with all of us, even the one he names as king. Maybe he's having second thoughts about abdicating."

Eli has a good point, and it makes me nervous. I feel my stomach start to swirl, and my heart is beating feverishly in my chest again.

"Rose, are you all right?" Tristan asks. "You don't look so good. I mean, you always look good, but you look pale."

I shake my head. "I'm not feeling so well."

"She should put her feet up," Shelby suggests. "When Dr. Pendergan is done checking Mark, she should check Rose, too."

It's a good idea. "I think I need some water, too," I say, and then suddenly, I start to feel weak. My vision is a bit dark around the edges, and my forehead feels clammy.

Could I have gotten poisoned vicariously through my love for Mark?

Tristan scoops me up into his arms, and I lean against his chest. We are almost to Mark's room, but I'm glad I don't have to walk the rest of the way, especially at this quick pace. My pelvis feels like it's ratcheting itself apart.

We enter Mark's room, and Reece lays him on the bed. Mark is still sweating, his brow damp, and his eyes are closed.

"Unbutton his shirt," Kelly insists.

"You unbutton his shirt!" Reece holds his hands up and walks away.

"Put me on the bed next to him, Tristan," I insist. As soon as I'm settled next to Mark, I unbutton his shirt. He groans a little. "Get a wet washcloth."

Kelly moves to the adjoining restroom to do as I've asked and returns with a cold, damp cloth, which I put on his forehead. He opens his eyes slightly and looks at me, and I lean down and kiss his cheek.

"I'm going to find Adam," Shelby says. "We need to figure out how deep King Gene is into this and what we can do about it."

"I'll keep you posted," Kelly says, and Shelby nods her thanks before she takes off out the door.

The other three Alphas are standing around, adjusting their weight from one foot to another, not sure what to do.

"Water!" Eli finally shouts and then rushes off to get me a glass of cold water. I appreciate it, and when I take a few slow sips, it helps a bit.

Soon enough, the doctor is there. She rushes in with her black bag to check Mark first, and I lean out of her way. She's brought one of the nice nurses with her, Harmony, and the other woman comes to check on me.

"How are you feeling?" she asks me.

"Uhm, tired… and nauseated. My heart is beating so fast." I sit still, being a good patient, while she checks my vitals.

"Your heart rate is a little high, but I think it's okay," she announces. "I'm sure this has been scary for you. Just try to relax, and Dr. Pendergan will check you as soon as she's done with Mark."

I thank her, and watch as Dr. Pendergoon starts an IV on Mark. "What are you doing?" I ask the healer.

"I'm going to give him some fluids," she explains. "It'll help push the drugs out of his system. He was definitely given something pretty potent, roofies or something, I'd say."

Another nurse comes in with a pole for the IV bag, and I see it's the mean one. I take a deep breath and look away from her.

I see the other Alphas standing across the room, conspiring about something, and I wonder what they are talking about.

I only hear one word: Emily.

Why are they talking about her at a time like this? I have no idea, but it makes my heart start thumping even harder.

"Calm down," Harmony says in a melodic voice that matches her name.

"Is he going to be all right?" Reece asks the doctor as I do my best to do what Harmony has instructed.

"Yes, in a few hours, he should be okay," she assures us. The doctor gets up and comes over to me as Reece goes back to confer with the other Alphas.

"Rose, you need to calm down, dear," Dr. Plentygas says to me as she rechecks my vitals. "You're getting too far along in your pregnancy to have these sorts of blows to your nervous system." She puts her stethoscope back in her bag. "I want you to rest for the remainder of the day. Only get up to go to the bathroom."

"Are the babies okay?" Tristan asks.

Dr. Picklegrasps checks my abdomen by pushing around a little bit and then nods. "Yes, the babies are fine. But for the babies to stay fine, the mama needs to be left to relax. No more stress, or else we're going to end up with four pups born way before they are due!" Dr. Pondergoose is looking at my men now.

"Yes, Dr. Pendergan," they all sing in chorus, looking ashamed, like they've done something wrong. I have visions of what my sons will look like when they do something naughty.

The doctor turns back to me and lightly instructs, "Get some rest. Eat well today. Vegetables, fruit, those sorts of things." Then she turns to the other Alphas and says, "You can leave her lying next to Mark, and I'll come and check on both of you in a couple of hours, all right?"

"Thank you," I tell her as she pats my hand. I am worried about my babies, but I know I will be well taken care of by these people who love me.

Dr. Poppinggator leaves, and I rest my head back on the pillow. I close my eyes, but when I open them a moment later, the light from the overhead lamp is blocked by a mop of dark curls. I almost jump with a start until I realize Tristan is leaning over me. "Yes?" I ask him.

"Are you okay?" He is looking at me with his bushy eyebrows raised.

"I was… until you gave me a heart attack." I narrow my eyes at him.

His face turns pink. "Sorry. We are going to go have a discussion, the three of us. And Shelby and Adam."

I look at Kelly. "I'll stay here with you guys," she says with a gentle smile. "I can't get Shelby to answer me on the mind-link, though. I know she found Adam. I told her you guys were okay and the doctor was here. Now, she's not answering." Since Shelby was the kingdom's Beta's wife, she had the ability to reach everyone via the mind-link.

Tristan rolls his eyes. "I guess we might be about to walk in on a real-life sex scene instead of a make-believe one."

"We could always just knock and wait," Reece suggests.

"Nah," Tristan says. "Walking in is always more fun."

I stifle a laugh as Eli spreads a blanket over me and Mark and then kisses my forehead. "We'll be back."

"Be careful," I warn.

"Don't worry," he assures me. "We will be. You just rest." He pats my baby bump, and then the three of my men who can walk right now head out of the room.

I put a hand on Mark's chest above his heart, feeling the thumping there and I close my eyes again, willing myself to relax.

CHAPTER 11: GENE MAKES UP HIS MIND

I wait in my cousin's office, pacing back and forth, my skirt billowing out behind me every time I turn around. It's a high-low, my favorite style, and it looks good on me. I can't believe I was forced to wear such drab outfits while I was at Alpha Stephen's mansion. The more time I spend in the castle, the more I can feel Emily coming back into herself.

As I wait for Gene to appear, I go over the conversation I had with Tristan. I think he bought it. I think he actually had some sympathy for me. I need to figure out a way to get him off by himself again so I can continue my sob story. I've thought of some other horrendous events I can tell him about. The more pathetic sounding I make myself, the better. I'm always in total control–even in the bedroom.

Well, except for control over Alpha Stephen's tiny peepee. No one could command that....

King Gene comes into his office with a huff and sees me, which stops him dead in his tracks. "What the actual fuck are you doing here?" he asks.

I'm not sure if he means in his office or in his castle. I'm certain he knows I came back to the castle earlier in the day. That information wouldn't have escaped him, though I was surprised at how easy it was for me to force my way back through the guards at the gate.

"Don't talk to me that way!" I bark at him. "You have a lot of explaining to do, cousin!"

"Me?" His eyes nearly pop out of his little head. "What the fuck are you talking about? I'm the king! I'm in control here! Why does everyone keep forgetting that?"

"I don't know what the fuck you're talking about, but we had a deal. A DEAL! And rather than honoring that, you bring that fucking bitch Barbara, of all people, here to give the crown to her?" I fold my arms and glare at him, tipping my head down so that I can look into his eyes.

He closes the door to his office like he doesn't want anyone to hear me dressing him down. "You were failing miserably at your task!" he chides. "Not only were you making it so that none of the Alphas wanted to marry you, but you were giving them all of the fuel they needed to conspire against me! Now, it's not enough that they wanted to hang on to that despicable Breeder after those children have crawled from her womb, but now, they are talking about dividing up the kingdom! Before I even declare one of them king! I will not have my lands, all that I've worked for, parceled up like slices of pie because you couldn't stay in your room and be nice, like a good little girl, you slutty little whore!"

My hand stretches out of its own accord, and a loud smack fills the office. As soon as I realize what I've done, I pull my hand to my chest with a sharp sigh. "Sorry!"

King Gene rubs his cheek, a look of hate on his face as he looks at me. "You colossal bitch!" he screams. "How dare you?"

"I'm just... Stephen called me all kinds of names thinking it was something I wanted to hear in the bedroom, and I didn't like it," I tell him, trying to cover. The fact of the matter is Emily doesn't let anyone talk to her that way.

But he's the fucking king, and he can do whatever he wants!

He pulls his hand away from his face and states firmly, "Barbara is here now. You have no place in my castle. All you will do is cause trouble!"

"That's not true!" I assure him. "I've already started making headway with Tristan. He believed the sympathetic story I told him earlier, and I have more tales to weave!"

"Unless by 'headway' you mean the head of his shaft is buried way up in your coochie, I don't want to hear it!" King Gene is practically standing on his tiptoes to try to look straight into my eyes. "You are the worst villain of all time! If this was a fairytale, you'd be... Prince John!"

I try to come back with a quick quip, but confusion at his words wash over me, and I ask, "Who the hell is that? Prince John?"

"You know. From Robin Hood?" He rolls his eyes at me.

I don't know what he's talking about, but I take it that his words are not a compliment. "I am the perfect villain when I want to be," I insist. "But that's not what I'm trying to do, dear cousin. I don't want to be a villain. I want to be a queen!"

"Yeah, an evil queen. Regina!" He is mumbling things that don't make sense to me anymore.

"No, a powerful queen! Like we discussed!" I hear a pleading tone in my voice that I can't stand, but I don't know what else to do. I feel this opportunity slipping through my fingers again, and I can't lose it.

Not to mention, if all of the Alphas are back here, that means that Stephen must be done fighting. So... he'll be looking for me. I doubt he'll show his face here after the other Alphas kicked his ass on the battlefield, but he may send someone to collect me.

To my cousin, I request, "Give me one week."

He folds his arms across his chest and glares up at me. He says nothing.

"You can't let that stupid bitch take what's mine!" I shout in frustration. "She's not loyal to you either, King Gene. She is fooling you into thinking that she is when she's not. Give me more time! I'll prove to you that I can do this!"

"Do what?" he argues. "I don't want you to do anything! I just want you to wait! You have to wait, like we discussed! I just wanted you to be here, in the castle, where you would be ready to take over as queen as soon as we knew who the king was going to be!"

"But then everything got fucked up, and you needed me!" I reminded him. "You needed me to work my magic on the Alphas to keep them from falling in love with that grotesque Breeder!"

"And you failed!" he shouts back at me. "You didn't manage to get even one of them to like you. You failed in getting them into your bed!"

"So has Barbara from what I gather! She managed to poison Mark but not give him the aphrodisiac, right? What kind of an idiot takes the aphrodisiac herself instead of slipping it to her target?"

A low growl comes through the back of King Gene's throat, and for a moment, I think he might shift. I'll have to shift, too, and we'll have a face-off in our wolf forms right here in his office.

Why is he defending her so much?

"It was an honest mistake!" he screams at me.

I take a moment to let him breathe, hoping he'll calm down, but he doesn't look like he's relaxing at all.

After a minute or so passes, I beg him, "Please, King Gene, dear cousin, give me another chance. Let me show you that I am the right choice as queen. You cannot trust her. Barbara makes me look like a fucking kitten. She's... a puma on steroids!"

With a loud sigh, he turns away from me and swears under his breath because he is fed up, and I suppose I can't blame him.

When he turns back to me, he states rigidly, "You have a week. But in that time, I do not want to see a single cat fight between you and Barbara! Your purpose is to show me that you can be the thoughtful, responsible queen I need to rule this kingdom when I step down. Show me you are Luna material, Emily, or I will let your sorry ass be betrothed to the man who is sulking around the walls of the castle gate, here to collect your pathetic bitch-self. If you can't, I promise you, I will never, ever see you again. The next time you show up at my castle, you'll find yourself with the very best view of the fields around the castle!"

I stare at him, confused, trying to figure out what the hell he's talking about. "View?" I echo.

He nods. "Yes. A lovely view. Because I will have my guards at the gate unceremoniously remove your fucking head from your fucking shoulders and have it placed on the end of a lance and propped up on the top of the castle walls for all of the fucking world to see!"

He speaks with such force that tiny flecks of saliva shoot out of his mouth and land on my face.

I don't wipe them away. It might look like I am being disrespectful again, and while I've never feared my cousin before, this time, I believe him.

I'd like to keep my beautiful head right where it belongs–not on the end of a lance.

"Thank you, King Gene," I say out of necessity, dropping my head as I show him respect.

His only response is, "One week."

CHAPTER 12: GOING AGAINST GENE

Eli

When we reach Adam and Shelby's room, Tristan reaches for the doorknob, determined to walk right in, as he's already forewarned us.

I grab his arm and pull it back while Kelly knocks, both of us giving him a stern look.

"What?" he asks. "I told you, it's more fun to just trot right on in. Why are we standing here, looking at one another like a bunch of ninnies who don't want to see a free show?"

I sigh and shake my head. "They're our friends, not a couple of porn stars. Why would you want to see them naked?" A shiver goes down my spine just thinking about it.

I definitely wouldn't want someone walking in on me and Rose having sex. It was nerve-wracking enough the time we had sex in the pond, out in the open, where people might appear from nowhere.

Before Tristan even has a chance to try to defend himself, the door opens, and Shelby is standing there, her hair a mess, her clothes wrinkled, and her blouse misbuttoned.

"Hello," she greets us, tugging down at her shirt and realizing her mistake. She can't fix it now without us all knowing what she's doing, so she shoves the front tails into her jeans and folds her arms under her chest. "What's up?"

She blows a strand of hair out of her eye, but it doesn't do anything but dance around a bit and land back over her eye.

I bite back a laugh as Tristan asks, "Where's Adam?" before he ducks his head into the room.

Shelby moves to block him. "Adam is… uh… coming," she says, and all four of us waiting on this side of the door break into laughter. Three of us try to hide it behind our hands, but Tristan tosses his giant head back and laughs like a lion roaring.

"Stop it!" Kelly says, smacking at the burly Alpha. "You're being rude. They're a married couple!"

Adam appears over Shelby's shoulder now, his pants unzipped and one sock missing, though he's wearing both shoes. "What's going on?" he asks, innocently.

"Tell you what," Reece interjects. "I'm going to close the door and count to sixty, and when we open it again, we'll start over, okay?"

"Better make it twenty or else they'll be going for round two," Tristan mutters.

Reece scowls at him and closes the door. Whether or not he's actually counting, I don't know for sure, but we wait awkwardly in the hallway, hearing the faint sounds of the two of them running around the room putting their shoes and socks on correctly, rebuttoning, and rezipping.

"Are you ready?" Reece calls after a moment.

"Yep!" Shelby says, and the door is opened to reveal the well-kempt couple we are used to seeing.

"Now, what do we need to discuss?" she asks, her hands folded in front of her.

"Can we go out into the garden where it doesn't smell like–"

I interrupt Tristan with a sharp elbow to the bicep, "Pine-Sol? I believe the maids are mopping the hall." The faint scents of lemon and pine linger in the air, but I don't know if that's from a current cleaning session or if it's just the smell the hallway always has.

"Sure!" Shelby walks between us and heads down the hall toward the exit to the outdoors.

We will need to keep our voices quiet out here. I wonder if Tristan has thought this through.

The six of us find a secluded place where we can see who is coming from both directions, and we make sure no one is hiding in the bushes or looking down at us from the balconies above us.

"What are we going to do about the king?" Tristan's whisper voice is almost as loud as his yelling voice.

"What about him precisely?" Adam asks. He's probably not whispering because he clearly doesn't see the point when we've already checked to make sure no one is around, and if he whispers anything like Tristin, they'll be able to hear him two kingdoms over anyway.

"Well, he's working with Barbara, obviously," Reece says with a shrug. "It seems quite clear he was a part of the drugging situation with Mark. If he hadn't been, maybe the plot would've actually worked. I got the impression whatever poison they were supposed to give Mark to make him wild and horny for Barbara actually went to her instead."

Tristan cracks up at this, and his laugh almost makes me laugh, but I remind myself this is serious.

"We know that King Gene wants to kill Rose. That's not a secret," Adam says in a rush.

"Whether or not he intends to let Barbara come in here and do that, or just take over her place, I don't know. Why would he want Barbara to seduce Mark? What was his end game?"

"To make Rose mad at him?" I guess. "So she will be upset and not want to be with him anymore? Maybe the plan was for Barbara to seduce each of us in turn so that Rose has a tiff with each of us, and we stop pining for her?"

"That could be it," Adam reasons with a shrug. "But if he wants to kill her, why would he care if the five of you aren't getting along?"

"Because he wants to make everyone miserable first!" Shelby exclaims, her hands flailing in the air. "He doesn't just want her dead–

he wants her to suffer before she dies. He's a horrible, miserable little man."

Kelly reaches over and puts her hand on Shelby's arm, and I am proud of my little sister for being so kind. Then she says, "That fucking bastard!" I am equally proud of my little sister for being so passionate.

"Maybe we need to fight crazy-ass fire with crazy-ass fire," Tristan suggests.

"What are you talking about?" I ask him, completely lost.

"If King Gene is willing to bring in some insane person to help him with his side of this battle, perhaps it's time we did exactly the same thing." Tristan gives us all a confident nod, his wild curls dancing around his smiling face.

"Say what now?" Shelby asks him for all of us.

"Yeah, so, he brought in Barbara, and she's clearly one butt-piece short of a loaf, so I'm thinking why don't we bring in our own wild card?" Tristan suggests.

"Butt-piece?" I ask.

"Yeah, the heel. The piece no one wants." He looks at me like I'm stupid for not understanding his analogy. I marvel at the fact that no one else looks lost.

Kelly leans over and whispers, "It's best to just let him think you understand." She smiles and nods.

"Who?" Reece asks. "I don't want just any crazy person brought into the castle. We already have our hands full enough with Gene, Emily, and Barbara."

"We need a crazy person who owes us one," Tristan says with a confident air about him.

"You're not suggesting we allow Alpha Morris to come back here, are you?" I ask him, a shiver of fear shooting down my spine.

"Why not? He owes us one. We can have him come in and take out Barbara or Emily. Maybe both of them. He's not averse to stabbing women."

"You can't be serious!" Shelby declares. "You want us to let the man who tried to stab Rose, while you guys were away at war, come back into the castle?"

"He's a changed man now," Tristan tells us. "He works for us now."

"He's not exactly the sort of secret agent I want to employ," Reece speaks for all of us.

"That's fine. He'll work for free," Tristan assures us.

"You're missing the point, Tristan. We don't trust him. There's no reason for us to bring back someone who could be dangerous to Rose!" I don't know how else to say it.

"Trust me on this one." Tristan winks at me, like I'm some chick in a nightclub he can charm to his way of thinking. "I'll make it work. Rose will be fine."

"I'm not sure I'm willing to completely trust you on that one, Alpha," Reece says, shaking his head, and I completely agree with him.

"In the meantime," Adam says, "I'll see if I can find out anything more specific about what's going on with Barbara."

"And maybe we can scare King Gene into thinking that you guys won't protect him should Kane attack again!" Kelly reasons, raising one finger in the air. I'm so proud of my little sister. She's so smart!

"That's a good idea!" Reece says, and I agree. "Then, maybe he'll give us more credit–"

"Or leave the castle," I chime in.

"Either one works," Adam reminds us, and we all nod. Everyone except for Tristan, who seems to be sulking that we didn't love his plan.

We don't need Morris here. I think that is a huge mistake.

And yet, I know in my heart that he'll do it anyway.

CHAPTER 13: KING GENE IS DRUNK

*ROSE

"You're so beautiful."

Mark's voice sounds hoarse and raspy as he tries to talk to me. He reaches over and caresses my cheek.

Neither of us have been awake for long. I opened my eyes first, a few minutes ago, and then watched as his eyelashes fluttered a few times, and now his blue eyes are locked on my face.

"How are you feeling?" I ask him, scooting toward him in bed so I can put my hand on his chest.

He coughs and tries to lift a hand to put it on top of mine, but he's so weak still, he gives up, and his hand falls back onto the bed. "I've been better."

I giggle, not because he's clearly under the weather still but because he is so adorable. "I wanted to murder you for a few moments," I admit.

His head moves up and down slightly, and I take it that that movement is supposed to be a nod. "I don't blame you. If you thought I was choosing to have sex with that awful monster, you should be ready to rip my heart out. But I would never, ever go behind your back to sleep

73

with another woman. I don't want to sleep with another woman. Not now, not ever."

I can't help but pull myself over to kiss him. His lips are a bit cooler than normal, and they aren't even a little damp. I assume it's from all of the sweat making him lose fluid. The IV bag is gone.

Puzzling over its disappearance, I ask, "Did Dr. Pe–uh, the doctor–come back in?"

"Yes, you were asleep. She just took my IV out. She said my fluids were better," he explains.

I glance at the clock and see we've been sleeping for about three hours. Or I have been, anyway. Apparently, he woke up at some earlier point.

"I don't know about that. Your lips are so dry," I tell him.

He awkwardly turns his head, and I see a glass of water on the nightstand next to him. I reach for it and bring it over to him, and he lifts his head slightly so I can put the straw to his mouth. He takes a long drink, and then I set the glass aside.

"Thank you," he says, and I nod with a smile in return. "Are you okay? Are the babies okay?"

"Yes, I'm fine. They're fine. I just needed to rest a little. Too much excitement for one day," I tell him, rubbing my abdomen.

"Good. I would hate to do anything to upset you or harm the babies." I can see the concern on his face as his brow wrinkles.

"I know that." I snuggle up next to him, careful to give him some room because I don't want him to be in any discomfort.

"I love you so much, Rose." He means it, and I know that even without the words.

"I love you, too." I kiss him again, and this time it seems more like normal.

"I was just trying to do what the king wanted, to keep him happy. I didn't think he would be so manipulative as to try to put me in that sort of a situation–again."

Another laugh escapes me. "I know," I reassure him.

"Where are the others?"

I am sure it's killing him not to be out there with the other Alphas trying to handle the situation. Personally, I'm used to sitting back and letting them take care of everything. I wonder if that will continue even after I'm done being pregnant, but I'm sure it will.

"They went to meet with Adam and Shelby to see what to do about Gene and Barbara conspiring, I believe." I think I'd heard that before I fell asleep.

A forlorn sigh escapes his lips. "I wish I could be there with them."

"Me, too," I agree. "But you need to get some more rest. She gave you a lot of whatever that drug was. I think they bungled that. I bet they didn't mean to give you so much."

Mark doesn't say anything. I assume he's just too tired. He rests his head back against mine, and his breathing evens out. I kiss his forehead and close my eyes, so glad he's still mine—and no one else's.

Reece

I have drawn the short stick…. I have to go talk to King Gene about this situation. I don't want to go at all, but Tristan is still sulking about us not agreeing with his amazing plan to call in Morris, and Eli and Kelly are up to something.

Shelby and Adam have gone back to their room to allegedly talk over what Adam should say to Gene since he's still pretending we don't know that the king intends to kill Rose, and Mark is still recovering.

So that leaves me….

I knock on the king's office door and wait for him to shout at me to come in. Rather than yelling, he actually opens the door for me, a glass holding three fingers of whisky in his grip, and it's clear to me that he's been drinking. A lot.

Maybe that will make this easier.

"May I come in, Alpha King?" I ask.

"Yes, yes." He waves a hand and retreats to his desk. I close the door behind me and take a seat across from him. He's so drunk, the amber-colored liquid splashes out of his glass as he drops into his chair. "What want you Reeceeee?"

I clear my throat, taking a moment to think about what he's said and decipher it. "We were just wondering... if we had done something to upset you. It seems like you and Barbara were trying to do something harmful to Mark, something harmful to all of us, and we want you to know that we are loyal to the crown. We want what's best for the kingdom."

He laughs, and it's so high pitched, it sounds like a little girl giggling as she pets a kitten. "You're not loyal to meee!"

"I didn't say we weren't," I reply. I didn't say we were either.

He sets his glass down and leans forward onto his folded arms, his eyes glassed over, and his head dancing around like a cork bobbing on the ocean. "Listen, here, you Alpha Reeceee, you!" He points an unsteady finger at me. "I heard you guys! I know you guys are after my throne! I know it!"

"But... that's why we're here!" I argue. "We are here because one of us will take over after you. What we do with the kingdom after you've retired is not your affair, King Gene–and I say that with all due respect." It doesn't matter that all the respect he's due is none.

"But you don't wanna do what I wanna you to do," he says. "You wanna have that nasty bitch Breeder as your Luna. And I don't wanna let her do that. And I only want one king. Not fooouuur." He holds up three fingers, looks at his hand, and then adds another one.

I shake my head. "That's not what we want. We just want what's best for the kingdom. And we need you to trust us. You chose us for a reason, after all."

"I chooosed you because I thoughteded that you would be the bestestes. But you're acting like little whiny baby giiirls!" He picks up his glass to take another drink and completely misses his mouth, the whisky splashing on his shoulder.

I guess it's fair to say he has a drinking problem... he's having a problem drinking.

"Okay, King Gene. I'm not going to argue with you." I hold up my hands. "But the thing is, you're going to be forced to make a choice here, soon enough. Either you can continue to trust us, and give us the liberty to do the appropriate planning for what needs to be done for the kingdom moving forward. Or... you can go ahead and let the only other Alpha who is strong enough to run things take over and see how that goes."

His eyes bulge from his head. "Only other Alpha who what? Do what?"

"I think you heard me," I assure him. "I know you're concerned that we won't continue to provide you with the protection you desire from our four packs, and I think it's a legitimate fear. So what happens if we stand down, King Gene? What happens if this tiff between you and the four of us becomes so big that we leave you on your own?"

He shakes his head adamantly. "That won't happen. It can't happen. You are... in my kingdom. I am the boss of you."

Again, I shrug at him. "Well, sometimes we can't make the troops do what they don't want to do, and they just run away from the battle-field!" I lift my arm and gesture as if I am shooing a bunch of warriors from the fight.

He swallows hard. "And if you won't defend me... that means...."

I nod my head. He gets it now. "That means you'll be overrun, and you'll become a captured king. The prisoner of the one and only–"

He interrupts me, the fear in his eyes obvious. "Alpha Kane!"

CHAPTER 14: A FAVOR

Tristan

Early the next morning, the day after Mark's poisoning, I am up before the crack of dawn and outside near the gate, down the road from the castle, pacing.

The other Alphas are busy, and that's for the best. They don't need to know what I'm up to. Not yet anyway.

Recently, the four of us have been acting like we have one head and can't make any decisions for ourselves. Every time one of us gets mildly "out of line," Mark throws a hissy fit like a little baby.

Well, he's still incapacitated, so this is the perfect time for me to take a bit of control of the situation.

But if this plan doesn't start to come to fruition in a few minutes, I'm going to abandon ship and head back to the castle. Mark might be out for the count, but Eli and Reece are going to figure out eventually that I didn't accidentally let Mr. Whiskers out into the north garden. They can only yell, "Here, kitty, kitty, kitty!" so many times before they lose their voices.

Besides, Emily or Barbara are likely to reply, anyway. I shake my head. They're looking for kitty, not pussy.

I hear a sound on the road outside of the gate and stick my head through the bars to look and see if anyone is coming.

"Sir, we can open that for you," one of the guards on duty says. I've been ignoring them for the most part. They're just Omegas. I don't like to put people into categories, but if there was a group of people that ranked right above boll weevil, it would be Omegas.

"I know that," I tell him. "I am an Alpha. I know how gates work. I'm just looking." In the distance, I see the person I've been waiting for. I know it's him, even though he's in his wolf form. He smiles at me, and I shoot a hand through to wave at him. Then, I try to pull my head back through the gate.

And can't....

I swear under my breath and try again, but all I do is smash my ears.

Visions of my head slathered in butter come to mind, as well as the angry faces of the other Alphas, and I twist my head one more time and wrench it out. My ears might've fallen on the other side of the wrought iron spokes, but I'm out.

"Open the fucking gate," I tell the guard who is laughing at me under his breath, and he does just that.

When he sees there are about thirty wolves pouring through, his eyes fill with alarm.

"Relax," I tell him. "These guys are here because I invited them."

He doesn't look any more calm.

I take in the group in front of me, and my breath catches in my throat.

"What the actual hell?" I ask, knowing that the Alpha in front of me can answer me with the mind-link since we are of the same rank.

"What?" he asks. "These are my best troops."

I look them over. One really is missing an ear. Another stops to scratch himself with a back leg, drawing blood from the flesh between patches of fur. Another has nipples so long they're dragging the ground, which makes me think she just had pups. Maybe as many as Rose is about to have....

No, this is not what I had in mind.

"Morris!" I yell. "When I spoke to you on the phone last night, you said you had an excellent group of warriors to bring with you!"

"No, Alpha, I said I had an excellent group of wolves to bring with me. I didn't claim they were warriors," Alpha Morris says via the mind-link. He is just as scrawny and awkward as a wolf as he is as a human.

I shake my head and grab a hunk of hair, nearly ripping out a handful of my signature curls. "Somehow, I totally doubt that."

"No, it's true," Morris argues. "What we lack in finesse, we make up for in intelligence. My wolves are far smarter than any others you'll ever encounter."

I look them over. One in the back has his paw shoved up his nose. He's literally trying to pick his boogers with his paw.

I want to point this out and tell them how stupid they are, but I did just get my head stuck in a gate.

"Besides, I know a secret about Luna Barbara, something that will blow your mind!" Morris says, his eyes widening.

I look at him skeptically as I hear in my head, "Tristan? Where are you? I can't find this cat anywhere!"

"I'm... still looking... by the purple flowers..." I tell Reece. They probably can't find him outside because Mr. Whiskers is in my bathroom.

"What do you know, Morris?" I ask with a huff.

He takes a step forward, like he needs to whisper in my ear even though he's using the mind-link. "Luna Barbara is working with... Alpha Kane!" he declares.

I roll my eyes and shake my head. "I told you on the phone that we were trying to convince King Gene of that, dumbass. It's not true!"

"No, it is true!" he declares. "And I can prove it!"

∿

EMILY

. . .

ONE WEEK!

I have one week to show my stupid ass cousin that I am queen material, and I have no fucking idea how I'm going to do it.

That little bitch won't even let me have my old room back! Instead, he has me in a wing of the castle completely separate from the Alphas. He says it's the best place for me. I can't fucking believe him.

Finished with stewing in my room, I decide to go out and see if I can find one of the Alphas. It's still early morning, and I'm usually not up this early, but I need attention. I hear some people walking around in the hallway near my room, so I decide to go and investigate.

"The rooms are nice," someone is saying, and I can't help but scoff. These rooms are not nice!

I step around a corner and nearly run into someone. When I see who it is, I leap backward.

"Alpha Morris!" I shout. "What the hell are you doing here? I thought the Alphas must've torn you apart for trying to kill their beloved Breeder."

"Nope. I'm here as a guest of one of the Alphas. He needs me for a secret plan. We're going to–" He immediately stops talking, realizing he's almost said too much.

"Help them with what?" I ask.

"Uh, uh, uh!" he wags his finger in my face, and I think about chomping it off. "I can't tell you. It's between me and my Alpha friend. He's my best friend."

I bite back a laugh. "Which one of the Alphas is your best friend?" I ask him.

He continues to shake his head like a little kid. "I can't tell you. My very best friend might get mad. He said I'm here on a secret mission. The keyword is secret. So I can't say anything that might make Tristan angry at me, you see."

I keep my face straight. The moron doesn't even realize that he's just told me.

Why the hell would Tristan invite this sorry ass Alpha back to the castle when I made him try to stab that Rose whore?

"Well, you should help me," I tell him, folding my arms. "I'm trying to take down Luna Barbara."

His eyes widen a bit and then he declares, "Oh, I know lots of secrets about her."

He's got my attention now, though I'm not sure I believe him. His secret is probably that she has to sit down when she pees….

"What secret do you know?" I ask him.

"Oh, I'd be happy to tell you, beautiful Miss Emily," he says with a twinkle in his eye that makes my stomach turn over.

"Go ahead," I urge him.

His head shakes so fast, I think he might lose it. I imagine it spinning off and lodging in the wall across from us. Then, he'd be out of my way again.

Problem solved….

"I can't tell you," he insists. "It's a secret."

"Because Alpha Tristan would get mad?" I ask, rolling my eyes.

He inhales so deeply, I feel myself being sucked toward him. "How did you know I was working with Alpha Tristan?"

"I'm a mind reader," I tell him.

"No, you're not. If you were, you would be able to tell me the secret about Luna Barbara!"

He's got me there. "Fine, well, I can only read minds that have something to do with the Alphas."

He nods, his mouth forming a perfect O, like he believes me.

"So you're just going to have to tell me what you know about Barbara."

His grin widens. "Sure. I'll tell you," he says. "But everything comes at a price."

I scoff at him. I've got plenty of money, but my purse is back in my room. "How much?"

He's shaking his head again. I hope no one walks by and gets hit with a flying head. "It's not money I want," he tells me, his head stopping so that he can wiggle his eyebrows at me.

"Then what?" My stomach tightens. I probably don't want to know.

He says, "Take my… virginity."

CHAPTER 15: CAT FIGHT–IN MORE WAYS THAN ONE

T<small>RISTAN</small>

After I sneak Alpha Morris and his misfits into the bedrooms in what I think is an empty wing of the castle, save Luna Barbara's room, I head back to my bedroom. From my bathroom, I hear loud mewing and wonder if the other Alphas just haven't come back inside.

How do they not hear that?

I open the door, and a ball of fur comes flying at my face. Claws sink into both of my cheeks as the cat hisses and screams. Blood streams down my face as I rip him, and a bit of flesh, away from my face.

"What the fuck?" I ask him, doing my best to manhandle Mr. Whiskers into a less dangerous position. I tuck him under my arm, but it's clear he's not happy. I get a glimpse into my bathroom.

Either it's been snowing in my bathroom or Mr. Whiskers murdered the toilet paper. I hope there's another roll under the sink. If I have to take a dump later, I'm not wiping with his shredded confetti.

"I got him!" I tell the other Alphas through the mind-link as I run toward the outside door.

I don't make it too many steps down the hallway before Reece and

Eli appear in front of me. Both of them look confused. Mr. Whiskers sinks his claws into my hand again, and I toss him down onto the stone floor. He takes off in a blur, hissing at me again.

"What the hell is wrong with him? It's like he's possessed by the devil!" I say.

"Your face looks like it," Eli points out.

I wipe the blood on my sleeve, and I am amazed at how much there is. Thankfully, it doesn't hurt anymore, and I assume that means I'm starting to heal.

"Where was he?" Reece asks.

"Oh, uh… near the flowers in the garden." I wipe at my other cheek and get just as much blood.

"Then why were you coming from that way?" Eli asks.

"I came in a different door," I say with a shrug. I should have thought this through better. They don't believe me.

"Tristan?" Eli asks.

"What?"

He puzzles over my face for a second and then shakes his head. "You're up to something. I don't know what it is, but you're up to something."

"I… am a perfect angel," I insist. "But I am insulted!" I stick my nose in the air and turn around, headed back for my room. I need to take a shower and then go talk to Morris. Maybe he has come up with a plan for how he can take out Luna Barbara.

After my shower, I begin to walk over to Alpha Morris's room. I think I hear someone crying. It sounds like a woman. It's high-pitched, and whoever is distraught is wailing like they can't get a handle on their emotions.

I think it might be Morris.

But it isn't coming from the room I told him to take, and before I can investigate, the bedroom door opens, and Emily walks out, swiping at her face. She stops and stares at me before she asks, "What the hell happened to you?"

"I was about to ask you the same thing," I admit. I wonder if my face still has scratch marks for her to be asking that. I think I smell the scent of sex lingering around her, flowing out of her room. "Who were you with?" I ask.

It couldn't be an Alpha. I just saw Reece and Eli, and Mark is with Rose.

She straightens up. "That's none of your business."

"You seem like you need someone to talk to Emily," I begin. "Maybe I can–"

"Oh, thank you, Alpha Tristan!" She latches onto my arm.

I was about to say find her a maid or something, but she seems to think I meant me.

"I have been dying to tell you more about what that dreadful Luna Barbara did to me."

"Wait!" I stop her, my forehead crinkling. "You were having sex with Luna Barbara?" Now, this is a story I can get behind.

Her eyes widen and she looks like she wants to scratch my face. "No! Gross! I hate that bitch. I mean, how she ruined my life!"

"Right...." I nod. I look around. I do need to talk to Morris, but it looks like Emily needs someone to talk to, and even though I don't believe what she told me before, I do believe in the idea that it's smarter to keep your enemies closer than your friends. "Wanna go outside?"

I don't need for anyone to think I'm up to something in Emily's room.

"Sure," she agrees, not letting go of my arm.

I find the nearest exit and take her out to a garden, where we have a view of a lot of balconies and everyone can see us. "What's the trouble, Emily?" I ask her.

She blows out a hot breath, finally letting go of me. "It all began five years ago...."

"Can I have the short version?" I ask her.

She turns and glares at me before she says, "Fine. Barbara stole my mate, my one true love, and she killed him. She also killed her own baby."

"Right," I said. "So I have heard."

"I don't think you understand, Tristan!" she exclaims. "Before I met

Barbara, I was a wonderful person. I was kind-hearted. I used to teach kindergarten!"

I tip my head to the side and stare at her. "I don't believe that, Emily. You're still the king's cousin. I can't see you taking a job that pays as little as a teaching position."

"Well... I did help the other kindergartners in my class when I was in kindergarten." She says this like it's the same as being a teacher.

Somehow, I even doubt that is the case. Maybe she helped them to glue their mouths closed or cut off their ponytails.

"Barbara did her best to have me killed! She sent a mass of warriors after me, trying to... take my virginity and leave me for dead! Thankfully, I got away."

"And you probably didn't have your virginity to take five years ago," I mutter.

She growls at me. "The point is, she tried to come after me! All because I was in love with Ivan."

"Wait... you were in love with her husband?" Ivan—Alpha Ivan—was Barbara's husband; the whole kingdom knew this.

Emily shrugs. "I didn't know that he was her husband. We met, and it was clear to me that he was my mate. So... we met several times, making love beneath a blanket of stars!" She looks up at the sky and takes a deep breath like she's lost in a memory.

I clear my throat. "You didn't know he was the Alpha?" I find that hard to believe. We almost always know when we're looking at an Alpha or a Beta. There's just an air of respect around them.

She bats her eyelashes a few times and says, "He told me he was a professional chicken sexer."

I stare at her with my mouth agape for a long moment before she moves toward me a little, and I'm afraid she is taking this as an invitation to kiss me. "A what?" I am imagining a grown man and a chicken in some awkward positions, and I have to shake my head to clear it.

"Don't be a pervert, Tristan," she warns. "A chicken sexer looks at baby chickens to see if they are males or females. You know... roosters or... regular chickens." She makes a face, like she knows that's not quite right.

"Hens," I tell her.

"Hence… I didn't know he was the Alpha." She thought I was segueing into another thought; I let it go. She still doesn't know that female chickens are called hens, and I'm okay with that.

"Well, Emily, it sounds like you and Barbara both have all the reasons in the world to kill one another. Tell you what, why don't we put you both in bikinis, get a big vat of Jell-O, find a couple of spare medieval mauls, and see what happens?"

She glares at me for a second before she says, "You know, I'd be happy to wear a bikini for you, Alpha Tristan." She winks at me, and my stomach turns over worse than it did when Mr. Whiskers tried to scratch my face off.

She didn't even get my name right. "No, thank you," I say. "Listen, I have to go talk to A—a friend." I almost said Alpha Morris, but I saved myself.

"Alpha Morris?" Her eyes are narrowed again.

"What?" I scratch the back of my head. I didn't know she was in that hallway when I picked those rooms.

"I know he's here," she declares. "Don't worry, I'm on your side. I won't send him after Rose again. Besides, he says he's completely loyal to you."

My forehead puckers as she looks forlorn again, and I remember she had been crying… and maybe having sex.

I have cried during sex before, so I understand. But I don't think Emily got any of her pubic hairs caught in a toy.

"He told you I asked him to come to the castle?" I clarify.

She nods, looking away. "Yes. He told me. He said he'd tell me a secret he has about Barbara, but he was just tricking me." She turns her head violently to look at me. "I don't like to be tricked, or… taken advantage of."

Things are starting to make sense now. Did Alpha Morris get Emily to sleep with him by telling her he'd give her a secret about Barbara? And then back out?

Was it the same secret he told me, that Barbara is really working with Kane?

"Well, you can't trust him, I guess," I say with a shrug, getting to my feet. "I need to go find him."

"All right. But remember, I'm at your disposal, Terrance."

I sigh, not even wanting to correct her. I give her a little wave and head inside, making my way to Morris's room.

I knock on the door, and a moment later, he answers with a wide grin on his face, whistling a happy tune.

He smells like Emily.

I don't think I can trust either one of them... I need to get this asshole into shape or else the other Alphas are going to be pissed I brought him here.

CHAPTER 16: PARANOIA

Emily

I sit in the garden for a bit after my talk with Tristan. I don't think that he believed a damn word I told him, and it pisses me off.

The other day, when I first got back, I thought that I might've actually had his ear. But now... he seems more worried about getting in there and talking to fucking Alpha Morris about their secret plan than speaking to me.

I have to wonder what it is that Alpha Morris thinks he knows that will turn this situation with Luna Barbara on its ear. He was supposed to tell me after the five minutes of awful sex we had where I took his virginity–though with that performance, I think he should still be labeled as a virgin, or at least half virgin–but he refused–laughing in my face.

I need to know what it is....

After a while, I get up off of the garden bench and head inside. I only make it about five steps when I hear a familiar tune being whistled and the clomping of footsteps.

It's the same song Morris was whistling while we were having sex.

I believe it's the theme of a television show. Just the sound of it makes me nauseated.

"Oh, hi there... lover," he greets when he sees me.

My stomach turns even more, but I don't correct him. I don't see the point in telling him we are anything but lovers at the moment.

"Hey," I say. "Well, I just had a conversation with your best friend. I didn't even have to have sex with him for him to tell me about your little secret." I roll my eyes. "It's not even that big of a deal, you know."

"Not a big deal?" He looks shocked. "What do you mean? Of course, it's a big deal!"

"You think?" I ask, shrugging my shoulders. "I bet King Gene already knows about it anyway."

"Well, he thinks he does because Alpha Tristan lied to him to try to get Luna Barbara in trouble, but King Gene doesn't know that it's true."

I clear my throat, thinking I almost have him. I just need to play nonchalant for a few more minutes, and this idiot will blurt out–

"Seriously, Miss Emily! It's a huge deal that Luna Barbara is really working with Alpha Kane to try to take over the kingdom!" He shakes his head at me. "Baby, I love you so much, but sometimes you can be dense."

Bile rises up in the back of my throat. Baby? He loves me?

"Shut the fuck up, Alpha Morris!" I shout, coming at him. He almost trips over his own feet as he backs away from me. "You're a fucking moron! Don't ever call me 'baby' or say you love me again! And stop whistling that goddamn song! No one cares about a stupid TV show!" I wheel around on him and start to walk away.

I get a few steps down the hall, walking over to Alpha Tristan's room, thinking I will check this theory out with him, when Morris shouts, "But wait... baby!'"

I ignore him and continue on my way, but as I am about to get to the Alpha's rooms, I notice that a door is ajar as someone is standing in front of it talking, and I pause.

"Listen, Shelby, I have to get back to the office. You're going to have to wait for Little Adam until later."

"Oh, there's nothing little about you, baby."

Again, I find myself thinking about puking as I stand there, eavesdropping on Adam and Shelby.

"I have to figure out what to do about this. We can convince King Gene to stand aside if he knows Kane is coming for the crown. He can hand it over to Tristan or one of the other Alphas."

"But baby–"

That is enough for me. I've heard everything I need to, and I know who I need to talk to next.

I take off, heading toward my cousin's office, thinking he will have to listen to me now. I've heard from two different people that Luna Barbara and Alpha Kane are after his head.

If he goes into hiding, I'll have a chance to convince whoever he puts in place as temporary king that I am the one who should be the next queen. I'll have to pretend that I will leave that stupid bitch Breeder alone, but that shouldn't be too hard.

I am the new Emily. I have turned over a new leaf….

King Gene's office door is open, so I make my presence known. He is slamming down the receiver on his phone and cursing.

Seems like a good time to invite myself in. "Hello, cousin."

He takes one look at me, drops his head, and says, "Fuck me."

"Listen, I'm going to tell you something you need to hear, and I need to make sure that I have your attention," I announce as I walk across the room.

"Emily, get out of here. I already told you, you have a week to do whatever it is you think you need to do to convince me to make you queen. You're wasting your precious time. You've only got six days left."

"What I have to say is more important than that, King Gene. It involves your safety. I have heard that Barbara is working with Kane!"

He rolls his eyes at me and scoffs, a maniacal giggle slipping from between his chapped lips. "That again? I've heard that one already, Emily, and I don't believe it! Why, just an hour ago, I called Luna Barbara in here and asked her if she was working with Kane, and she told me no."

I stare at him, waiting for him to tell me some further proof, but that's it. That's all he's got.

Her word… against everyone else's.

"She's lying to you, cousin!" I exclaim. "If she was trying to kill you, do you think she'd announce it on the evening news? Listen, you need to go into hiding! He knows exactly where you are, and he has an assassin in your building, one he tricked you into inviting here!"

"I invited her because I wanted to!" he shouts back at me.

I shake my head. "That's what he wants you to believe! Maybe he's controlling your mind, slipping thoughts into your dreams! You don't even have any foil on your head!"

King Gene reaches up and places a hand on his head. "Foil?"

I look up at the ceiling, and my eyes trace all around the room. "You never know what methods he'll use!"

He opens his mouth and then closes it. "I don't know, Emily. Let's get the Alphas in here and see what they think."

"Well, I don't know how you'll have a meeting without Kane knowing," I say with a humph.

"What? You think he can see into my office?" Gene spins around, looking for some sort of a sign of infiltration.

"It won't be obvious. You'd better get some foil!"

His eyes are wide as he stares back at me.

A few moments later, a maid rushes in with a roll of aluminum foil. Quickly, my cousin tears off a piece and wraps it around his head, including his face.

"Well, that's a good way to suffocate," I mumble. I consider just letting him pass out, maybe actually die, but I decide against it. "Let me help you." I bite back the word "idiot." I make him a little hat of tin foil, and he puts it on his head.

"You have to wear one, too!" he says.

I refuse to do any such thing. "Alpha Kane can't hear me!" I insist.

"Why not?" Gene folds his arms, looking ridiculous. I have sculpted a long pointy top to his hat that looks a bit like Stephen's floppy penis, but bigger.

"Because… I have a vagina," I tell him.

His eyebrows knit together, and I just nod.

"You wanted to see us, sir—what the hell?" Tristan stops mid-sentence when he comes through the door, followed by all three of the other Alphas. Mark looks a little under the weather. I've heard that Barbara tried to kill him—or something. "What's that on your head, King Gene?"

"Shhhh!" Gene hushes, grabbing pieces of aluminum foil for all four of them. Without speaking, he directs them all to make similar hats. They look at me, and I shrug. It's clear the king wants them to do it, and none of them feel like arguing, so a moment later, they all have foil penis hats, and I am trying not to laugh.

"Why don't you have on a tin foil hat, Emily?" Mark asks me.

"Because she has a vagina, you moron!" Gene yells at him. "Now, listen up! I have heard that Alpha Kane is working with Barbara, and they are trying to kill me! Emily says he can hear every word I say!"

"And your every thought," I chime in.

"Unless you have a floppy-looking dildo on your head made out of reflective material?" Tristan says, unamused.

"What do dodo birds have to do with anything?" Gene asks. "Listen, she thinks I should go into temporary hiding and let one of you idiots be king for a while!"

All of them light up at this prospect. "I didn't say just any of you, though," I remind them. "I think Tristan is the man for the job."

He arches an eyebrow at me.

"What do you think, Alpha Tristan?" King Gene asks. "Do you have it in you to run things while we send our armies out to squash Kane?"

Tristan salutes the king. "I swear on my life as an Alpha, I will not disappoint you, sir."

I try not to laugh. It's a little hard to take him seriously when he's wearing a big schlong on the top of his head.

But when Gene says, "Fine. Then… I've got to figure out where to hide," I know the score this round is Emily one, King Gene the idiot, zero.

CHAPTER 17: WE HAVE EACH OTHER'S BACK

I can't reach my snack, and I don't know what to do about it.

About ten minutes ago, Kelly brought some sliced pickles and peanut butter into my room and set them on the nightstand.

The only problem is, I was reading at the moment, and I didn't reach for them right away.

Now, she's gone out into the hallway to speak to Shelby, and my arms must have shrunk because they don't quite reach....

And... scooting isn't really an option at the moment. I've tried reaching as far as I can without moving my bottom, and I nearly rolled onto my side. Visions of my large pregnant self rolling onto the floor, maybe rolling out the window, down the roof of the floor below me, out into the garden, and on, and on, forever come to mind, and I don't think that's a good plan, so I sit still for now, willing Kelly to come back and hand me my snack.

I could use the mind-link, but that would make me seem like a big baby.

That word brings my hand to my abdomen, and I find myself rubbing my little fighting champions. They are all very kicky today. I imagine what it will be like when they are on the outside. Will they just run up to one another and kick each other for no reason?

Sadness washes over me as I realize I may never know....

As much as the Alphas are fighting for me to be able to stay with my babies, there are no guarantees. I still may have to let them go.

I can't imagine doing that, not when I feel like I know them already.

A soft knock on my door draws my attention and gets me excited. My mouth begins to water. Even when Reece sticks his head in, I'm not longing for him in a way that I normally would have before all of these babies invaded my body. I'm just glad he's more mobile than I am.

He can get my pickles and peanut butter for me!

"Hey, darlin'," he calls softly from the door. "Can I come in?"

"Of course, you can," I say, forcing myself to stay centered on the fact that I am happy to see him. He sits down next to me and kisses me, and while I'm doing my best to focus on him, as soon as he releases my lips, I say, "Can you hand me that?" and point to my snack.

He was already leaning in for another kiss, so he freezes awkwardly, lips puckered, to open his eyes. His eyebrows raise. "Your pickles?"

I nod. "And the peanut butter. Please. I can't reach it."

He chuckles under his breath as he hands me the little tray it was brought in on. "Silly girl. Why didn't you call for help? Kelly is standing out in the hallway talking to Shelby."

"I know," I say, already dipping a juicy slice of green pickle into the peanut butter. "I didn't want to bother her."

He still thinks this is funny. "Do you need anything else?"

My jug of ice water and my book are on the bed next to me. "I'm good. Thanks."

He smiles back at me as I give him a mischievous grin, and then he snuggles up beside me, wrapping his arm around me and the babies. "How are you feeling?" he asks, his head on my shoulder.

Between bites, I tell him, "All right. Still a little stressed. But not as bad as before. Has anything important happened?"

The soft groan that comes out of his mouth answers my question before he even starts to speak. "Yeah," he says. "So... King Gene is going into hiding for a while."

I stop with a bit of pickle in the air, near my open mouth, and turn my head to look at him. "What? He is? Why?"

"Because we've finally convinced him that Luna Barbara and Alpha Kane are working together to kill him. He's decided it would be better for him to go off somewhere and hide and let one of us Alphas be the temporary king until we can kill off Kane."

My face scrunches up. "But... he invited Barbara here, didn't he? Thinking she should be the next queen since Emily left?"

"Yeah, he did invite her, but apparently, Barbara really is working with Alpha Kane, and Barbara does want to be the next queen, either by hooking one of us or by overthrowing Gene, overpowering us, and bringing Kane in to be her king. I don't know, Rose. Everyone is scheming at this point. We thought we had made up the rumor about Barbara and Kane working together, but Alpha Morris is certain it's true."

Again, I find myself pausing mid-bite. "Alpha Morris? That nasty, rail-thin man who tried to kill me?"

Reece's head rocks back and forth, and I can tell by the expression on his face, he didn't agree with whoever decided to bring him back either.

"What is he doing here?" I can't help but shout.

"Tristan thought it would be a good idea. We all told him it wasn't, but he said that the man owes him one, so he brought him in. Now, the rest of us are dealing with it."

I hold his gaze for a few seconds, not sure what to say to that. I do trust Tristan, but at the same time, I'm not sure this is the best idea the man has ever had. "Perhaps Tristan's ego has gotten the best of him," I murmur.

"Well, yeah, maybe so. And now that he's temporary king...." Reece shakes his head, his voice fading away.

"Tristan is the temporary king?" I ask. He acknowledges me with a nod. "How did that happen? I always felt like King Gene favored Mark or you over him."

"Emily suggested it, and King Gene just went with it. I'm sure Emily just thinks he's the most easily manipulated."

She probably thinks she can act all sexy and get him to do her bidding. Thinking of her trying to seduce one of my men makes my appetite fade. I shove the last bite of pickle I already peanut buttered into my mouth and hand the tray to Reece, who sets it back on the table. Once I'm finished chewing, I ask, "Are you okay with that?"

He nods. "It'll be all right. Though, I did hear him singing, 'If I Were King of the Forest,' a little while ago when I walked past his room."

I almost laugh, imagining Tristan dressed up like the lion from *The Wizard of Oz*.

"Don't worry, darlin'," Reece says, leaning over and kissing my temple. "We'll take care of you. Don't be afraid of stupid Alpha Morris or anyone else. I know firsthand that these guys won't let you down when you need them, and neither will I."

I smile at him, but I'm confused. "What do you mean?"

"I mean...." He grows quiet for a moment, his eyes glazing over slightly, like he's remembering something he doesn't want to. "When we were out there battling against Alpha Stephen, I was attacked by a much stronger wolf who was fresh to the battlefield. For a moment, I really thought I was going to die. But then, out of nowhere, the wolf went flying off of me, and Eli was there. He just seemed to appear out of thin air. He knocked that wolf off me, and then the big guy was dead. End of story."

I can tell from Reece's expression that he's still shaken up about this, and I am so thankful that Eli was there to keep him safe. Some people might've stood back and watched Reece die, thinking it would make the situation easier for them, but none of my men would ever do that.

"I'm so thankful you both came back to me unharmed." I drag my hand down his cheek, and he pulls me in for a kiss, a deep, passionate one that lets me know he's thankful he's still here, too.

I can't help it when my body starts to meld to his. I don't want to try to have sex when my belly is so big. It's worked recently, but I've had too much stress. Mark and I kissed quite a bit while he was in here, but not much more than that. When Reece's hand slips beneath my top and bra, and he finds a breast, I lean into him, moaning a bit.

But I have to tell him, "Can we... not go too far?"

He grins at me. "I'm here to do whatever you want, gorgeous woman." I smile back at him, and he kisses my neck, his hands continuing to roam my body. He feels so good; I might be begging him for something else later, but for now, I'm content just to let him touch me, kiss me, and remind me that I am loved.

CHAPTER 18: QUEEN EMILY

EMILY

As I stand in front of the full-length mirror, I can't help but smile at the reflection of perfection beaming back at me. Shaking my hair, I watch as the curls fall around my shoulders like soft velvet ripples.

Although I had no doubts about the success of my mission to get my idiot coward cousin out of the castle, I know I still have a lot of cards in my deck to play. He is probably hiding out in his plush emergency bunker somewhere far away, sitting on his swamp ass with a silly foil wrapped around his head out of concern that Alpha Kane is monitoring him or listening to what he's thinking. How much of a fool could a so-called king possibly be?

I look around the empty room and feel my heart drop just a notch. I wish there was someone around I could boast to about how clever I've been. I wish my posse was here so that they could marvel at how awesome and great I am.

I sigh. I don't need their validation, though. Soon they will be curtsying to me when I am their queen. I will wave them away as they all scramble to kiss my feet as their illustrious ruler. My king will be by my side beaming at Emily, his beautiful and clever wife.

Speaking of king, Alpha Tristan was really making my whole plan a bit difficult. Getting him to bend to my will seemed easier in my head than in real life. The curly-haired gorgeous giant isn't budging. He is cleverer than I anticipated. Maybe I should have suggested that King Gene put Alpha Mark as temporary king instead. I mean, he had been foolish enough to spank me that one time.

Alpha Tristan has even refused to assign another chambermaid to me. Who does he expect to brush my precious tresses? Or lay out my clothes for me? Who is going to tear up the perfect-sized piece of toilet paper for me to use when I go to the bathroom? Argh, the man is so handsome, but he is really going to be a hemorrhoid in my backside when it comes to my mission.

I need to find a servant around the palace to do my bidding, not just running my usual errands of cleaning my eyebrow spoolie brush, or telling me I'm pretty, but to go check where Barbara is. I need to get rid of my competition now before my cousin returns.

I would have gone after the dirty Breeder that has started looking like a barrel with her bulging belly, but I can never gain access to her. She has people watching over her every minute of the day. I have even heard she has people accompany her to the toilet now. Is it all because of little me that they have her so heavily guarded? I am really a force to be reckoned with then.

And they say Emily can't be queen....

Besides, attacking the Breeder now would put me on the wrong side of the battle line with the Alphas. I need them to continue thinking I am a good girl now.

"Be a good girl, Emily. Make them like you, Emily. Show them you are queen material, Emily. Yada-yada." Even with my idiot cousin so far away, I can still hear his irritating voice in my head.

I can't go ask Beta Adam for help. His wife has him under lock and key. She's so overprotective of her husband. Who would be interested in stealing such a boring man? Even if he was free, I wouldn't want him. He is cute, but definitely not a wretched Emily type. I think Shelby is just so insecure it's pathetic. Maybe if she was giving him some good head, she wouldn't have to be so worried about him straying or something.

I will have to go after Barbara. If I kill her, no one will miss her. I will have done everyone a huge favor. Heck, they might even hail me a heroine. All hail Queen Emily, the hero.... Now, that has a nice ring to it.

I walk over to the door leading into the hallway. As I poke my head out into the hall, I smile when I see a maid carrying a mop and bucket walk toward me.

"Hey, you. Come here," I say. She looks at me, and I think I see her scowl before she bows her head and comes over.

"You called, Lady Emily?" the maid asks with her head still bowed.

"I need to send you on an errand," I say.

She doesn't raise her head as she says, "King Tristan says we aren't to take direct instructions from you, my lady. Anything you need is to go through him first."

I suck my teeth as I feel the rage bubble in my chest. King Tristan this, King Tristan that... hogwash!

"I will pay you," I add.

"With all due respect, my lady, I can't disobey the king's orders," the maid says.

"Do you know who I am?" I ask as I inch closer to the servant.

"Yes, everyone knows who you are," she responds. I get a feeling she isn't even intimidated by me in the least.

"If you value your job, you will do as I ask. I am the future queen and can have your head for this insolence!"

She bows ever so slightly and begins to walk away from me without responding.

"Hey, come back here!" I yell, but she doesn't give me another glance.

"I won't be another Tara," I hear her mutter as she walks away.

Dang! It looks like I have to do all this by myself. I walk down the hallway in the direction of Luna Barbara's room. As I near the door, I glimpse two guards. Great! It seems Alpha Tristan has everything and everyone on lockdown. Why had I assumed the giant was as brainless as his blow-up sex dolls?

I stop, unbutton the top of my blouse, and purposefully stride up to the guards. As I near them, I can see them turn to look at me. I straighten my neck and push my chest forward, hoping my cleavage will do much of the convincing rather than my words. I fan my face with my palm and run my hand from my neck down to the exposed flesh of my upper breast. Their eyes follow my every movement, and I can't help but bask in the attention.

The first guard I stand in front of is shorter than me. He looks plain, pinched, and uncomely. He looks at me nervously, and I am amused to see his eyes wander down my blouse and to my chest in quick succession. Well, who can resist such perfection? I put my palms under my breasts and lift them just a little as if I am adjusting them. The action makes the guard visibly swallow nervously.

Oh, sexy, gorgeous Emily never disappoints.

"Open the door. I need to see Luna Barbara," I demand.

"My lady we–" he pauses as he tries to collect himself. Once composed he starts again, "I'm sorry, my lady. We are under King Tristan's instruction not to let anyone in."

"Oh? Even little me?" I ask as I pull the front of my skirt up, exposing a large amount of milky white thigh flesh.

Again, the guard follows my movements and visibly gulps. "I... I'm sorry. No one can enter. Luna Barbara is a prisoner; no one enters and no one exits."

I let go of my dress. I am tempted to move closer to him and nestle his head inside my bosom to try to seduce him into opening the door, but I am not about to touch that dirty guard.

I turn around and frog march back to my bedroom. I need to think of another way to gain entrance into Barbara's living quarters. The window of the room that Alpha Tristan is holding Luna Barbara prisoner in is so tiny that I could never climb through it. The only way into the room is through that heavily guarded door.

Luna Barbara has to cross the world of the living border to meet her maker today, and I am going to give her the passport to do that one way or another.

When I see the sun setting, I tip-toe down the hallway again. I see new guards stationed at the door. It doesn't take me long to shift into my wolf form and charge at the unsuspecting guards.

I pounce on the first one with my front paws. The force pushes him into the wall behind him and unfortunately, he is impaled into one of King Gene's art deco wall spikes. Oh, well.

Who puts spikes on their walls anyway?

The second one unsheathes a knife as he turns toward me, so I spring forward and grab his neck between my teeth. The metallic taste of blood flows onto my tongue.

Who would have guessed that a mere dirty guard's blood could taste this... sweet?

CHAPTER 19: CAT FIGHT IN WOLF FORM

Emily

I shift back into my human form to retrieve the keys from one of the dead guard's pockets. I am naked, but I have never been one to shy away from my flawless birthday suit. I love how I look without the unnecessary distraction of clothing. It's a pity we are always expected to put on something to look decent.

The attack on the guards was swift. I hope I didn't make too much noise. I want to catch Luna Barbara unaware and ill-prepared; after all, she is a stronger wolf than I am. I need the element of surprise on my side to cause enough damage to her so as to kill her.

As I slowly unlock the door and walk in, the sound of leisured clapping fills the dimly lit room.

"Evil Emily. I was wondering when you would be coming to visit your old pal. I have been waiting for you. Do you need to borrow some clothes? Just looking at your naked body is giving me pink eye," Luna Barbara says with a bite. I can see her sitting in a rocking chair at one end of the room. She picks up a champagne flute and takes a sip.

I blink as I look at her. How was she being given champagne, yet I was denied even a glass of awful prune juice? Is she not a prisoner? Do prisoners get spoiled with champagne? On the small table next to her I glimpse a little bowl of caviar and an open box of chocolates with empty wrappers strewn around it. What is this, prison or some romantic hideaway? What am I going to see next? A semi-nude muscular hunk feeding her strawberries and whipped cream?

How had she anticipated that I would be coming? As if reading my mind, she says, "Wondering how I knew you would come? Oh, Emily. I know every move you will make before you even think of it. After all, you learned your best tricks from me. Remember when you were my lap dog? 'Oh, Barbara, teach me your ways. Oh, Barbara, how can I get Ivan to look at me with puppy dog eyes? Oh, Barbara, you are awesome, I wish to be just like you.'"

"You were just as poisonous back then as you are now," I spit out. "I knew you were busy trying to get Ivan for yourself, bitch. I too could see you for who you really were underneath all that layered make-up: a dried-up sour raisin. You are so lucky to see me naked like this... such perfection in human form. Isn't it nice seeing what you don't have anymore–a young body without wrinkles? Wish you were me, huh?"

She scoffs and places the champagne flute back on the small table. "Emily, Emily. You are still delusional. If your body was that beautiful, wouldn't men be lining up to claim your hand in marriage? Even Ivan couldn't be serious about you. One wonders why he ended up being MY husband instead of yours. Maybe he was more into experienced classics than a wannabe-has-been like chewing gum that has lost all its flavor."

I can taste the bile rising in my throat at the discussion of Ivan. Luna Barbara can't see how Ivan still affects me. "Ivan is dead and gone. I don't even care about him anymore. Besides, I'm glad you took him. He was never the type of man to satisfy me," I lie.

"You mean he couldn't satisfy the black hole you call your va-jay-jay? So if he wasn't man enough, who is? Alpha Stephen? I had no idea that evil Emily is now into deflated clown pencil balloons. Is it really true he has a problem with his...." She makes a whistling sound as she points at her pelvis.

I suck my teeth. "Why do you care? Want to steal him too?"

Luna Barbara throws her head back and laughs. "Steal who? Alpha Stephen? Bitch, please. Been there, done him. Besides, if I wanted him, I could just have him. Unlike you, I am actually a master in the art of seduction."

I roll my eyes. "Really? Is drugging a person into submission one of your master skills in seduction?"

Luna Barbara glares at me but doesn't respond. I guess she wasn't aware that I knew about how she had tried to drug Alpha Mark.

Finally, she says, "What the fuck do you want, Emily?"

"Your head on a fucking platter," I answer.

She snarls as she regards me. "And you are going to take my head off my shoulders I suppose?"

I shrug. "Maybe I will or maybe I'll just leave it attached to your lifeless body. After all, your pack might want to take your body in one piece to their burial grounds. I could be nice enough to at least give them that much."

"How considerate of you. I'm not sure I will show you the same kindness, but I can try," Luna Barbara answers as she stands up. She is about half a foot taller than me. I swallow but try to hide my fear from her.

I watch her push the silk gown she is wearing off her shoulders. It glides to the floor, revealing her naked body beneath it.

She shakes her head and stretches her arms above her head. Her breasts push up as she does, and I snort. There is no way in hell she could have such perfect boobs. I'm certain she's had work done, as I know her breasts should be hanging on her chest pathetically like used condoms at her age.

As she begins to shift, I do the same. Her jet-black wolf stands and looks down at me.

"Let's do this bitch! I promise to make your death swift and fast," she says to me through the mind-link. Her wolf growls at me as we circle each other. I snarl back as I prepare to pounce.

Attacking her as she sees me coming would be stupid. I need to distract her for just a minute. Maybe I could make her think someone important is coming through the door. That probably wouldn't work, though, unless she thinks it's one of the Alphas.

"Did you say something?" Luna Barbara asks.

"No," I say, wondering if somehow she has read my mind. Should I have worn a dildo foil hat on my head too?

I crouch down and go for her forelegs. Maybe if I knock her down a few inches it will be easier to subdue her. She anticipates my move and leaps up as I advance. Her long sharp claws slice painfully through my shoulders. Before I can react and retreat, she has her paws pinning me to the floor.

"Stupid Emily. Didn't I tell you that I know your moves before you even think of them?"

I wriggle trying to get free, but she is so powerful. As I struggle, I realize it only causes her claws to dig deeper into my chest. "Bitch!"

"Aw, are those going to be your parting words, bestie? How about 'I will miss you?' Don't be sad, though, you will finally be with Ivan in three... two...." She bares her teeth, and I close my eyes, waiting for her to rip my throat open.

"Stop!" a voice booms from the door.

A huge shadow appears through the doorway; the person strides over and yanks Luna Barbara off me like she is a little kitten. I wince from the pain as her claws are extracted from my chest. I can feel a thick, warm liquid gush from my shoulder and chest.

I look down and see that I'm bleeding heavily. My head feels a bit dizzy, and everything goes cold. Oh, Moon Goddess, I don't want to die. What would the world be without Emily in it? Miserable, that's what.

Alpha Tristan stands in his human form and looks down at both of us. Even in our wolf forms, the dude is huge.

"Help," I manage to whisper to him through the mind-link as I try to will the pain away.

"What the hell is going on here? Who killed the guards?" he demands.

"Luna B... Barbara was trying to escape," I swallow and bite down on my inner cheeks as pain ripples through my chest. "I saw her killing the guards… I rushed over to stop her."

"Emily killed the guards. Even on the brink of death, you are still a lying bitch. I would have thought you would want to at least confess your sins before your miserable end."

How does she know what I told him? Or did she just guess?

I turn my head to see that Luna Barbara has shifted back to her human form. She is standing tall, naked, and proud with her hands on her hips. Yes, that body has definitely had some work done. I can tell a tummy tuck when I see one. I'm sure that if I squint hard enough I will be able to see the liposuction marks.

Throbbing pain surges through my shoulder and chest again, and I wince. I am finding it hard to breathe now. The figures in front of me are getting blurry.

"Beta Adam, get Doctor Pendergan to Luna Barbara's room, stat." I hear Alpha Mark's voice say from somewhere distant.

Luna Barbara crouches beside me and smirks, "Look what you made me do."

Oh, wow. She's going to kill me and get away with it. I was a fool to come in here. Everything around me turns dark as I slip into nothingness.

CHAPTER 20: DISTURBANCES

MARK

The sound of feet marching around outside the door is making me restless. My groggy head and dry mouth aren't making it any easier to relax. I get up and walk to the door. I need to find out what the ruckus is all about.

"Do you think the palace has been invaded?" Rose asks as she clutches her belly protectively.

I stride back to her and lift her chin with my palm and smile as I gaze into her eyes. Looking into her eyes is like getting lost in a cave full of fireflies on the night of a full moon. Beautiful.

"If we were under attack, I'm sure we would have known about it by now. Besides, we have a strong defense force set around these walls; no one can get in. If they do, the four of us are all here to protect you, baby, so don't worry about anything."

Rose smiles and nods softly. I can tell she's still shaken and I plan to go investigate what's happening. The door bursts open and Kelly storms in. She has a small box in her arms that she sets on the floor.

"Have you ever heard of knocking?" I ask.

She looks at me and rolls her eyes. "Knock-knock," she purrs as she crouches beside the box.

I shake my head. "What's going on out there?"

"Emily and Barbara were fighting. Eli says you should make your way to Barbara's room," she answers as she sorts something inside the box.

"Oh, okay. What do you have in there?" I ask curiously.

"Weapons of mass destruction," she replies without raising her head from the task of going through her box.

I raise my brow. "Weapons?"

"Uh-huh." She doesn't offer any more details.

I kiss Rose on the head as I prepare to leave, then stroll over to where Kelly is crouched in front of the box. As I peer inside the box, I frown.

"These are just nun chucks," I point out, puzzled.

"Not just any nun chucks, Alpha Mark. Ten of the most deadliest type of nun chucks ever created. I can take out an entire wolf pack with these," Kelly says with an air of pride.

"I really don't see that happening, Kelly, but if this is your weapon of choice, so be it," I tell her, shaking my head.

Just then, Alpha Morris walks into the room. I move to stand in front of him. If Emily and Barbara's fight was a distraction to get us all to leave Rose at his mercy, he has another thing coming.

I have to look up as I regard him. The guy is very tall, yet so scrawny. If he were to eat a bit of protein and put some meat on those bones, he would be quite a fierce-looking giant.

"What are you doing here?" I bark at him.

He moves back a few steps, opens his mouth, and closes it again. It looks like he has lost his ability to talk.

"Alpha Lanky is with me. He'll be on guard duty outside the door. King Tristan's orders," Kelly says.

I look down at Kelly and raise my brows at her.

"Say what? The man who tried to kill Rose is going to be guarding her?"

Kelly smiles and shrugs. "Alpha Lanky isn't all that bad. Besides, I'll be here with Rose. He will be outside. If he tries anything stupid, I will shove so many nun chucks so far up his ass, he might just look like he got a Brazilian butt lift."

Alpha Morris winces and then nods his agreement. "I'm a friend. One of you now."

I shake my head. One of who? I move closer to him. "If you try anything funny, I will tear every one of your limbs from your pathetic body."

My voice sounds menacing, but it doesn't help that my head is level with his chest as I speak. Damn, the guy is tall.

"Take care of her," I tell Kelly. "You, come with me," I say as I take Morris's arm and lead him out of the door. I leave him outside the now-closed door and make my way toward the East wing.

I speed walk down the hallway toward where Barbara is being held. As I get there, I see two bodies lying on the floor covered in red blankets. Well, that was easy. It seems the two witches took each other out.

"No one gave me the good news," I announce as I enter the room.

The three Alphas all turn to look at me with frowns on their faces.

"What good news?" Tristan asks.

"I heard Emily and Barbara were fighting, so I assume they took each other out," I nodded toward the bodies. "You know… met their maker. Kicked the bucket."

"Alpha Mark, I had no idea you would call my death good news. Do you hate me that much? After what we shared a couple of nights ago?" I hear Barbara's voice.

I jerk my head to my right side and see her sitting in a rocking chair slowly unwrapping a piece of candy. She is naked and smiles when our eyes meet. What the hell?

"Do you see her too?" I ask.

Eli and Reece roll their eyes.

"See who?" Tristan asks.

I point at Barbara. Tristan looks in the direction I'm pointing and then back at me.

"Are you feeling all right? Maybe the drugs aren't completely out of your system. Do you have a fever?" Tristan steps toward me and puts the back of his hand to my forehead.

"I'm fine. But I promise you, Luna Barbara is sitting right there. Can you all see her? I think she's haunting me." I add in a whisper, "And she's naked."

Tristan lets out a loud belly laugh.

"I think he is going mad," Reece adds.

I look from one Alpha to the next. Did this mean they all couldn't see her?

"I am telling you, Luna Barbara is sitting right there," I insist.

"Of course, I am, darling Mark. Where else would I be? This is my room after all," Luna Barbara explains.

I stagger back. "Guys, do you hear her at least?"

I'm hoping Emily won't be haunting me too. Her ghost will torment me to no end, begging me to spank her.

"Earth to Mark. We can all see and hear Luna Barbara. She isn't a ghost. She is very much alive... unfortunately," Tristan clarifies.

Phew. They had me going there for a bit... or did I have myself going? I look at Tristan as my mind tries to process everything.

"So, if she is alive, who are those dead people out there? Please tell me one of them is Emily," I ask.

"Wouldn't that be nice? I'm sorry to say it, but Emily is a cockroach; she doesn't die. Even if you spray some pesticide in her face, you'll still see her stick legs kicking," Luna Barbara says.

"One of them killed the guards that I had keeping watch over Luna Barbara's room," Tristan says.

"What? Which one of them killed the guards? Those men had wives and families." I clench my fists as fury engulfs me.

"For crying out loud, Emily killed those guards. How do you suppose I killed them? The door was locked from the outside, and the guards were outside. If y'all think I can glide through doors or keyholes, you are giving me too much credit. Or do you all think I really am a ghost? Walking through walls and shit? Use your fucking heads to think," Luna Barbara says.

"We know your story, Barbara," Eli says. "We're just confirming that one of the guards didn't unlock the door for you, then you killed them, and let Emily in."

"Where's Emily? If she killed two innocent men, I hope she is dead too," I say.

"No. She was taken to the infirmary. Dr. Penderghan is tending to her injuries. She has a torn shoulder ligament, a chest wound, a few broken ribs, and a punctured lung," Tristan narrates.

I look over at Luna Barbara. She shrugs as she pops a candy into her mouth. "All I did was touch the bitch and she fell apart."

"So tell me again why a murderer needs medical attention? Why didn't you just let her die?" I direct the question to Tristan.

"We never leave a wolf wounded. Besides, she has to be in her best shape to face the punishment that's coming to her. I have a few ideas on the best torture gadgets to use on her. I promise you, Emily has a slow, painful, and humiliating death waiting for her."

I nod. I do want to see Emily suffer for her crimes.

"Emily doesn't deserve a quick death. That would be too easy. She needs to stew and suffer," Reece adds with a distant look in his eyes.

Emily has spilled so much innocent blood for her own selfish needs. I agree that she needs to suffer. I think of the poor cook and her family.

"As for you, Luna Barbara, you can't stay here. You aren't innocent either. You drugged Alpha Mark, and we know about your alliance with Alpha Kane," Tristan declares.

Tristan calls some of the strongest men from his pack and instructs them to take Luna Barbara to the dungeon.

We all go to Eli's room. When we get there, Tristan pours out drinks for all of us.

"Well, thank you, Your Majesty," Eli says. He bows slightly and grins as he accepts the drink.

"We need to get rid of Barbara," Reece adds.

"Yeah, maybe we can ship her to another realm or something," Tristan says.

I frown. "If only it were that simple."

"Then find a witch to cast a spell that will put her in that book. She just has to go far, far away," Tristan declares.

Just then the door bursts open. I guess no one knocks anymore.

Shelby charges in; she looks like she has just seen a dementor and is breathless.

"R... Rose is in labor!"

CHAPTER 21: WE'LL LAUNCH THE ATTACK

Each contraction brings with it a pain that consumes my entire existence. There is only pain and fear in these moments, and they seem to last forever. I can hear voices around me, but I don't pay any attention to them since I'm trying to concentrate on how I'm feeling.

This can't be right, can it? It should be a few weeks before the babies arrive. What's happening?

The pain disappears, but only temporarily, for only about a minute. I breathe deeply while keeping my eyes closed because I don't want to reconnect with life outside of my body. With the awareness I have, the room might as well be empty, but still, I can hear people talking.

In fact, I think I can hear the voices of my Alphas in the room.

"Rose, dear, can you hear me?" I open my eyes slightly and I see Dr. Pendant standing beside me with a stethoscope. She proceeds to put it on my abdomen, and when she does, the crippling pain returns. I push my head back into the pillow and clench my jaw.

I can feel someone reaching for my hand. I smile as I think it is one of my men trying to comfort me, but then I feel a stabbing pain in my wrist. I try to pull back the hand, but it is held firm.

"Stay still, dear. I need to get this IV into your arm," Dr. Pentagon is saying. Soon the IV is in.

My eyes remain closed as I hear her feet shuffle toward the foot of the bed. I feel it as she lifts my nightgown slightly with what I assume are gloved fingers probing my folds. What the hell? Was she doing this with all those people I hear in the room?

"Okay, she isn't dilating. I think what she had were just Braxton-Hicks. She isn't going into labor yet, but she needs to rest and keep hydrated. I've given her an IV with something to help relax her," the doctor explains.

"You hear that, little flower? No more listening to Toni Braxton. See what happens when you do?" Tristan says. I can hear the relief in his voice.

I open my eyes and lean my head to the side to look at him. Reece and Mark stand holding each other's hands. When they realize how they've been clutching each other so tightly for comfort, they let go and pretend it never happened. I can't help but chuckle. Men are so funny. What is so wrong with holding each other's hands for comfort? Shelby, Kelly, and I hold hands all the time.

They all move closer to the bed and gather around me. Kelly looks at me with tears still streaming down her face. I guess even her nun chucks were useless against the Braxton-Hicks.

"So, doctor, should she not listen to any music at all or just the Braxton sister's songs? Can she listen to Mariah Carey or Janet Jackson, or will she get Carey and Jackson hicks? Could we have a list of the safest music she can listen to?" Tristan asks. He's just being silly. We all laugh, glad he's broken the tension

Dr. Pentecost frowns at him. She doesn't seem to get that it's a joke. "This wasn't caused by music, King Tristan. It's a natural occurrence. Take it as practice for the real thing. Braxton-Hicks is just the name for it."

Tristan nods, then turns and winks at me, probably deciding to just let it go. The other Alphas look relieved. Maybe if they had read some of the birthing magazines I gave them without being afraid of seeing a picture of a woman pushing out a baby through her vagina, they would be a bit more informed and not so scared.

I wonder why they don't want to see the truth about how babies actually come out of a woman. How do they think their children will exit my body? Do they think I'll sneeze and they will fly out of my mouth or nostrils? That would be ideal, really.

I hadn't expected Braxton-Hicks to happen now... or I had just hoped I didn't have to go through them.

"Emily's surgery went well. She'll need to be on oxygen for a while until her lung heals," I hear the doctor tell the Alphas.

I can't help but wonder what happened to her. Did someone spank her a bit too hard?

After the doctor leaves, my men, Kelly, and Shelby all sit around the bed. Some are on chairs and some are on the bed.

"I heard the doctor talking about Emily. What happened to her?" I ask.

"Oh, she almost died," Shelby says.

"Emily almost died?" I ask.

"Yeah. Luna Barbara kicked her bony ass. I heard Luna Barbara's wolf was levitating around the room like a ninja, and she practically knocked the bitch tendencies right out of Emily," Kelly adds.

I think my eyes look like flying saucers as I look at Kelly. Everyone laughs and I think she's exaggerating.

"They were fighting and Emily was beaten," Tristan says. "I guess they have bad blood. But I don't think you should be worrying about Emily or Barbara, little flower. Just focus on your beautiful self," he assures me, and he leans in to give me a peck on the lips. Then he deepens the kiss, letting his tongue taste every corner of my mouth.

"Ew!" Shelby exclaims and giggles. Mark smacks Tristan on the back of his head.

"Get a room," Reece orders.

"We are in a room," Tristan says.

An eruption of laughter envelopes me and makes me feel warm all over. I am surrounded by love. This feels so right. This feels like home.

~

Barbara

"So you ran away from the palace because you bought the lies they told you?" I ask King Gene through the mind-link.

Dang! This place smells as if a dead rat had a baby with a skunk's fart. Terrible. How dare Alpha Tristan throw me in here? This wouldn't have happened if King Gene was here. The coward! I would still have the luxury and freedom to roam as I wish. The only restriction would be the stupid dog collar, but I would take that over this horrid place.

"I know you're working with Alpha Kane, Luna Barbara," King Gene says. "I thought you came here to help me with my mission to cause confusion among those idiots and get rid of the Breeder."

I roll my eyes and fend off a fly with my hand. "I think you are the idiot in this equation, my king, with all due respect. They sold you a story and you bought it. Why would I work with Alpha Kane? This is the same man who once attacked my pack. You know I hate him just as much as you do. How could you let those Alphas get rid of you so easily?"

There is a bit of silence for a moment. "But Emily said she knows for a fact that you are working with Alpha Kane. My head is even itchy from wearing a foil hat on it every day."

I pause. Why would he be wearing a foil hat? I mean, he does look like a turkey, but why would he want to be roasted in a foil wrapping willingly?

"I don't know anything about the foil, but I do know you need to get back here. They are conspiring to turn everyone against you. Also, why would you believe anything Emily says?"

I pause before continuing.

"This is the same girl who once made you give her a thousand dollars every week because she said she needed to buy premium grade hand-weaved chocolate flavored tampons. She told you they would help absorb the rebellion out of her when she goes on her periods. I admit that periods can make a woman cranky, but no special tampon does what she claims. Also, women don't have a period every week. There is no such thing. She is just as sneaky and knows she can manipulate you whenever she wants. She's now very close to the Alphas, by the way, and she's going to help them get rid of you as revenge for sending her away to Alpha Stephen."

"Are you sure you aren't working with Alpha Kane?" he asks.

Goddess, this man is just stubborn. "Of course, I'm not. I want my revenge on that bastard just like you do. Also, the night my child went missing was the same night he launched an attack on my pack. Coincidence? I think not."

"Those idiots really thought they fooled me. Well, I'll show them," King Gene finally relents.

I sigh in relief. I cut the mind-link to King Gene, and I try to sniff my underarm. I can still smell the faint fragrance of my roll on. Any smell is better than the rancid air in this dungeon. This place is uninhabitable.

I try to wrap the flimsy silk robe around me that I managed to grab when I was manhandled by Tristan's man. The Alpha could have at least allowed me to get some decent clothes on first.

I manage to form another mind-link to the one person who can get me out of here.

"Hey, babe. I think you should prepare the troops for the takedown," I say as soon as I have his attention.

"Did the idiot Gene buy your story?" the voice on the other end of the mind-link asks.

"I'm very persuasive when I want to be. Besides, why would he ever have reason to think that I'm lying? It's time to take over this palace."

"That's my girl. I miss you so much. I'll prepare the troops and we will launch the attack. Just hang in there, sweetheart. Daddy Kane is coming."

"Hurry!" I say and cut the link.

CHAPTER 22: SOMEONE HAS TO DO SOMETHING

Tristan

Barbara is up to something, and I know it. I put her in the dungeon, hoping that she would be able to keep herself from stirring up things too much while she's down there, but I know I can't prevent her from using the mind-link.

Not even if I put a foil hat on her head.

I pull the Alphas together in Eli's room. "We need to be ready for anything," I tell them. "I think Barbara really might be plotting with Alpha Kane. Since I'm temporary king, I'm temporarily in charge of the scouts for the castle guards as well, and I've told them to let me know if they see anything strange."

"And... have they seen anything strange?" Mark asks as he pours a drink of whatever booze we are all passing around today. It's too bad it's hard for any of us to even get tipsy since we're all shifters and larger than most human men.

"They have," I reply as I pour my own drink.

"What's that exactly?" Eli asks as he takes the bottle out of my hand to top himself off.

"Well, they are organizing on the outskirts of the forest near the north of the castle again, and I can't be sure, but I do think that Barbara's helping them one way or another," I explain to them.

"Helping them how?" Reece asks. "Do you think she intends to tell him when we are all distracted and have him attack then?"

"Maybe she'll wait until we're all in the bathroom," Eli jokes, and they all laugh.

"Alphas!" I shout. "Be serious! We need to get our acts together. We can't keep acting like a bunch of fumbling idiots! Rose had false labor not long ago. That means we're all on the verge of being fathers."

They all sober up quite a bit after that. I've been trying to be more of a grown-up lately… and while I'm not batting a perfect record just yet, I am batting over three hundred.

That's good, isn't it?

"Sorry," Mark says on behalf of all of them. 'So what are we going to do?"

"We are going to get ready for an attack," Tristan says. "And I think we should consider sending Barbara out of the castle while King Gene is away. She's causing all kinds of issues, and if she's gone, things will be a lot more calm."

"And Emily?" Eli asks, dragging his hand down his chin.

That makes me sigh. I want to say let her die in the hospital, or I'll put her to death for what she's done, but the honest truth is, I don't want to answer to King Gene for her death. She is his cousin, after all, and for the moment, I'm only temporary king.

"I think we should wait until she's well and then send her back to Stephen. Maybe that will distract him from attacking us, and we can focus on the true enemy, which is Kane." Those are my thoughts on the issue anyway.

"As I see it," Reece begins, leaning forward on the couch, his hands folded between his knees. "This is our chance to get things cleaned up around here while Gene is gone. We can send Barbara off, send Emily away or kill her off, and we need to do something about that ridiculous Morris."

"Morris is a good guy now," I remind him. "He's doing my bidding."

"Yeah, until he's not," Mark says with a scowl.

I glare back at him, but he does have a point. So far, Morris has done what I've ordered him to do. "Let's just leave Morris out of this for now."

"Is that by order of the king, or just Tristan talking?" Eli snickers like he's trying to be funny, but I don't find it humorous. It is irritating to me.

"Who's with Rose right now?" Reece asks, looking either puzzled, worried... or constipated.

"Shelby, Adam, and Kelly are in there," Mark assures him. "Rose is sleeping."

"That's good. I don't like it when all of us are away from her," Reece explained. "It makes me nervous."

"She's fine," I assure him. "Can we stay focused on the matter at hand, please? This is what I want to do. There's a secret prison in the north, near that large snow-covered mountain range in Snowfall pack."

"Everything is covered in snow in Snowfall pack," Mark says in an irritating voice.

"Yes, I know, but the mountains are large, and the prison is secret, so that will make it all the harder for her to escape," I reply.

"But how the hell would we even get her there?" Mark wants to know. "We'd have to go right through Kane's line of soldiers in order to get her to prison, and there's a good chance that he'd attack whoever is transporting her."

"That's a good thing," I remind him. "It could potentially draw Kane away from here. Not to mention, I have it on good authority that Barbara's own army is beginning to form lines as well. They're situated to the west of the castle."

"And Stephen's coming from the southeast?" Eli asks.

I nod. 'We are essentially surrounded–almost. So we have to do something. With Gene gone, we have a small window of opportunity to act. We need to take advantage of it. He'll figure out soon enough that no one is reading his mind, and if Kane and Barbara really are working together, he'll think he needs to be here to do something about it. So, let's act while we have a chance to do it." I try to sound convincing, calling on all of my inner-king skills.

They look at me like they think I've lost my mind. Or maybe they think all of this power has gone to my head.

"Maybe we just need to see what it is that Barbara wants," Eli says with a shrug. "I don't think she actually wants us, like Emily. I think she wants something else. Like power."

"Ha!" Mark scoffs. "I don't think you'd feel that way if you'd been drugged and nearly... taken advantage of!"

I do feel bad for him about that. "But the only reason she's here is because Gene wanted her help! So why would we support that by leaving her here?"

"He's going to come back and wonder what we did, and when he finds out, he'll just bring her back!" Reece exclaims.

"Well, we're out of options, aren't we?" I ask. "We can't leave her here, and now you're saying we can't send her away! What else can we possibly do?" I am exasperated.

Mark doesn't miss a beat. "Kill her."

We all turn and look at him. Normally, Mark is passionate but fair. At the moment, he seems so angry about what Barbara did to him, what she intended to do with him, that he's not thinking straight.

"That's a bit... drastic, don't you think?" Eli asks, but Mark immediately shakes his head.

"No, I don't think so. I'm tired of women taking advantage of me. And I'm not going to stand around and pretend it didn't happen!"

"Emily didn't take advantage of you," Reece says. "You spanked her. So instead of women, you should say woman."

"Emily was trying to take advantage of me." Mark's piercing eyes are narrowed in anger.

I'm not sure what to say. I think killing Barbara is a bad idea, even though she tried to take advantage of Mark–and she also tried to take advantage of me.

I think it will backfire on us, and when Gene shows up, he'll be angry.

Not to mention, her pack may very well attack us, and we'll have even more enemies wheeling in on the castle.

"No," I say, shaking my head. "I'm not going to do that. We can keep her in prison here or transfer her to Snowfall pack, but we're not going to kill her, not for that."

Mark's gaze narrows even more. "Maybe you don't mind when women try to drug you and force you to do things you wouldn't normally do. Or maybe you would normally do them, but I wouldn't, and I am offended. I want justice!"

With that, Mark gets up and walks out of the room. All I can do is stare after him for a few moments, not sure what to do or say.

Once he's gone, I clear my throat and say, "Well... that went well."

Eli and Reece only stare at me.

Being king is harder than I thought it would be. Maybe I'm not very good at it.... Maybe I shouldn't have thrown my hat in the ring for this.

But I'm king now, and there are at least three packs amassing outside of our gates, so someone has to do something.

And in my experience, generally speaking, when someone has to do something, it's usually me.

"Let's start small," I say. "Let's get rid of one of these bitches. That's easy enough."

"Emily?" Reece asks.

I nod. "Who wants to return the bride to the bridegroom?"

Eli replies, "I'll do it."

CHAPTER 23: NIGHTMARES

Rose

I lay in my bed, staring up at the ceiling, listening to Kelly and Shelby talk about…. Well, I don't even know what they're talking about.

I'm really not paying any attention to them at all. I'm thinking about the babies.

The Braxton-Hicks contractions have subsided, thank goodness. I'm not in any pain, though I'm still uncomfortable. Dr. Pepperglass says that I'll probably be in discomfort for the rest of my pregnancy. After that, she says there's a good chance I'll be uncomfortable for about eighteen years.

I think she has forgotten that I won't be with my babies for the next eighteen years, and she's thinking I will be the typical mother who doesn't get any sleep because the babies are crying and are up constantly worried once they start walking because they might wander off or fall in a lake or get swallowed up by a sinkhole….

Maybe she was under the impression I would be one of those moms who are constantly worried about how my kids are doing in school. Are they learning fast enough? Are they learning too fast, and now they're bored? Are they making friends? Are they making so many friends that they're talking during lessons?

What about high school and dating and all of those things? Would I be the sort of mother who would cry the moment she saw her daughter... daughters... in her wedding gown? Will I approve of my children's mates?

Someday, my children will have children of their own. Would I be a fun grandma? Would I give them too much ice cream and let them stay up too late? Or would I lecture my kids that they're too lenient, and the grandchildren are spoiled?

Yes, I can see Dr. Papergat saying I would be uncomfortable for the next eighteen years if I was going to be raising four beautiful lives for eighteen years and be responsible for keeping those beautiful lives living.

But... at the present... that's not what's supposed to happen.

I'm supposed to let go of these little cherubs in a few short weeks and hand them over to others to worry about them.

Then... what?

I rub my abdomen as a tiny foot kicks against my rib cage, and tears collect in my eyes. What if the person who is supposed to be worried about them on my behalf isn't worried about them at all?

And... what about me?

I'm just supposed to go back home and forget that somewhere in the world are four tiny people who are half me and half these men that I love now and will always love?

I'm supposed to let go of the eight people I love most in the world and just go on about my business as if I don't really care that I am the only one missing everything that is wonderful and lovely about the everyday lives of my children.

"Rose?" I hear Kelly say with much concern in her voice. "What's the matter?"

"Nothing," I say, swiping at my tears. A box of tissues sits on my nightstand, but there are so many things on my nightstand right now that I don't reach for it because I'm afraid I might make a mess.

Kelly and Shelby both come over and sit next to me on either side of the bed. Shelby plucks a tissue out of the box and hands it to me, and I dab at my eyes, trying to keep my tears at bay. I feel like a baby myself, crying all the time. But I've read in my books that it's normal for me to be emotional.

"It's okay." Kelly rubs my arm. "The babies are safe. Dr. Pendergan said that it's normal to have these practice contractions. It's just your body getting ready to have the babies."

"And even if the babies were born right now, which they won't be," Shelby continues, "they're all large enough to survive on the outside."

I nod, knowing that that's probably true. They would all be teeny tiny, but they'd be okay.

I'm honestly not worried about the safety of my babies right now. I think they will all be healthy, happy children when they are born and will grow up well-loved and taken care of by their fathers, who will all four raise them as if they were all their parents.

But their mother? Since I am not supposed to be allowed to fill that role, who will?

Emily? My children might be eaten alive.

Barbara? They will all grow up to be pole dancers.

No, I can't imagine either of those women being their mothers, and if the Alphas are allowed to choose their own wives, well, they could end up with all kinds of step-monsters.

Tears sting my eyes again.

"It's all right!" Kelly brushes my hair back from my eyes.

"Tristan is king now," Shelby reminds me. "I'm sure that he will make sure that nothing can happen to you, dear."

"I know," I say, but I don't know. Tristan is only a temporary king. King Gene will be back soon enough, and when he arrives, who knows what will become of me?

"You should try to get some rest," Shelby encourages me. "Go to sleep, and when you wake up, you'll feel better."

I shake my head. "I don't think that I will. I don't think I'll feel better until the babies are born, the king is decided, and I'm assured I'll be allowed to stay."

"Don't you know that even if King Gene forces you away from the castle, the new king will be able to bring you back?" Kelly continues to brush my hair away from my face, trying to make me feel better.

But I'm not sure it's working.

I do manage a nod.

"Really, Rose. You have four strong, brave, strapping men who will make sure nothing ever happens to you. You'll be fine." She gives me a sympathetic smile, and I manage to smile back at her.

Suddenly, I do feel tired. I decide to close my eyes for a bit and go to sleep.

I hear Kelly and Shelby get up off of the bed, and one of them tosses a blanket over the top of me.

I pull it up under my chin and I try to think of happy moments to dream about, like... my Alphas... and my grandmother who used to bake cookies for me when I was little... and that horse that lived in the field behind our house when I was in high school....

I'm walking through the forest, wearing a long white gown. My feet are bare, but I'm in my human form, not my wolf. It's a cool day, and the wind rustles the leaves above me. In the distance, I know someone is waiting, but I don't know who it is.

Maybe it is more than one person.

Maybe... there are several.

I continue to walk, hurrying my pace in my haste to find out who is there, but I have to be careful not to trip over any of the exposed roots that jut out from the ground along the trail I follow between the trees.

I hear the sound of children laughing. They are calling to one another. Their names make me smile, and I know who these children are.

Rounding a corner, I walk out from between two large pines and see a beautiful meadow filled with butterflies. The azure sky above is a lovely contrast to the white fluffy clouds that flutter by.

"There she is!" a familiar voice calls, and my eyes land on a picnic blanket in the center of the carpet of green.

There they are!

All four of my Alphas are here. Mark and Tristan are sitting on the blanket while Reece is playing a game with the children and Eli is flying a kite.

It's the picture of a quaint happy family–if all families contained four fathers.

My children–two girls and two boys–laugh and cheer as I come closer to them. Now that I'm in the meadow, there aren't any roots to trip me up. I gather up my dress and begin to run.

The distance shouldn't take that long for me to cover, but it seems like I am running in slow motion. No matter how hard I try, I can't seem to get there.

And the scene in front of me is changing....

The sky grows dark, storm clouds gathering quickly above the meadow, lightning bolts splitting between clouds like daggers as angry rain begins to fall. All eight of them freeze, the kite falling from the sky, their faces frozen in panic and fear but they aren't looking up at the sky.

They are looking at the forest behind them.

That's when I hear it.

The thunder isn't loud enough to completely drown out the cacophony of what sounds like hundreds of wolves tearing through the trees, running straight for me–straight for my family.

As the first glimpse of fangs becomes visible between the trees, I scream.

It's an earth-shattering shriek intended to somehow frighten the wolves off so that they cannot harm my family.

But all it manages to do is wake me up.

I sit up straight in bed, my heart pounding in my chest, sweat dripping off me.

My room is dark, but across from me, I see a pair of eyes.

And I feel like screaming again.

CHAPTER 24: WHERE DID SHE GO?

Rose

"Wh-who are you?" I stammer as I continue to lock eyes with the stranger standing at the foot of my bed.

Now that I'm fully awake, she doesn't look quite as menacing. My eyes have adjusted to the light, and I can see that she is a tiny older woman, and while she's creepy, I think I can take her, even in my very pregnant state.

She doesn't answer my question, only continues to look at me in a menacing way. Her beady eyes narrow even more, and I think she looks a bit like King Gene.

I never imagined anyone could be shorter than him, but this woman is even more tiny than he is.

"Are you her?"

Her voice creaks and cracks as she speaks, assaulting my ears. I have no idea what she's talking about, and I wonder if I should call for help. Who is supposed to be guarding me and isn't here? Who let her in here, anyway?

I am still convinced that I can beat her up even without Kelly's nun chucks, so I don't try to alert anyone that I've been infiltrated just yet.

I just ask her the natural question that anyone would ask in this situation.

"Am I who?"

"Her!" she barks at me, a bony finger jabbing out as she walks around the side of the bed.

I want to lean back further into the pillows, but I am already crammed against the headboard.

Shaking my head, I say, "I'm sorry, but I don't know what you're talking about, ma'am. Perhaps you are in the wrong room or need help. I can call for some–"

Before I can finish my sentence, that bony finger juts out into my face. "You are her, aren't you?! You're that miserable little bitch who took my GeGe away from me! He loves you more than he loves me, right now, and that makes me very, very angry!" She makes a fist with her hand and slams it down into her leg and then winces at the pain, and I wonder if she'd snapped her old bone in half.

"Listen, ma'am," I say, my eyes flickering between her tiny body and the door for a moment until I realize I have to turn my head away from her to look at the place where help is located. "If you're speaking about King Gene, I can assure you, he doesn't love me at all."

Using the mind-link, I reach out to the Alphas. We're not in the same pack, but since they're Alphas, I should be able to reach them this way, and we are close enough in proximity and in our relationships that they should hear my distress cry. "Hey, guys? Who's guarding me? I have... a problem."

"No!" the old woman screams at me. "He does love you! And I won't tolerate it! I won't stand it! I will not stay in my room and behave any longer!" Turns out all of her fingers are bony as she reaches out and grabs my cheeks, squeezing them and giving me a good shake.

Her nails dig into my skin, and I wince at the pain, thinking she's likely broken the skin, and I'll have lacerations on my face. I reach up and grab her arms to try to pull her away, but she's stronger than she looks, and I'm afraid if I pull too hard, one of her twig arms might snap off.

"I am," I hear Eli say in my head. "I'm right outside the door. You were asleep so…."

"Can you come here?" I ask him, glad that I can speak with my mind in a clear voice. I bet if I tried to move my mouth right now, I'd sound like a clown.

I somehow manage to free her grip from my face and give her a little shove without knocking her down. She growls at me, and I brace myself for another impact when I hear the door open.

Turning to look at Eli, I see a confused expression on his face as he looks at me, his head tipped to the side.

"Thank the Moon Goddess!" I say. "Help me get her calmed down, please."

His forehead crinkles even more as he quietly closes the door behind him and walks over to the opposite side of the bed from where Miss Angry Britches is standing. "What?" Eli asks, looking around the room. "Rose, baby, what are you talking about?"

"Her!" I exclaim, pointing at where the woman is standing. "She's accusing me of taking GeGe away from her and trying to dismantle my face!"

He doesn't look any less confused as he follows my finger. "Rose… the woman in that picture on the wall isn't going to take your face off, and she's not talking to you. What's going on?"

"Not her!" I say remembering the portrait on that wall of a grand looking woman holding a book. "This weirdoooo!"

I turn my head and realize….

She's gone!

"Wh-wha–whe–where did she go?" I finally get out as I twist around on the bed, looking for her.

"Rose, there's no one here," he says, concern in his voice.

"Yes, there is!" Even though I don't see her now, I know she was here. She didn't go out the door. She has to be right here.

Eli casually walks over to the door and flips on a light switch. I can clearly see the entire room now, even though my eyes sting a little from the assault, and he's right.

There's no one here.

"I don't understand," I admit. "She was right here!" I lift my hands to my cheeks. I can still feel the burn from her grabbing them, but when I pull my palms away, they're not bloodied.

Eli sits down next to me, a hand on my shoulder, and before he even speaks, I know what he's going to say. "You must've been dreaming, Rose. I was right outside the door the whole time, talking to Adam, since I switched shifts with Tristan about an hour ago, and he was in here with you and said you were so sound asleep, you probably didn't even know he was here. Before that, Shelby and Kelly were in here, and that's when you fell asleep. Whatever you saw, it couldn't have been a real person."

"Do you think she was a ghost?" I ask him, a shiver climbing up my spine.

"No!" he says quickly and with great conviction. "I don't believe in ghosts. It must've been part of your dream leftover when you opened your eyes."

"But I didn't just see her, I felt her when she touched me. And I definitely heard her old, creepy voice."

He snickers, probably because I admit she was creepy, and now he thinks I really was having a bad dream. "Well, whoever she was, she's gone now."

"I can see that," I say, though I wish I wasn't carrying four people around because I wanna check under the bed, in the closets, and in the bathroom.

The more Eli runs his hand along my arm, the more amorous I can tell he's feeling. Normally, I would respond to his touch by reaching over and touching him right back, but the idea that the old woman is in her somewhere watching me, or that she is an apparition and is watching me from another world, makes me think twice.

When Eli leans down to kiss my lips, I pull back. "I'm super hungry," I tell him.

A look of disappointment takes over his handsome face. "Okay," he says. "But I think you should lay off on the pickles and peanut butter. Maybe it's giving you bad dreams."

I glare at him, but the only words I can think to say to him are, "Those are fighting words."

He chuckles and gets up. He'll have to go get my food himself because we aren't letting just anyone prepare it after the chef incident.

That means I'm about to be left alone again. I've spent countless hours alone in this room, but as my eyes flicker to the woman in the picture, I have to wonder... does she know something I don't?

CHAPTER 25: THE BREEDER MUST DIE

King Gene

I'm steaming with anger as I reach the palace gates, to the point where I'm even feeling physically heated, as though it's not anger overheating me at all.

"Do you think you should remove that, Your Majesty?" asks one of my guards. Only a few of my most trusted men had accompanied me to my hideout... er, had gone with me on my top-secret mission. Of course, I'd left my Beta behind. Adam needed to keep an eye out around here.

I look at my guard with my brows knitted together, and the man nods toward me, his eyes on the top of my head.

Lifting my hand to my crown, I hear the loud crumbling of foil... and I realize I'm still wearing that ridiculous foil hat Emily had talked me into making.

Obviously, the damn thing doesn't work since Barbara mind-linked me right through the useless piece of shit. It certainly will do me no good against Kane. I rip it off my head, crumble it into a ball, and throw it to the ground as my guards hold the door open for me and I reenter my beautiful palace.

Ah, home… this is where I belong. I am the king, and I will regain my proper place today with glory and fanfare.

First things first… I need to find that Tristan fellow and formally excuse him from his temporary duties as king. He had a thing for that filthy Breeder, so I start toward her quarters hoping to find the Alpha there.

Well, there is an Alpha there standing outside her door, but it isn't the one I am looking for. "Mark, boy!" I call to him.

"Alpha Mark," he says, looking down at me with his brows raised as though he's startled. I can't imagine why he would be startled to find the king walking the halls of his own damn palace.

"Whatever," I say. "Where's that Tristan lad?"

"Alpha Tristan?" he asks.

"Yes, that's the one," I say. Isn't that what I just said?

"I… I'm not sure," he tells me, still looking like he's staring at a ghost. "What are you doing back already? What about Alpha Kane?"

"To hell with Kane," I holler. "I am the king. I belong in my palace, and that's where I shall be, enemies be damned. Now, where's Alpha Tristan?"

"Um… I think he went out somewhere in the gardens," he says.

"Now why the hell would he be out in the… never mind, I'll find him," I grumble. "A lot of help you are," I add with a mumble. But then I turn on my heels and look up at him again. "How's the woman… the Breeder holding up?"

"She's doing really well," the Alpha says with a smile. "I don't think we'll be waiting too much longer to see the new heirs to the throne."

Not the news I was hoping for… I force my lips into a smile. "Fine, fine," I say, spinning back around and heading off to the… where was it? Oh, yes. The gardens, Tristan is in the gardens.

I walk off without another word. There's no sense in making small talk with the wrong Alpha. Although I have a vague recollection in my mind about the group of four Alphas not helping me with Kane if I did something. Or didn't do something. What was it? Eh, it probably isn't important right now.

After a long walk taking great strides, my guard beside me inexplicably requiring fewer steps than I, I arrive at the gardens.

They're empty.

The sides of my mouth sink to a frown as I spin around and walk just as quickly back to my quarters. I'll find the man later. What I need now is a long shower and a return to my own luxurious bed.

All the while that I'm walking... and it takes quite a while to navigate these hallways... I start to think more about the Breeder. Alpha Mark said she was getting closer to those babies crawling out of her. I didn't see the woman for myself. Maybe I should have.

Regardless, it seems her crawling time is coming, or whatever you call it, so I'd better enact my plan. For that, I'd need my Beta. "Adam!" I holler through the mind-link.

"S-Sir, Your Majesty," he says with a sputter in my head. "You sound close."

"Of course, I'm close, you idiot," I say. "Meet me in my quarters."

"In the palace?" he asks.

"Of course, in the palace. Where else would my quarters be?" I ask.

I've finally reached my room, and I command that the guard wait outside and let only the Beta enter.

Ah, a rush of fine fragrance greets me. I'd instructed the maids to keep fresh flowers in my room at all times so that when I return, I can bask in their luxurious scent. Now that's true loyalty; I'll have to reward the maids for a job well done.

Moments later, my Beta walks through the door, looking completely disheveled.

"Were you out in the garden too?" I ask him.

"Garden?" he asks. "No, why do you ask?"

"It's not important right now," I say.

"Your Majesty, forgive me, but why have you returned already?" Beta Adam asks.

"I live here!" I say in a booming voice. From his startled jump, I can see that my tone was effective. "I can come and go as I please. I'm the king!"

"Yes, of course, you are, Your Majesty."

That's better. I can't stand a mouthy Beta. "What I'm doing isn't important," I say. "What is important is what's been going on here since I've been gone. Are those infants about to crawl out of that woman or not?"

"Not quite yet," my Beta says. "We had a bit of a scare, but she's fine now with some rest. The pups should be just fine."

I grunt and head over to my wet bar. The maids keep all my bottles of fine whiskey underneath the bar where I can reach them, and I pour myself a glass. I pause for a moment, watching the one-hundred-year-old liquid swirl around in the sparkling crystal before I gulp it down. Perfection.

"Your Majesty?"

I hear the words and open my eyes. Apparently, I'd closed them to enjoy my drink. "What?"

"You were asking about the Breeder's condition," he says.

"Condition, yes," I say. "How close would you say it is to the crawling day?"

"The crawling day?" He says it as though it's a question, but then his eyes open a little wider as though he's realizing something. "Ah, the day of the birth. We have a little time left, but I do think it's approaching soon."

"No good, Adam," I say. "That's no good."

"Why not, Your Majesty?" Adam asks. "That means it's closer to when she's going to leave. I thought that's what you wanted."

"You idiot!" I say, nearly spilling my drink while slamming it down on the bar. It's a shame to waste a drop of this fine whiskey. "When those babies crawl out, one of those scheming Alphas will expect to lay claim to the throne. Or rather, all damn four of them are planning to take over! Why would I want them to have any hold over what's rightfully mine?! I swear I have no idea why I let you talk me into this whole arrangement in the first place."

"But I didn't—"

"You didn't think, I know!" I say. "We'll have to rectify this mistake right away."

"Rectify?" he says.

"You're repeating things, do you know that, Adam? I need my Beta to be in much better command over his mental faculties, you know," I say. I pour another glass and walk over to relax in my favorite chair. I have to scoot up a bit to climb into it, but it makes me look tall and regal.

"Your Majesty, my mind is perfectly fine," he says.

"Good! Good," I say. "You'll need to really use your noggin to hatch the perfect plan to get it done."

"Get it done?" Adam asks.

He's really starting to get on my nerves with all these questions. I thought I made the task he was to accomplish perfectly clear. I look at him, a bit more even with his eye level now since I'm sitting in my favorite chair. I really do love this fine piece of furniture.

"My boy, don't tell me you've forgotten your task," I say.

"No," he says, with a nervous twitch in his eye. "I haven't forgotten what you want me to do. But the pups, Your Majesty. The Breeder is far along in her pregnancy...."

I hold up my hand. "I don't want to hear about the disgusting technicalities of pup bearing," I say. "All that messy stuff is for women to discuss. You and I have a far different matter at hand, something far more important to me... er, to my kingdom."

"But I just can't—"

"Dammit!" I scream. "You're my Beta, and you're here to follow my commands without pause! You're to carry out my plan immediately before those Alphas have any cause to lay claim to my throne! Kill that nasty Breeder woman immediately! I expect to hear the news that she's dead by sunrise."

CHAPTER 26: WHAT THE KING STOLE

BARBARA

Kane must be dead.

If he isn't, he will be soon enough.

It's been more than a day since our last mind-link conversation, and he still hasn't arrived at the castle to save me from this shithole.

Now, he isn't even answering me on the mind-link! It's like he was trying to come and free me and got into a serious battle outside of the castle with the guards or one of those fucking Alpha's forces and was dispatched.

As I pace back and forth in my tiny little cell, the stench of mildew continuing to burn my nose, I ask myself where I went wrong. How did I fail to seduce a single Alpha? How did I fail to convince Gene that he should go ahead and declare that I would be the next queen? How did I fail to convince Kane to storm this castle and free me from this horrible place?

It seems like my knight in shining armor has rusted and gotten stuck somewhere out in the woods.

Walking over to the bars, I take hold of them and give them a shake. Of course, nothing happens except I get rust all over my hands. In frustration, I shriek and rest my head on bars.

"I'm going to have to figure out how to get out of her myself!" I growl.

"Hee, hee, hee!"

I hear a creepy laugh from the darkness to my left and freeze. I know there's no one else in this cell with me because I've paced back and forth a thousand times. I would've tripped over the person by now!

"Who's there?" I demand, glaring at the solid stone wall between my cell and the next one over, which is where I'm assuming the giggler presides.

"Oh, no one," a male voice says. He sounds old and tired, despite his chipper attitude.

Walking over to the wall, I fold my arms under my chest. "You've gotta be someone to be laughing at me like a fucking hyena," I growl at him.

"Nope. I'm no one," he insists. "I've been no one for close to thirty years. I just sit down here, eat my three meals a day, piss in a bucket, take a dump wherever, and sometimes dream about the past. What's the point in having an identity when that's all there is to your existence?"

"So you're a fucking psycho then?" I ask, rolling my eyes. There's no point in me standing here and talking to someone who didn't even let me know he existed until a few seconds ago when I've been here for days.

"Oh, I might be," he says with another chuckle that basically confirms it. "But I used to be someone, a long time ago." He sighs, and I think I hear a bit of sadness in it.

"Well, I apologize that I don't have time to feel sorry for you right now," I growl, sinking down onto the floor with my back to the wall. "I'm a little busy trying to figure out how the hell to get out of here."

"You can't," he says. "Not unless King Gene comes and lets you out."

"Shows what you know," I say, scoffing. "Gene isn't even king right now. Tristan is."

"Tristan is only temporary king," he tells me like he's a reporter for the fucking daily news. "Gene is the true king, and he'll be back soon enough. If he wants you here, this is where you will rot. And this is where you will die."

"Maybe that's the case for you," I tell him, picking flecks of dirt off of my bare leg. "But I have connections to the outside world. I'll be sure to get out of here, probably in the next couple of hours." I look at the gate as if I expect Alpha Kane to be standing there with a big smile on his face and the keys in his hand.

But of course, there's no one outside of my cell. There's hardly anyone outside of my cell–ever. About three times a day, a guard brings a bowl of slop and slides it through the grate without a word, and it's usually accompanied by some brownish water. That's the only time I ever see anyone.

"I thought the same thing." The man's voice isn't so cheerful now. "I thought for certain that someone would come soon to let me out. I mean, I had friends! I had mind-link capabilities. Why wouldn't they come and release me? It's not as if I'd done anything wrong."

I try not to even listen to him because I know that it will only make me feel worse about what is happening to me, but his words continue to seep into my ears.

"For the first few days, my friends assured me that they were on the way, that they would be here to get me out as soon as possible. I waited patiently, trusting in them. Getting into this cell so far under the castle is no easy feat."

"I guess you're still waiting?" I ask, sarcasm dripping from my voice.

"No, no," he says quickly, like I was serious. "I gave up on that a long time ago. No, whether my friends decided it was better not to go against the new king or they decided they weren't quite my friend after all. Ultimately, after a few weeks, I realized no one was coming. So... instead of waiting for rescue, I started to wait for a trial, to be judged and have a punishment handed to me."

"And how did that go?" I brush my fingernails over my shoulder, bored but also a bit frightened to hear his answer.

He clears his throat, all of that joy now gone from his voice. "It never happened."

I sit up a little straighter. "You never had your trial?"

"No, I was just… forgotten. Left here. So, now, instead of waiting for a trial, I'm simply waiting… to die."

His last words send a shiver down my spine. I don't want to sit here until I die. I have to convince myself that that can never happen to me. "Did you ask what the deal is? Why you hadn't gotten a hearing with the king?"

"Ask?" he says with that same chortle I heard when he first began to speak to me. "Ask who? It's not as if King Gene wanders down here to have a look around every couple of hours!"

He has a point. I'm not sure who I would ask either. The guards who bring our food sure the hell aren't going to respond to us begging to speak to someone.

I don't want to admit it to this guy I can't even see, but I am starting to get a bit worried. The idea of spending the next thirty years of my life down here makes me want to vomit, but there's nothing in my gut to throw up because I haven't eaten anything since I arrived here.

"What did they lock you up for, anyway?" my neighbor asks me.

I sigh loudly. I don't want to get into it, but I have nothing more pressing to do. "Originally, I was a captive in the castle. King Gene and I came up with a scheme where I would pretend to attack the capital so that I would be arrested. But I was supposed to be free to roam about the castle. I was supposed to be helping him with some-thing. " I don't think I should say aloud what it is I was supposed to be doing.

"And it was Tristan who put you here? When Gene temporarily gave him the throne?" he asks.

"Yes," I reply quickly. "For no damn good reason at all!" I figure the fewer people who know I almost killed Emily the better. But in my defense, she had attacked me first.

I was just defending myself!

"Well, I hate to burst your bubble, girly, but I think I'd just start to get used to it if I were you. People like us... we don't get second chances."

"Speak for yourself!" I tell him quickly. I don't know how he's lumping me into the same group as him. He was probably a petty thief or something. "What are you in for?" I ask. "Did you steal something from King Gene?"

"No," he says, his tone more serious than ever. "Not at all."

"Then... why are you here?" I repeat.

"King Gene stole something from me." I can hear the bitterness in his voice now.

My forehead crinkles as I try to determine how the hell he is the one in prison if King Gene stole something from him. "Like what?" I ask.

He is quiet for a long moment before he replies, "The throne."

CHAPTER 27: THAT WOMAN HAS TO GO

"Where's Eli?" I ask. Three of my four men are in my room, looking at me with furrowed brows and expressions of concern.

"He's... taking care of a problem, little flower," says Tristan. He sits next to me on the bed and feels my head as if I have a fever.

"I'm not sick," I say. They've all been looking at me like I'm crazy ever since I'd seen that frightening woman in my room. I don't think any of them believe me when I tell them she's real. But she was here, standing right in front of me, her eyeballs searing into me as she threw around those wild accusations.

"We know that, little flower," Tristan says softly.

I love the sound of his voice when he's talking to me with love in his eyes, but I really want my men to believe me. "I wasn't dreaming," I say. "She was real."

"I'm sure she seemed very real, darlin'," says Reece, who is standing on the other side of my bed.

Mark is in the corner. I'm sure that Eli had told all of them that I was going crazy.

"It's probably just the pregnancy making your dreams seem so real," Tristan says.

He could be right, but I don't think so. I know what it's like to have realistic dreams, and even my most vivid dreams are clearly just that —dreams—in the light of day. I'm not so sure about this.

"You're so close to delivering our children," Mark adds, coming closer. "It's natural to have all kinds of emotions and dreams and confusing thoughts during a time like this, especially since you're having four pups."

"I'm not emotional just because I'm pregnant," I say. "I know what I saw." Frankly, I'm not sure I'm convinced of it myself. If someone told me what I was trying to tell them had happened, I'd probably think the woman was a bit loopy from an advanced pregnancy, too. I need to go easy on them all. They're all so loving and just trying to help.

"Well, I know what I'm going to do," says Tristan, standing up and walking over to the far wall. "This painting is outta here."

I giggle a little. My men definitely know how to make me feel better.

"It definitely is creepy," agreed Reece.

Tristan takes the painting off the wall and literally throws it out the door. "Now, little flower," he says when he comes back to my bedside. "We have some business to attend to. Kelly, Shelby, and Adam will all be here to protect you for a couple of days while we're gone. If you need us for anything at all, know that we'll be back here in a flash, okay?"

I don't like that they are going off dealing with 'business' at a time like this, but I know it's important to keep the kingdom running, especially when there's a temporary king in charge. I trust my men with my life, and I know everything they do is to protect me and our children. I wonder if Eli is off getting a head start on that business.

I smile and am about to speak when the door bursts open and Beta Adam runs in. He pauses for just a moment to catch his breath— apparently, he'd been running—and says, "We've got a problem."

EMILY

My head aches, but the pain isn't half as powerful as the rage I'm feeling. That bitch Barbara put her filthy claws on me and ripped my flesh. If it doesn't heal quite right, I might even have a scar.

Can you imagine? A scar on Emily's flawless skin is a sin against the Goddess herself.

I don't like that doctor, either. She and her snotty little nurses probably didn't even disinfect the wound properly before they bandaged it. Luckily, I heal quickly, though, so hopefully, there won't be a scar.

To make matters worse, I'm chained to the bed in this awful room like a common criminal. I'm not in the hospital anymore, thank the Goddess—I don't know how much longer I could stand being around those annoying women.

But my situation isn't much better yet since I can't even get a hand free to check under the bandages to see if there's any permanent damage. Not to mention, the room I'm in is mediocre, at best, with so much dust everywhere that I desperately need a shower.

Emily always looks her best. Don't these imbeciles know that?

Finally, I hear the door creak open, and before the servant can walk into the room, I say, "It's about damn time. Now, get these cuffs off me and draw me a bath! I've been waiting for—" I freeze mid-sentence when I look over the gorgeous hunk of manhood who just walked in.

"Alpha Eli," I say in the sweetest voice I can muster. I'm so good at thinking on my feet! Or lying down, as the case may be now. "I do wish you'd let me know you were coming. I would have had the maids prepare a special dinner for us."

"Shut up, Emily," he says.

I can't believe the rude insult. I'm being so sweet! "Well, that's no way to talk to the cousin of—"

"Of the king." He finishes the sentence for me, and I swear, he seems a bit testy. It's not like he's the one lying here injured and in handcuffs. "I don't have time for your games, Emily. I'm here to make sure you go home."

"Home?" I ask. "But the king needs me here in the castle for—"

"For nothing," he says. Boy, he sure is rude today, cutting me off. "Alpha Tristan is acting king, and he's ordered you out of this castle. You're to go back where you belong, back to Alpha Stephen."

I gasp in shock, dramatically, and I'm very good at that. "You can't send me back," I say, trying to force tears into my eyes. I think about how much my shoulder hurts and try to get the waterworks going that way. It's no use, though. I'll have to try a different angle. "Tristan is not the king," I say. "I know for a fact that my cousin is back in the palace. I have mind-linked with him, you know."

"He hasn't transferred power yet, so officially, Tristan is still acting king," Eli says firmly.

"Oh?" I ask. "I'd like to speak to him right away. Tell him to come to my room."

Alpha Eli laughs. He has the gall to laugh at Emily! "That's not going to work," he says. "He's not coming here just so you can call your cousin to come transfer power."

Shit. So this Alpha has brains as well as brawn. I'll have to switch tactics. "Then maybe we can talk about you and me, huh?" I say, batting my eyelashes. "I'm already chained up." I gently rattle my handcuffs in a seductive manner. No man can resist my charm, not even an Alpha. "Why don't you come over here, and I'll see what kind of magic we can make together?" I smile, showing my fluorescent white teeth.

"Save it, Emily," he says.

I'm shocked and insulted, and I can't even recognize what other feelings I'm having, but I know for a fact that I don't like the way this Alpha is ignoring my advances. He must be made out of steel or something. What has that filthy Breeder got that lovely Emily doesn't have? Why, I run circles around that bitch. This Alpha doesn't know what he's missing.

Suddenly, two guards appear in the doorway. Are they taking me now? I can't go back to that limp, lifeless Stephen. I'd rather die fighting. Well, the two guards don't look bad. I'm sure I can take them with my wolf form. I'm the cousin of the king, for fuck's sake!

"Don't get any stupid ideas, Emily," Eli says.

I look back over at him. "Whatever do you mean?" I ask, still batting my eyelashes. If I do this long enough, I'm sure it'll work. He's a man, after all. Men have insatiable needs.

He gives me a straight-lipped look, as if he's getting bored or something. Imagine being bored in my presence—Emily, cousin of the king and world-class beauty!

"I mean that Dr. Pendergan gave you something that'll keep you from shifting, so don't even think about trying to escape," he says.

I feel my heart sink into my stomach. No!

"And my best men here are going to personally escort you back to where you belong, where your 'loving husband' can keep you out of trouble," Alpha Eli says. "Of course, hubby may be a little late for dinner since he seems to be wanting to cause a little trouble of his own first. So, my army will deliver you a package just as soon as they can."

My eyes brighten. Maybe they'll kill the worthless man, and I'll be free of him!

"Oh, don't worry," he continues. "We'll make sure Alpha Stephen is nice and 'healthy' so he can keep rocking your world every night. That is, after everyone's done spanking you just for fun."

Panic overwhelms me. "You can't do this to me!" I scream.

"I can… we can, and we will." He nods to his men, who come at me while I kick and scream… but they both hold my legs while Alpha Eli ties them together and then grabs a silk tie from the curtains and has the gall to wrap it around my mouth.

I grunt as loudly as I can—it's the only sound I can make with that dusty piece of cloth stuck in my mouth—and whip my body around as the men grab me and pull me toward the door. I shimmy around trying desperately to somehow slip my tied feet around something, anything that will keep me here and away from that horrible, limp, depressing Alpha Stephen.

Vases crash to the floor and lamps go flying as the guards drag me, still grunting and fighting, all the way out of the palace.

CHAPTER 28: SCHEMES AND PLANS

BARBARA

"What do you mean he stole your throne?"

I think my neighbor here has to be some sort of a crazy person. He thinks he's King Edward, King Gene's father? Everyone knows that King Edward and his wife, Queen Marcella, retired to a large palace in the east of the country a few years before they both caught an illness and died within days of one another. Though they had been very reclusive once they moved away, they weren't locked up in the castle. That was preposterous!

Besides, Queen Marcella was a nut job. She was crazy from the time she was married to King Edward, so it wasn't as if she would have been able to function if she was locked in the dungeon. Either she would've keeled over dead from her own delirium, or the guards that worked down here would've lost their minds.

"I mean what I said," my neighbor says in a casual voice that makes it sound as if what he's saying isn't that big of a deal, like imprisoned kings are the every-day norm. "My son took the throne from me. He locked me up here. I've been here ever since. It's a pity, really, since I would've gladly just stepped aside and let him have it if he wanted. But... he wasn't patient enough for that, so he took it."

"And locked you up down here?" My voice is full of sarcasm, but I can't help it. I have to let this guy know I'm not buying what he's selling.

"Yes. My wife at least was locked in one of the towers. So at least she'd be comfortable. I do miss her…."

"Queen Marcella?" I question him.

"She was such a beauty. I love her so much. I hope she's still alive. I think she is. She was my true mate, you know. I didn't just marry her because she was beautiful or because she was a good asset coming from a dangerous pack that wanted power. No, I loved her. That was back when people still believed in true mates."

I listen to him ramble, but his talking of true mates makes me angry. Very few people are lucky enough to find their true mates these days, and those who do don't appreciate them. I think of stupid ass Emily and my own husband, who were allegedly mates. I didn't believe that a mate bond was strong enough to break up a marriage.

But apparently my husband and that skanky bitch disagreed.

"Listen," I say to him. "You're not the fucking king. You're just some crazy old dude who has been locked up for so long you don't remember which way is up. When my boyfriend breaks me out of here, which better be soon if he wants to stay my boyfriend, I'll take your sorry ass with me."

He laughs. It's the laugh of a man who has gone more than a little insane.

I'll get him out of the cell, but then he's on his own.

With a sigh, I reach out with the mind-link again. "Kane?" Again, there's nothing. "Kane! Goddess damn it, answer me right now, or so help me, as soon as I see you again, I'll cut off your balls and shove them up your nose!"

"Barbara."

I hear my own name in my head spoken in a soft, soothing voice from the man that I think I love, and I take a deep breath, hoping he has good news for me.

"Where the fuck have you been?" I can't help myself. Anger courses through me. "It's been days!"

"I am fighting to get into the castle. It's surrounded by the forces of four other Alphas and the king's guard. This is no easy task. I shall be there as soon as I can be."

"You'd better get me out of here, now!" I scream. I hang my head and grab two hunks of hair in my fists, threatening to pull it out.

I stop myself, though. I don't want to be bald. I decide to wait and bottle up my rage to let it all go on Kane when I see him. He might be my lover, but he's not my mate.

So I can hurt him and not have to worry about the consequences....

~

Mark

"WE HAVE to do something about Gene now that he's back." I close the door to the library and take a quick peek around, seeing no one. We aren't meeting in Eli's room because he's not here. He volunteered to take Emily back to Stephen.

It shouldn't be a very hard job since Stephen's troops are amassing on one side of the castle. Kane's are on the other. They are trying to surround us, but our troops outnumber them greatly, and we have each sent for more warriors from our packs. They will come in behind our enemies, and soon enough, we won't be the only ones surrounded.

I am slightly worried about Eli, though. I don't think he took enough forces with him. I think he might end up getting himself into trouble, but he felt confident he had it under control.

"Here's what I think we should do about Gene," Tristan says, leaning casually on a bookshelf. My eyes float over the titles and notice that they are all books about human waste. "How to Poop When You're All Backed Up," "Your Large Intestine and You," "What to Do When You're Expecting a Bowel Movement—and Nothing Happens." I almost laugh, but I hold it back.

Tristan's forehead wrinkles as he stares at me, but he continues. "Unless and until King Gene and I meet in person, I'm acting king. So I'll just avoid him."

"How are you going to do that?" Reece asks, a very serious expression on his face that tells me he doesn't notice shit.

"Simple. I'll run. If I see him coming, I'll spin around and go the other direction. If he summons me, I'll make an excuse."

"Like what?" I ask Tristan. "You're taking a dump?"

"Yeah, maybe," he says, still straight faced. "That does take a long time."

"Perhaps I can interest you in some literature on the subject?" I gesture toward the books.

He looks down and slowly shakes his head. "You're such a little boy, Mark," he chides.

"Me?" I can think of a hundred examples of him acting like a child, but I don't argue.

"Anyway, that's the plan. And then... we can organize to just get rid of him altogether," Tristan says.

"How? We aren't going to kill him, right?" Reece asks. "I don't want regicide on my rap sheet."

"No, no, we'll just have him declared insane. Shouldn't be too hard. His mother was declared insane before he moved her to Shady Pines Chateau."

"He moved her?" I ask. "I thought his father retired and the queen went with him?"

Tristan's shoulders go up and down again. "I've heard a lot of rumors. But anyway. That's the plan for now. Sound good?"

"Well–" Reece begins.

"Don't argue with me! I'm the king!" Tristan barks in a teasing tone.

"Acting king," I correct him.

"Tomato, potatoh," he says, and I roll my eyes.

"Fine. That sounds like a plan. Now, I think one of us needs to go check on Rose, and I volunteer," I tell them.

"You spent an awful lot of time with her when you were poisoned.

I think this is a bit unfair," Reece says, folding his arms and sulking a bit.

Somewhere behind me, I think I hear a strange creaking noise. Before I can answer Reece, I turn and look over my shoulder.

I swear I see a picture on the wall swing slightly. How strange.

"Fine," I tell Reece, thinking I should investigate. "You go ahead, and I'll catch up with her later."

"Well, that was easier than I thought it would be," Reece says.

I'm already out of my chair. With a shrug, I walk toward the wall. I've got something to look into."

I glance behind me to see Tristan has pulled one of those poop books off of the shelf and is looking at it intently. He turns the book slightly as if there's an illustration that doesn't look right in its current direction. I shake my head and move on.

Walking to the wall where I saw the picture moving, I feel around. At first, it seems like an ordinary wall. But then, I realize there's a slight separation between panels.

This doesn't seem right. Looking at the bookshelves close by, I begin to tip books up, looking for the strangest ones first, the most worn ones, the biggest ones.

I pull on a book that says, "How to Win at War," and I hear the creaking noise again.

The wall opens up.

It's a secret passage.

CHAPTER 29: NO SUCH THING AS GHOSTS–RIGHT?

GENE

"These fucking incompetent people!" I holler, speaking to no one in particular except myself. Not a Goddess-damn one of these imbeciles I call servants can tell me where the fuck Alpha Tristan is in this blasted place. It's my own damn palace; people should be bowing to me, not to that idiot! I need to find him now to transfer power officially so that I can take control again.

This kingdom is mine, and mine alone!

"You!" I scream at the nearest butler, and the weak-minded little moron nearly jumps out of his skin.

"Y—yes, y—Your Majesty?" he mumbles.

"That's right, I'm Your Majesty, not that idiot Tristan," I holler at him. "And I need to find the useless Alpha now so I can get on with my... majestying!"

The moron just stares at me as if I hadn't just issued a perfectly clear command, and he doesn't say a word.

"Well?!" I screech into his face, close enough that I can see my own spittle landing on his chin.

His hand rises as if to wipe it off, but then he sees the look in my eyes, which I'm sure inflicts sharp pangs of terror deep into his soul, so he thinks the better of it. "I—I haven't seen Alpha King Tristan, Your Majesty."

The sound of the formal title in front of anyone's name but my own sends me over the edge. I reach up my hand and slap the imbecile across the face, sending him hurtling into the door jam.

The useless servant. I'll find the oversized Alpha myself.

All those blasted Alphas have such a hard-on for that lowlife Breeder that they can't stay away from the woman, so my next stop is to try her room again. If I go there often enough, I'll be sure to catch him.

I love my palace. But getting around in here is time-consuming. It's a long walk to just about everywhere from just about anywhere I can be, and it seems to take me longer than anyone else to get where I'm going around here.

It's ridiculous.

As I walk toward the Breeder's quarters, I run into a few dozen other servants, and they all act as if they can't even see me. They must fear me. I don't bother asking any of them about Alpha Tristan because I doubt any of them know anything.

Clueless. They're all absolutely clueless.

Finally, I reach the Breeder's corridor. If she's unguarded, I'll probably have to take care of Adam's task myself. It might actually feel satisfying. I am starting to get bored around here.

Rose

I open my eyes from a brief nap, and Kelly is standing over me... again. She's been watching me like a hawk ever since I saw that frightening woman. Everyone still thinks I was dreaming.

"Did you do it again?" she asks as soon as my eyes focus on her pretty face.

"Do what?" I ask.

With the pregnancy so advanced and so many tiny little pups inside me, I'm feeling pretty low on energy. Sometimes I think that's making me a bit forgetful, so I'm not sure what she's talking about. Maybe that's something I should look up in my pregnancy books. I wonder if multiple uterine horns affect your memory.

"Dream," she says, smiling at me. "Did you dream about that scary woman again?"

"Kelly, you're a wonderful friend," I say. I don't want to make her feel bad. "But I didn't dream about her. I saw her with my own eyes."

"Rose, dear," she says, sitting on the bed beside me and patting my hand. "I know it felt real, but it just couldn't be true."

"But it was!" I say, trying to be very firm and insistent using my new, confident tone of voice and hand gestures.

I've been working on my assertiveness training lately based on a book I'm reading. I have a lot of time on my hands since I'm on bedrest all the time, so I've been reading self-help books a lot. I'm going to be a mother to four pups, and even if the worst possible thing happens—that I never get to raise them myself—I still need to become a stronger person so if they ever do need me sometime in the future, I'll be able to be there for them.

I think it worked because the look in her eye changes just a bit as if she's taking me more seriously. I really do need to read that book a bit more.

I keep going, speaking slowly, firmly, and calmly. "The last place I saw her standing was right over there." I point to the corner near where the painting of the woman used to be, which Tristan had ripped off the wall. I really don't mind that he did since it was a little creepy.

Kelly walks over to the spot and holds up her arms. "So, right here?" she asks.

I nod. "Yes," I say. "She was over there ranting and raving, and Mark came running in, and then she was gone."

I'm still so confused about what happened. I'm not one to believe in ghosts, but this whole palace is a little creepy sometimes, and with all the death that's happened from all the wars in this land, I guess anything is possible. But she didn't seem like a ghost. She wasn't transparent. She was real.

Kelly spins around a couple of times, looking like she's examining the area, including the ceiling and the floor. "No trap door here," she says with a grin.

"Well, there must be something," I say. "I'm not crazy, just pregnant. Very pregnant."

Kelly giggles and looks around some more, but then she stops giggling suddenly and she's looking at the wall, in the same place where the creepy painting used to be.

"What is it?" I ask.

She shakes her head. "I'm not sure," she says. She walks over to the wall and touches it. "There's some sort of crack here."

"A crack?" I ask. I hope the whole palace isn't crumbling down. I'd hate to be trapped under falling timber when I'm this pregnant.

"It's…." She stops talking and feels around. "There's a lever here in the corner!" she says.

"A what?"

"A lever," she says again. "It's…. Oh!"

And just like that, a section of the wall opens up about a foot. I'm not crazy after all!

She turns to me and smiles, and we both giggle, but we're interrupted by some yelling outside.

"It's King Gene!" Kelly says in a whisper.

"Um… close that opening!" I say. Instinctively, I surmise that this is something we're not supposed to know about. The less King Gene knows about what Kelly and I know, the better.

Besides, if it's a secret passage that leads around the palace, it'll be the perfect place for Tristan to use to get away from King Gene so that he can keep control of everything. If Tristan remains king, then Gene can't force me to leave my babies and the four men I love more than anything.

I hear some arguing between Gene and Beta Adam, who is

standing outside the door guarding us while my men are away. I don't know what the king wants with me, but he's probably just looking for Tristan, and he won't find him here, so everything should be fine.

I miss my men so much when they aren't around, and they haven't even left the palace yet. I pray that when they do go off and do whatever 'business' they're planning, that they'll be safe.

"I... I can't," says Kelly. "I can't close this thing all the way. This is going to have to do." The door—or whatever it is—is still open by a crack. She comes back over and sits on my bed. "Maybe he won't notice," she says.

I nod in response.

As if on cue, King Gene bursts through the door then and stares at us for a split second. "My Goddess, woman, you're huge," he says.

"King Gene?" asks Kelly. "Can we help you with something?"

"Help me?" he says, still looking a little in shock. I guess he doesn't often see pregnant women, especially ones carrying four pups, and as far along as I am. I'm used to it, but I guess for other people it can be a little... different to see it.

He snaps out of it. "I'm looking for Alpha Tristan," he says, sounding a little annoyed. Well, he actually sounds a lot annoyed.

Kelly shakes her head and holds up her arms. "He's not here," she says.

"Well, I can see that he's not here," Gene says. "I need you to tell me where he is. That's an order!"

"Your Majesty," says Adam, walking up behind him. "The ladies don't know where the Alpha is. Let me help you look for him. We'll split up."

"I am the king!" King Gene says with a boom. "I'm not a fucking search-and-rescue dog! I expect the people of the palace to cooperate with me! We will not be 'splitting up' and looking for the man. You go look for him, and you'd better find him soon!"

"Of course, Your Majesty," Adam says.

King Gene furrows his brow and turns around, then he stops cold. He eyes the wall across the way, and even from my perspective on the bed, I can see his face turn as white as a porcelain sink, as if he's seen a ghost, and as if he's very afraid.

He's looking right at the crack in the wall.

"Your Majesty?" asks Beta Adam.

Without a word, King Gene turns on his heels and runs as fast as he can out of the room.

CHAPTER 30: EVERYTHING IS JUST FINE

Eli

Moving a wounded wolf shifter who doesn't want to go is not easy in human form, and it would be even more difficult in wolf form. Thankfully, I have a large enough team of shifters in my group who are willing to stay in their human form that we are managing to get Emily slowly back to where she should be... with Alpha Stephen.

He seems to be retreating though. Ordinarily, that might be a good thing, but it is taking us forever to get her there. I didn't want to use a vehicle to alert them of our approach because I thought that might be detrimental to our cause, so we are literally carrying Emily to her demise, strapped to a stretcher, going as fast as the shifters in human form can walk over rough terrain while she screams and bucks and tries to get herself loose.

So far, she's still stuck to the stretcher, but she's managed to turn the damn thing over three or four times and landed on her face on the ground each time.

It hasn't stopped her from continuing to try again.....

We trek on.

I have considered sending a messenger ahead to Stephen's troops to let him know we're coming, but I don't know whether or not he'll accept someone even under the flag of truce, and I don't want that person to get killed because Alpha Stephen is a douche.

So… the twenty of us are moving on together.

And every time we start to get within a few miles of Alpha Stephen and his warriors, they move.

They aren't necessarily retreating, I suppose. They are actually just moving about around the same amount of miles from the castle as they were when we started this dance.

I've even tried reaching him on the mind-link, but he won't respond.

It's almost as if he doesn't want her back….

"Put me down, you fucking cock suckers! I swear to the Moon Goddess, I will tear you limb from limb and use your own bleeding arms to beat the shit out of you!" Emily screams behind me.

I can't imagine why her fiancé doesn't want her….

Finally, after a couple of days of this nonsense, I decide I've had enough. While we are camping for a couple of hours, giving everyone a chance to catch their breath, including the screeching banshee tied to the stretcher, I announce my plan.

"I'm going to run on ahead," I tell them.

I watch everyone's eyes widen.

I am currently in my human form, wearing a pair of shorts, like everyone else who has shifted back to human and is sitting around, eating and drinking some water to make sure they are able to continue on the journey.

But they all stare at me like I'm nuts.

"Listen, we need to get word to Alpha Stephen that we have her. Whether he wants her or not, he's taking her." I see them shaking their heads as I explain.

"It's too dangerous, Alpha," Trevor, my Beta, says. "You could get hurt. Not only are Alpha Stephen's troops running around here, but so are Alpha Kane's. There could be other rogues and rebels out and about as well. Alpha, sir, with all due respect, I don't think it's a good idea."

"I don't see any other alternative," I tell him. "We've been trying to catch up to him for a couple of days now, and he won't wait for her, and he won't respond to my mind-link messages."

"Maybe he doesn't want her back," Cora, one of my seasoned warriors, says as she takes a bite out of a piece of beef jerky. Still chewing, she says, "I can't imagine why."

Emily is situated under a tree a little bit away from where most of us are sitting, but we can definitely hear her. "Fuck off, you assholes! I'm going to rip your dicks off and shove them into each other's throats!"

"She's delightful," Cora finishes.

I have half a mind to just leave Emily here and let Stephen know where she's at, but then I have a different idea. "We are about twenty miles from Alpha Stephen's main village. You guys just take her there. Dump her off in the city center if you need to. I don't care. In the meantime, I'll go let His Floppiness know that his love interest is being deposited back on his property."

"But... why don't you just come with us?" Trevor asks. "It would be safer."

"I'll be fine," I assure them. I think of all of the battles I've been through. I can't even count them all. I'm certainly not afraid of Alpha Stephen, and I'm confident I can outrun anyone else who tries to get in my way.

"Alpha, maybe you should take a few of us with you?" Cora suggests. "There are more than enough of us to make sure the witch gets home."

I shake my head. "I need you guys to protect the warriors in human form. They won't be able to shift that quickly if someone comes out of the shadows and attacks, especially not while they're carrying that holy terror." One of the shifters guarding Emily tries to give her some water, but she spits it all over him.

Yeah, I am seriously considering leaving her here... in the forest... with these giant ants crawling all over the ground... with honey spread all over her body.

"I know you're an intelligent Alpha, sir, and I don't mean to be

177

disrespectful," Trevor continues, "but I think you might not be thinking clearly right now because you want so badly to get away from her."

I laugh. "I do want to get away from her, but that's not why I'm doing this. Trust me. I'll be fine." Thoughts of Rose and my unborn child come to mind. I wouldn't do anything to jeopardize my chance at seeing my baby or of spending time back in Rose's arms.

I can't convince them, and I don't need to. I grab my bag with a few supplies in it, including some protein bars and water, and tell them, "I'll be in touch via the mind-link. Just head to the village."

"Yes, Alpha," Cora says, but she's shaking her head.

"You two are in charge," I add, looking at Cora and Trevor, and they both acknowledge my command with the sign of respect.

With that, I step deeper into the woods, take my shorts off and put them in my bag. Then, I shift and work the bag onto my back.

Ready to go, I set off in the direction I know Alpha Stephen's troops are located in because I can pick up their scent.

It seems to me that I can run full speed over to them and deliver my message quickly enough that I can meet back up with my warriors and actually be there when they take Emily to the village. I don't think that Stephen is more than five or ten miles off in the opposite direction.

I lope along as the sun begins to descend, and even though I can tell by the scent that Alpha Stephen's troops are shifting again, they can't detect me as easily as they could my entire entourage, and I can adjust where I'm going more easily than they can because there's just one of me.

After a few hours, I see them come into view in the distance. I see guards at their post, doing their best to protect the camp that still seems fairly mobile at the moment.

"I need to speak to Alpha Stephen," I say from a distance.

"Halt!" the guards bark in my head. "Alpha Stephen isn't taking guests."

"I have his fiancée," I tell them, "and I'm taking her to his village. I need to tell him that himself. I am an Alpha, and you will show me respect."

The guards cower slightly. They can't help it, even if I am their enemy at present.

"Wait there!" one of them shouts.

I have no reason to argue with him, so I do.

I wait. And wait. And wait some more.

Almost an hour passes before I see Stephen in the distance. He is in his human form, with large wolves on either side of him. Standing a good twenty yards away from me, he shouts. "I don't want her!"

I almost laugh because no one seems to want her. "Well, I'm dumping her in your village, so you do whatever the fuck you want to with her, but I'm not keeping her. And by the way, you do know you're on the wrong side of this war, right?"

"Don't you dare dump her!"

I have delivered my message, and he hasn't responded to the part he should have, the part about switching sides. I decide I've done what I can, and I turn around and take off at full sprint through the forest, heading toward Stephen's primary village.

An hour or so into my run, I sense that Alpha Kane has troops nearby. I can tell by the scent and the way the air has shifted in the distance. I can't really explain it, but I decide to change my course slightly.

I run through a small meadow and out the other side when a strange smell hits my lungs.

It's skunk—and a lot of it.

It smells like a group of skunks had a stink-sack squeezing orgy, and it makes me want to vomit.

"What the hell?" I think to myself.

Running out of there as quickly as possible seems like a good idea.

I sprint between two large pine trees and see a strange sight in front of me. It looks like a trap that's sprung, and inside of it is some sort of a large animal, struggling to get out.

I find the entire situation odd, so I slow down to try to evaluate it.

BELLA MOONDRAGON & OLIVIA BHELLE KILDARE

That's when I feel a rush of wind on my left followed by a sharp prick in my shoulder.

Looking back at my own body, I see a red dart sticking out of my upper arm. "What the fuuuu–"

Everything goes black.

CHAPTER 31: THE SECRET PASSAGE

ROSE

Beta Adam, Kelly, and I are all staring at each other, wondering what scared King Gene so much. It had to have something to do with the secret doorway that Kelly had just discovered.

Kelly was the first to speak. "Okay," she says. "Whatever's in there is clearly something that spooked him." She looks at me. "Describe that woman again?"

"Well," I begin. "Something about her looks like King Gene. I can't place it though. She's tiny, shorter even than he is. She has skinny arms and bony fingers. She was wearing old, ragged clothes that looked like they didn't even fit her anymore. And she was babbling something about her 'GeGe,' something about him not loving me? It was strange."

"Hmm," says Beta Adam.

Kelly looks at him. "Hmm what?" she says, although her tone is more like a statement.

"It's probably nothing," he says. "But she sounds like she's describing Gene's mother, Queen Marcella."

"Why would she be around here?" asks Kelly. "I thought the old king and queen from these parts had gone off to live quietly in the east, and that later they had died."

"That's what I thought, too," Adam says. "That's the rumor I heard, anyway."

"Do you think she might really be alive, and that she's back here visiting?" I ask.

Adam shrugs. "I suppose it's possible," he says. "Sometimes rumors are wrong. She could still be alive. But it's weird that she's sneaking around here in your room."

Kelly moved over to the wall and felt around the same place where she'd opened the door.

"What are you doing?" Beta Adam asks.

"I'm opening the secret passage," she says. "I'm going to go find her and see what's going on."

"Secret passage," Adam says.

I realize that he doesn't know about the door yet. "Kelly found a crack in the wall that opened some kind of door," I say. "Just before King Gene walked in. He was looking at it before he ran off."

"That has to be how the queen came and went from Rose's room," Kelly says. "And if she can get in, so can anyone else. We need to secure her better, so I'm going in to find out where this passage leads."

"Kelly, you can't go by yourself," I say. I know she's a strong warrior, but I'm worried about her. Who knows who's wandering around in there?

"We can't both go," she says, looking at Beta Adam and then back at me. "I'll be fine. I'll be right back."

Before I can say anything else, she pulls open the door and steps through it. I'm hoping she doesn't go far as it's probably dark in there, although her wolf eyes can likely adjust to it.

It's really hard to lay in bed and let everyone else do dangerous things to protect me. I know it's important that we keep the pups safe, but knowing that doesn't make it easier to watch my friends take risks. I look over at Adam.

"Where are the Alphas?" I ask. "And what was that 'problem' you'd told them about before?" The last time my Alphas had been with me,

Beta Adam had run into the room and said there was a problem, then insisted on talking about it out in the hallway.

"It—it was nothing," he says. "Just a military issue, and I didn't want you to worry."

"Military?" I ask. "They're not going off to war, are they?" I try to scoot into an upright position on the bed.

"Relax, Rose, please," he says calmly, moving toward me like he's afraid I'm going to go into labor right then and there, just because I'm upright.

"I can't relax if they're in danger," I say.

"Your Alphas are all very strong. They all lead very powerful and sophisticated packs," he says in a calm voice. "They are all accustomed to occasional military skirmishes. I'm sure they've already taken care of the problem."

I nod, but looking him in the eye, it feels like he's not telling me something.

I do need to trust my men, though. He's right—they're all strong and powerful, and they're used to fighting. I just want them to be safe all the time.

I'm sure they're okay.

Turning my head, I look toward the open door in the wall. I have to trust Kelly, too. I know she's strong enough to take care of herself. It's not like I could go after her anyway, so I decide to just lay back down and wait for her.

I close my eyes and take a deep breath. This pregnancy thing is tough, and it seems like it's taking forever! I just want my children in my arms and the arms of their fathers.

KELLY

It doesn't take long for my eyes to adjust to the dark tunnel. Surprisingly, it's a lot bigger than I thought. I had expected to end up in a room next to Rose's, but here I am walking through what amounts to a maze in the wall.

It's a whole series of tunnels that lead—well, everywhere.

I haven't gone that far, but I am a little worried. I shouldn't keep Rose there long with only Adam to guard her. Beta Adam had told me and all the Alphas that King Gene was ordering Adam to kill Rose immediately, so the Alphas had gathered together to figure out what to do with Gene while I guarded Rose.

I just absolutely boil over in anger whenever I think of how that man wants to murder an innocent woman—especially since she's pregnant with four pups! I can't even imagine how the Alphas are feeling right now and how they're keeping themselves calm.

Personally, I think a little regicide wouldn't be a bad thing right now.

I need to focus though so I don't get lost in this labyrinth of tunnels. This is really a fantastic place and a great idea for the inside of a palace, but for us, it's not so great since someone's been sneaking into Rose's room.

I look behind me, and it all looks familiar, so I make a note of the scent, turn around, and keep going just a little bit farther.

I reach a spiral staircase and go up; it seems like it's a few stories high. Finally, I reach the top, and there's a hallway. I look back down the stairs and still hear the muffled voices of Adam and Rose echoing in the passageway.

Knowing she's safe, I keep going. Around the next corner, there's a light, so I peek around. It's a small room, and it's tucked away on the side of the path I'm on. I can see a flickering light, which must be a candle, and I briefly wonder why there isn't any electricity. But I guess if they constructed the tunnels secretly—and that seems to be the case —they would have never wired the area for electricity.

I look back in the direction of Rose's room and wonder whether I should get some backup before going forward. I dismiss that idea quickly because we can't leave Rose alone, and I'm certainly not going to let her try to get up and follow us down this hall and up these stairs in her condition.

I pause for a moment while I wonder if I should just go back right now. Beta Adam is certainly trustworthy, but if King Gene comes back, he'll expect him to follow through on his murderous command. No—the way Gene had high-tailed it out of there looking like a ghost had just tapped on his shoulder, I'm sure we don't have to worry about him going back into Rose's room anytime soon.

Why is he so afraid of his own mother, if that's who that woman is? Maybe the rumors are true, and she really is dead. Could this be a real ghost?

I decide that that's ridiculous, and I push forward and find out who is in the room, but I'm taking it slow. Across the room from the open doorway where I'm standing is a large bookshelf that takes up the entire wall. It's full of books, and they're not dusty as I'd expect in this creepy secret passageway, so it looks like someone has been here recently.

I take one last deep breath, and I'm about to step inside, when I hear a voice. It's a woman.

"Oh, my GeGe, you've been a bad boy," she says. "Yes, yes, it's a bad boy you've been. How long have you ignored your mother? You need to obey, obey your mother and be a good boy once again. GeGe should be a good boy when his mother is around. Be a good, good boy."

It's almost like singing, and some creaking sounds are accompanying the voice. I take a silent step into the room and see a woman in a rocking chair staring at something in her hand.

She doesn't even notice me as she keeps rocking and singing and staring at the object, which looks like a photo of some kind. She looks exactly like Rose described her—old, tiny, and thin, and wearing raggedy clothes.

I take another step and accidentally kick some pebbles on the ground, which makes a noise just loud enough to make the woman look up.

She stands up suddenly and yells, "It's you! You must be the one who poisoned the mind of my GeGe!"

CHAPTER 32: CAPTIVE

Eli

My mouth feels like I've got an old sock shoved in it, even though I know it's empty. I can move my tongue around freely. I've had a gag shoved into my mouth before, so I know what that feels like, and this isn't it.

It's close, though.

I can't see anything. I have some sort of a blindfold tied around my head. From the smell of it, someone or something has urinated on it recently. Either that, or wherever the hell I'm being kept just smells like a toilet.

Maybe a little from column A and a little from column B.

I feel wood against my back and my legs, so I have a feeling I'm in some sort of a cabin or a small house or something. It doesn't feel like a large space, but then, I'm not sure. I wish I could shift into my wolf form, but it's clear that the bindings on my wrists have silver in them. Not only do they sting a little, but they're preventing me from shifting.

I was in my wolf form when I was drugged, so they must've given me something to force me to shift back. I think they at least had the decency to put a pair of shorts on me because it doesn't feel like I'm completely naked, but still, I have no shoes and no shirt, and I'm sitting in squalor with a desert in my mouth and the smell of bodily fluid filling my lungs.

These folks are a class act, that's for damn sure.

I try to listen to their voices as they talk across the room. I'm pretty sure I'm in a small place because if it was big, they'd move away from me, right? So far, I don't recognize any voices, but that doesn't mean it wasn't Alpha Stephen's men or Alpha Kane's who had grabbed me.

"They'll pay top dollar!" I hear a male voice say. He sounds older and like he thinks he knows everything. "All we need to do is ask!"

"But I heard that King Gene is trying to get rid of all of the Alphas now, all four of the ones from the contest," another male, this one a little younger, says. "Why would they pay for him if that's the case?"

"Trust me on this one! I've known Gene a long damn time. He's not going to change his mind now. He'd have to admit he was wrong, and Gene don't ever admit he's wrong." That's the first guy again.

I hear what sounds like a female, judging by the way she's making noises in the back of her throat like she thinks they're both idiots.

She's probably not wrong.

But she doesn't say anything, and then we're back to the second guy again.

"I think we kill him, make a statement, put his head on a lance, and leave it outside of the castle. That's the best way to get our point across." He chuckles under his breath and adds, "Literally."

No one else laughs. The first guy is even more irritated now. "Since when are you in charge of this operation? I'm the Alpha. I'm the boss. We're doing things my way. End of story!" Then I hear what sounds like a blow and a gasp from I'm assuming guy number two, who I am not a huge fan of after his last suggestion.

"All right, all right," he says. "We'll write up a ransom note, Goddess!" the second guy says, apparently recovered from being struck by his alleged Alpha. "Who do we address it to?"

"I swear to the Moon Goddess herself, you are the dumbest fucker I've ever met in my life, Melvin!" the Alpha shouts. "King Gene, you moron!" I hear another whack and know that Melvin just got hit again.

I don't know who Melvin is, but I do have a feeling this so-called Alpha is actually a rogue. I have heard that there are some rogue packs situated between Alpha Stephen and Alpha Kane's territories, so I'm guessing I was apprehended by one of them.

I wanna swear myself. I remember how confident I was that I could do this mission on my own and how my team tried to dissuade me from it. Now, here I am being held against my will in Goddess knows where….

"Alpha Eli? Can you hear me? Where the fuck are you?"

Trevor's voice enters my head, and I know that he doesn't actually expect a response or he wouldn't be cussing. He must have been trying to reach me for a long time, but I was unconscious, which means he wasn't able to find me.

"Hey, don't talk to me like that!" I say, half-joking.

"Alpha?" Trevor's voice perks up. "Oh, thank the Goddess! We thought you were dead!"

I add everyone who was on the assignment with me into the conversation. "Yeah, well, I'm afraid I have no idea where I'm at. I've been apprehended by a pack of rogues. At least, that's what I think they are. I'm in some sort of a little cabin or something. All I know is that the second in command's name is Melvin." I think he's the second in command anyway. "They're going to send a ransom note to Gene to try to get me back, but if that doesn't work, they're going to put my head on a lance."

"Where were you when they picked you up?" Cora asks me.

"They shot me with a dart on my way back from Stephen's lines. I'd say I was probably halfway to the village." I can't remember exactly, and my head hurts just trying to think. That's thanks to the drugs they darted me with, I'm sure.

"Okay, we'll go back and trace your scent. I take it you're restrained?" Trevor asks.

"Well, I'm not sitting here on the floor pretending to still be out because it's fun. Be careful. You might need backup from the other

Alphas." I don't want Cora, Trevor, or any of my other guys getting hurt because I'm a dumb ass and tried to do something on my own that I shouldn't have.

"Don't worry," Cora says. "We'll be careful. Just try to keep your head where it belongs in the meantime, Alpha. I'm pretty sure your beautiful Breeder likes your head still attached to your body."

I think about adding, "Both of my heads," but I keep those thoughts to myself.

And then I hear the female say, "I think our Alpha is awake."

"What makes you say that?" Melvin asks. "He ain't talkin'."

"He isn't talking to us, but he's breathing more normally. Skull-mark! You were supposed to make sure he never woke up, Goddess damnit!" the Alpha shouts.

"Uh... sorry 'bout dat boss," a voice nearer to me says. I take it that is Skullmark.

I try to slow my breathing so they think I'm still out, but it's too late. I must've lost track of that while I was talking to my team.

"They're knocking my ass out again," I say to my rescue party as I feel another prick in my arm. There's no point in trying to struggle when I can't even see what I'm fighting and the silver is burning into my flesh.

"We'll find you!" I hear Cora say, and that's the last thing I hear before everything goes black again.

Cora

"We need to hurry!" I tell Trevor. "Let's go back in the direction Alpha Eli was going in when he was headed to the village."

"Yeah, come on everyone," Trevor agrees. "Now that we've deposited that bitch, Emily, we can run twice as fast to find the Alpha."

190

"I sure hope they don't decide to kill him," I mutter, and Trevor gives me a sympathetic look.

In my mind, I am having a completely different conversation, though. "You fuck ups!" I say to my team back at the cabin. "You let him wake up long enough to contact his entire team! Now, we're all racing back toward Alpha Stephen's men to try to pick up on Alpha Eli's scent. Please tell me you were at least smart enough to do something to mask it?"

"Don't worry, baby," my mate, Alpha Pike of the Rogue Forest pack, says in my head. "We did plenty to mask it. Even the keenest bloodhound ain't gonna be able to find this poor bastard's scent."

"Yeah, well, if you're going to negotiate, you'd better get it done fast because Trevor's nose is pretty good, and he's liable to find out exactly where you took his Alpha, you dumbasses." I'm the Luna and the real one calling the shots around here. My mate only thinks he's in charge.

"Watch your mouth!" he says, as if that's going to set me straight. "We're doing this on my time schedule table, not yours!"

I roll my eyes. Every single one of these guys is a genius. "I'll keep you posted. Just… don't do anything else stupid!"

"Don't you worry about me and us," Pike says. "We don't do nothin' stupid around here. And as for the bloodhound, well, if he gets in the way… take him out."

"Yeah, sure. I'll just kill the guy in charge of the mission in front of a bunch of other wolves from Alpha Eli's pack. No problem." Again, my eyes go up. "Just be ready to hide again if you have to."

"Yes, Luna," everyone says except for the Alpha. He says nothing because he knows I'm right.

I glance at Trevor, who is running full speed in his wolf form. Can I take him out and make it look like an accident? We just might have to find out. My pack of rogues has worked too long and hard for this opportunity to let anyone get in the way.

CHAPTER 33: THE GHOST IS ALIVE!

Tristan, Reece, and I are all just sort of standing here, staring into what can only be a secret tunnel that's leading out of the library. The doorway seems to have been activated by removing a book about war, so maybe this is a secret place for the king to hide if enemies infiltrate the palace.

There's a long pause while we each assess the situation.

Finally, Tristan speaks. "Should we investigate?" he asks.

"We should, but maybe that's something we should save for later," I say. "There's a whole hoard of troops amassing out there, and I'm also worried about Eli. Has anyone tried to mind-link with him lately?"

Both Tristan and Reece shake their heads.

"He's a competent Alpha," says Tristan. "We don't need to babysit him. But we do need to deal with Kane and Stephen before they get too comfortable. This passage though," he reaches over and opens the door a bit wider, "is... interesting. I think we need to find out whether Gene is using it to listen in on our conversations. We also may be able to use it to find out what he's up to."

Reece nods. "I do think we should look into it," he says. "But I also think at least one of us should back up Eli. And I can do that." He pauses for a moment, and I can tell he's using the mind-link. "He's not answering," he says. "I'll get my warriors mobilized."

"We'll join you soon," says Tristan. "This shouldn't take long. If you need more backup in the meantime, let us know."

"Thanks, Reece," I tell him.

Reece nods at us both and heads out. I'm worried about Eli, but I know that Tristan's right. He's a strong warrior, and he's smart. I'm sure he's got everything under control and he's just too busy to answer right now. I'm so relieved that Emily is out of our hair, and that Barbara is safely locked away in the dungeon. But even so, I don't think it's a good time to let down our guard around Rose and our children. I'm sure the other Alphas feel the same way.

There's a flashlight on one of the bookshelves nearby, and though it seemed out of place moments before, now it makes sense. Even if it's pitch-black inside, our wolf eyes can adjust, but I still don't mind the extra help just in case, so I grab the flashlight as we head through the doorway.

It takes a second to adjust to the dark, but I don't want to use the flashlight just yet just in case Gene is in here. I'd rather sneak up on him than the other way around.

We're silent as Tristan and I move forward, communicating only in the mind-link.

'It's bigger than I thought,' he says in my head.

'I'm guessing this covers the entire palace,' I say.

The corridor is very long and seems to split off in different directions. I imagine it leads to about every room in the palace.

We go forward for a while, choosing a straighter path so we can find our way back. Eventually, we hear voices and see a faint glowing light. Oddly, it seems like it's coming from above us. It doesn't take long to figure out why; there's a wide path in the hallway that holds a winding staircase. It looks fairly high up, a few stories high, then it looks like it leads to an opening.

'Do we have time to check that out?' I ask Tristan.

'I'm sure Reece and Eli will alert us if they need anything, and we can mobilize our warriors fairly quickly,' he says. 'I think it's safe to take a few minutes to see what's going on up there. I'm definitely hearing voices.'

'Me, too,' I say. 'Let's go.'

We wind our way up the staircase toward the landing above. Whatever Gene is up to now, he's not going to get away with it.

KELLY

"I haven't done anything to anybody," I tell the strange old lady. She's taken a few steps toward me, so I hold up my hands as both a defensive move and to show her that I mean her no harm. At least not yet, I don't.

Instead of coming any closer, she seems to fall back into a state of emotional despair and backs up, plopping ungracefully down into her rocking chair. I take a few steps closer as she sits there sobbing.

"Who are you?" I ask. "Are you okay?"

The woman shakes her head, still sobbing uncontrollably. She's so frail, and her clothes are so tattered and torn that I feel sorry for her, but I'm not sure what to do. I assess that she's not dangerous; I could take her down without even trying, so I go with a gentle approach. I move closer and stand beside her, gently patting her back.

"It'll be okay," I tell her. "Please tell me who you are, and what you're doing here all alone like this."

That seems to have made things worse because she erupts into even louder sobbing, so I keep patting her on the back, hoping she'll calm down. I won't try mentioning being alone again, that's for sure.

Finally, her sobs slow down, and she looks up at me. "You're nice," she says. "No one has been nice to me in such a long, long time."

"Well, I think we can change that," I say. "I have a lot of friends, and we'll all be nice to you. Let's start by introducing ourselves. I'm Kelly. What's your name?" She seems so frail that I'm talking to her slowly, as if she's a child. I doubt she's talked to anyone in a long time.

"I—I'm Mar—Marcella," she says.

I blow out a breath. Now I have to figure out whether I'm seeing a ghost, dreaming, hallucinating, or seeing something real. "The queen?" I ask. "Queen Marcella?"

She nods, then she blows her nose on an old piece of cloth that looks a bit too dusty for that kind of thing. "I was queen once," she says. "It was wonderful."

"What are you doing up here?" I ask. I'm hoping that now that she's opening up a little, that I can find out why she's here. I've already decided that she's not a ghost, so Gene must have done something awful to this poor woman, his own mother! I swear, every time I turn around, I'm learning something about that slimy toad of a man that pisses me off more.

"Oh, I live here," she says. "GeGe told me—he said that it's not safe out there, that I have to stay hiding here. He promised me that as soon as it was safe, I could see him again."

"Him?" I ask, but then I smell a familiar scent. It's two of the Alphas, and they're not far away. I back out of the room with a few steps and see them coming up the last of the stairs toward the landing. I hold up my finger to my lips, hoping they'll realize that means I need them to approach quietly. They seem to take the hint and hold back a bit.

I go back into the room, motioning for them to follow me, carefully. They nod and approach, waiting just outside the door.

"How long have you been here?" I ask Marcella.

She looks up at me with a blank stare. "Oh, you look nice," she says. "What's your name?"

"I'm Kelly, remember?" I say.

She furrows her brow a little and frowns. "I don't know a Kelly," she says. "Are you the new maid? My room could use a cleaning."

"Well, don't you remember?" I ask. "I just introduced myself a moment ago."

"There hasn't been anyone in here in ages," she says, and I can sense a little irritation in her voice.

I guess the Alphas sensed it too since they came around the corner. Marcella stood up and looked angry again.

"It's okay," I say to her softly. "These are my friends. They can be your friends, too."

"They look mean," Marcella answers gruffly. "You look nice, though."

I smile pleasantly. "Thank you," I say. "My friends are nice, too."

Marcella backs up and sits down on her chair, returning to her rocking and sobbing.

"Marcella?" I ask. "Are you okay?"

"Marcella?" whispers Tristan.

I nod in his direction.

Marcella looked up. "Oh, hello," she says. "When did you get here?"

I smile. Clearly, the woman has some memory issues, so I decide to go talk with the Alphas out in the hallway. "I'll be right back," I say.

But Marcella doesn't answer; she just rocks in her chair and returns to sobbing. I motion for the Alphas to step out of the room.

"That's Queen Marcella?" asks Mark in a whisper.

I nod. "Apparently so." I keep my voice down. "She seems to have some memory problems, and I haven't been able to get her to tell me much more than her name. And she looks just like Gene, so it has to be her."

"I thought she had gone off and retired with the king and passed away," says Tristan.

I shrug. "That's what everyone thought, and yet here she is," I say. "What should we do?"

"Well," Tristan begins, "this could work in our favor. I think we need to watch for a bit and see if Gene is here looking after her."

I laugh without meaning to. "If anything, he's hiding from her," I say, then I briefly explain how Gene had run, terrified, out of the room when he saw so much as a crack in the door.

"This could still be—" Tristan begins, but he's suddenly cut off by the sound of Beta Adam's voice screaming down the hallway downstairs.

"Kelly!" Adam hollers. "Come quick! It's Rose!!"

CHAPTER 34: WHO'S THE BETRAYER?

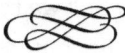

CORA

They moved him.

Even though the others that I am working with are morons and can't seem to get anything right, at least when I sent them a mind-link message that Trevor had gotten information from Eli about where he was, they had the intelligence to move the Alpha.

They also used an awful skunk spray to try to cover up his scent, and we crossed through it several times in the woods when we were trying to figure out where Eli had gone to. It's revolting, and I'm pretty sure Trevor is smart enough to realize that the scent has to be fake; unless an entire family of skunks was killed by farting to death....

I am glad that we're still lost in the woods so that I don't have to start killing these guys. I think it might get suspicious after a while if every time I go off in one direction with a single wolf, that wolf ends up meeting an unfortunate ending, like falling off of a cliff or tripping and accidentally breaking their neck.

That might work a time or two, but probably not eighteen times.

"What should we do?" Trevor asks me using the mind-link as we continue to search through the area near where Alpha Stephen has been captured.

"I'm not sure. I haven't been able to reach Alpha Eli through the mind-link." I don't tell him I haven't tried. I have been able to reach my friend Darla, who is with the morons watching the Alpha, and she tells me he's still out. I am making sure that they are keeping an eye on him this time since they have done a piss poor job up until now.

"I haven't been able to get in touch with him either," Trevor admits. We continue to search, but we're just going in circles now. He shakes his head like he's swearing, but wolves can't talk. "I don't know what to do, and I don't want to tell the others."

At least he will admit it when he's lost, not like a typical man.

"Maybe we should go back to the castle and let the other Alphas know?" I say, using a tone that makes him think I might be unsure of whether or not that's a good idea. That's actually exactly what I want. My job is to make sure our little group isn't discovered by this group, not to have to kill any of these knuckleheads or otherwise harm the Alphas back at the castle.

Of course, if I could help facilitate the demands of our Alpha, that would only work in our favor....

"Yeah, you're right. This is a job for a bigger team than just us," Trevor finally says, shaking his head. I can tell he feels like a failure. I pretend to give him a sympathetic look, but I'm actually rejoicing on the inside.

We "reluctantly" turn around and head back for home. I can tell Trevor is trying his best to get in touch with Alpha Eli as we go, but he won't be able to reach the Alpha, not for a really long time.

My friends will make sure of that....

~

GENE

. . .

It's dark beneath my desk, but I can fit right up against the side with the drawers hiding me from the side where my chair is currently pulled all the way in. It's a tight squeeze, even for me, but I had to hide somewhere.

How did this happen?

How did she get out?

And what the hell is she going to do to me now?

My lips tremble slightly as I think about it. When I was a little boy, she was the most wonderful person in the world. We used to have the best times together. Even though she was the queen, she used to bake cookies with me and sing songs. She read me a bedtime story every night from the time I was born until I was twenty-two.

She was the best mama ever.

But then I realized that my father was not going to retire anytime soon, and I had to take matters into my own hands.

I had to get rid of them—both of them.

Well, I could hardly have them killed. After all, the Moon Goddess would frown upon someone committing regicide. So instead, I simply had them disappear. By the time I had all of my father's close followers either turned against him or murdered, it wasn't too hard to just make up a story.

We had a nice going away party that my father was "too ill" to attend and my mother was too far gone with dementia to notice, and then we waved at an empty car leaving the grounds. The driver thought he was in on all of it until a few of my henchmen took him out on a bridge about twenty miles from the castle, and he went down with the car.

When they returned to the castle to report they'd taken care of the driver, I had them taken care of.

And so it went until anyone who had any idea what had gone on was dead, and the lunatic in the dungeon who claimed to be the king was ignored by the one guard I allowed to bring him meals. Now, no one pays anyone in that portion of the prison any mind.

"We've got him in our custody," my informant's voice comes

through the mind-link. "And the ransom note is on the way to the castle."

I am surprised I am able to pick his mind-link messages up from here. "You should be too far away by now to communicate with me," I remind him.

"Well, there's been a bit of trouble getting the others to do what we need them to do. They still think we're in this for the money."

I sigh. Why can't anything just go right to begin with?

"Well, it would be nice to get the money and finish the job," I tell him. "Whatever you do, don't let them know that I'm working with you. That's the most important part. I can't be accused of being in cahoots with the likes of rogues. Besides, if this blows up in my face, I don't want to be responsible."

"Of course, King Gene. No one has any idea that I'm double-crossing them. They all think I'm some sort of a moron."

I can't help but chuckle under my breath. "Well, it might have something to do with your name."

"It's a nickname, Sire!" He says "sire" like it's a curse word. "At any rate, I'll take care of the Alpha and make it look like an accident, but you've got to be willing to deliver on your end of the deal."

"Of course. I know your situation," I say. "I know that your wife can't have kids. You will get exactly what you've asked for. As soon as this mess is all behind us."

The door to my office creaks open, and a shiver goes down my spine. Is it her?

"King Gene?"

It's one of the guards. I say nothing, and the door closes. I can breathe again.

"Sire? Did you hear me?" the voice in my head says, clearly annoyed this time.

"What? No, I didn't hear you. I'm the king! I'm busy doing important... royal business."

"I said, please make sure it's a boy. That's important to me."

"Yes, yes," I say dismissively. "She's having a whole litter. You can have your pick. Just make sure Eli doesn't come back to this castle alive." That will leave me with only three Alphas to take care of.

"Don't worry. I'll dispatch him," my informant says, and I can't help but smile.

"That's all I need to know, Skullmark."

ALSO BY BELLA MOONDRAGON

One Night with the Billionaire

Shared by the Sexy Billionaire Twins

The Alpha King's Breeder series:

Bought by the Alpha: The Alpha King's Breeder Book 1

Loved by the Alpha: The Alpha King's Breeder Book 2

Lost by the Alpha: The Alpha King's Breeder Book 3

Luna of the Alpha: The Alpha King's Breeder Book 4

Legacy of the Alpha: The Alpha Kings's Breeder Book 5

Daughter of the Alpha: The Alpha King's Breeder Book 6

Descendants of the Alpha: The Alpha King's Breeder Book 7

Shadow of the Alpha: The Alpha King's Breeder Book 8

The Luna's Vampire Prince series:

The Culling

The Kingdom

The Conquered

Pregnant With Four Alphas' Babies

Chosen As the Breeder

Mated to Four Alphas

Threats Against the Breeder

At War for the Breeder

The Stolen Breeder

Four Alphas, Four Babies

Becoming the Luna Queen

Descendants of the Breeder (releases 9/1/2024)

Desired by the Devil series

Whispers of the Devil

Bantor of the Devil (coming soon)

The Mafia Kings series

Indebted to the Mafia King

Sign up for Bella's newsletter here.

Follow Bella on Facebook here.

www.ingramcontent.com/pod-product-compliance
Lightning Source LLC
Chambersburg PA
CBHW072236190626
46809CB00018B/2523